PENGUIN CLASSICS

TWO SPANISH PICARESQUE NOVELS

FRANCISCO DE QUEVEDO, author of *The Swindler*, was born in Madrid in 1580. He studied at Valladolid and at Alcalá, where he obtained his degree. He was a prolific writer of prose and poetry and was closely involved for most of his life with politics in Spain and Italy. In 1611 he moved to Italy after killing an opponent in a duel, and his life subsequently was a mixture of success and disaster; he spent some time as a prison governor and towards the end of his life was imprisoned in a monastery as a result of his writing. He died at Villanueva de los Infantes in 1645.

The authorship of *Lazarillo* is uncertain, though it has been attributed to Diego Hurtado de Mendoza, the satirist, poet, historian and humanist.

•

Michael Alpert took a degree in modern languages at Cambridge and a doctorate in history at Reading. He is Principal Lecturer in Spanish and the History of Spain at the University of Westminster. He has published several books and articles on Spanish history and is now preparing a new international history of the Spanish Civil War. He has also translated *The Three Cornered Hat and Other Stories* by the nineteenth-century Spanish novelist and short-story writer Alarcón, for the Penguin Classics.

TWO SPANISH PICARESQUE NOVELS

>—<—>—

Lazarillo de Tormes
ANON

The Swindler (El Buscón)
FRANCISCO DE QUEVEDO

>—<—>—

Translated from the Spanish by
MICHAEL ALPERT

PENGUIN BOOKS

PENGUIN BOOKS

Published by the Penguin Group
Penguin Books Ltd, 27 Wrights Lane, London W8 5TZ, England
Penguin Books USA Inc., 375 Hudson Street, New York, New York 10014, USA
Penguin Books Australia Ltd, Ringwood, Victoria, Australia
Penguin Books Canada Ltd, 10 Alcorn Avenue, Toronto, Ontario, Canada M4V 3B2
Penguin Books (NZ) Ltd, 182–190 Wairau Road, Auckland 10, New Zealand

Penguin Books Ltd, Registered Offices: Harmondsworth, Middlesex, England

This translation published in Penguin Classics 1969
17 19 20 18 16

Introduction and translation copyright © Michael Alpert, 1969
All rights reserved

Printed in England by Clays Ltd, St Ives plc
Set in Linotype Juliana

CONTENTS

INTRODUCTION

Lazarillo de Tormes (published 1554) and *The Swindler* (called in Spanish *La Vida del Buscón*, written in about 1608, and published 1626) are among the first picaresque novels. The word picaresque derives from the Spanish *pícaro*, which means rascal or crafty good-for-nothing, and is used to describe the hero of a similar novel, *Guzmán de Alfarache* (1599). I say hero, but in fact picaresque heroes are anything but heroic. These two are criminals, Lazarillo mainly from bad luck, but Pablos clearly by choice. The *pícaro* is usually a cynical youth, brought up the hard way and determined to treat others as cruelly as he has been treated himself. His aim is to *burlar* others: to deceive and play cruel tricks on them, and indeed cruelty is one of the dominant motifs of these novels, which reflect a world where the rule is 'every man for himself'. The *pícaro's* goal is respectability, which means money, and of course he is keen to make the best showing he can in the world; Spaniards traditionally are.

On his wanderings, which can lead through several towns or even countries, the *pícaro* meets and pits his wits against a variety of people, and in this way the writer builds up a portrait of contemporary society. The incidents might be – and in some cases they are known to be – taken from the author's own life, and perhaps that is why the narrative is usually so very convincing. It may also be why Quevedo's highly educated and sophisticated mind can sometimes be seen through the basic though intricate character of Pablos.

Part of the importance of *Lazarillo* lies in its being the first ever picaresque novel, quite different from the novel of chivalry, the literary type in vogue at the time. A novel of chivalry had a real hero, a very perfect gentle knight like Palmerín de Inglaterra or Amadís de Gaula, who lived in an unreal world, never had a base thought, idealized women, and performed incredibly brave (and impossible) deeds against ghastly odds. The style of these novels is wordy, the sentences long and relaxed, and the language sometimes deliberately archaic. But they were obviously very much read: when he wrote *Don Quixote* more than fifty years later, Cervantes found them a fit target for satire.

Three editions of *Lazarillo* date from 1554, and it is thought that there may have been an earlier one. The three appeared in Burgos, Alcalá (near Madrid), and Antwerp (then part of the Spanish Empire), and the book was immediately so popular that in 1555 a sequel appeared, *The Further Adventures of Lazarillo*. By 1560 a translation into French had appeared, and others followed into English, German, Latin, Italian, and Dutch. The first into English was by David Rouland of Anglesey, published in London in 1586. In 1559 the book was banned by the Inquisition, but in 1573 an amended version appeared which omitted some of the more violently anti-clerical comments as well as the tale of the pardoner and the account of the friar of the Order of Mercy.

Lazarillo is anonymous and has been attributed to many, but it seems most likely that the author was the versatile Diego Hurtado de Mendoza, satirist, poet, historian and humanist. But there are rival claims. One for a member of the famous Valdés brothers' circle, based on the supposed Erasmian quality of the anti-clericalism, was scotched by Marcel Bataillon, the great authority on Erasmian ideas in Spain. It was also once thought that the author might be a *converso*, a descendant of Jews turned unwilling Christian to escape banishment or death at the stake, but this thesis is not in favour now.

The story of the book concerns a small boy whose father dies in war after being banished by the law and whose mother, unable to support him, sends him off in the care of a blind beggar. In the service of this blind man he learns to bear hunger and exposure, and to look after his own interests. Later in the book, he acknowledges his debt to this master, whose cruelty forced him to desert, after taking appropriate revenge. The boy's only teacher is the blind man, unless one includes his next master, a priest in whose house only ingenuity keeps him alive. He soon finds himself attached to a penniless gentleman, and then really has to make use of what he has learnt. The gentleman's otherworldly pride brings still greater poverty to the poor boy who, instead of being supported himself, now has to support his master by begging. The author often plays on the irony of criticizing others without spotting one's own defects; the gentleman cannot see that, while he 'suffers for his honour what he would not endure for the sake of God', he is but a beggar at one remove. The author satirizes at the same time the traditional Spanish preoccupation, *quedar bien*: to impress, to make a brave showing in the world. No one can have failed to notice it who has been to Spain and seen how apparently poor people dress impeccably and spend their money freely.

Among the incidents which follow is one which, though barely mentioned, throws a great deal of light on Lázaro's character. He is given a steady job, but leaves it as soon as he has saved enough money, and goes looking for an easier life. So though he has 'never had a chance', we are not apparently to sympathize too much; his character has the flaw which makes him a true *pícaro*. *Pícaros* from later novels are sometimes born into respectable families, but none the less choose the criminal way of life (for instance Mateo Alemán's Guzmán, who recounts his life from a bench in the galleys). Others at least recognize their faults (as does Pablos – somewhat unexpectedly it is true – at the end of *La Vida del Buscón*). Lázaro does not spot his faults at all, but that is the author's particular irony, brought to a striking climax in the last chapter of the novel, where Lázaro marries the mistress of a priest and as a result is preferred to the post of town-crier. (The blind man had prophesied that he would have much to do with ropes and horns.) As town-crier he accompanies condemned criminals to their deaths, proclaiming their misdeeds. This is criticizing with a vengeance. But Lázaro himself is now a cuckold. In fact he is more than just a cuckold, more than a *mari complaisant*, he is what the Spanish call a *cabrón*, a man who permits his wife's infidelity not only shamelessly but for his own profit. It suits Lázaro very well not to know what is happening, and his treatment of the friends who try to warn him is brilliantly rendered. The irony pulls the threads of the novel together. It was Lázaro himself who was criticizing his

9

brother in chapter one: 'How many people must there be in the world who run away from others because they can't see themselves?'

Though the book's construction – particularly its conclusion – seems hasty, the unevenness is sometimes concealed by the story's inevitably episodic character and the racy terseness of its style. There are only about 20,000 words and every one of them counts. The descriptions are pithy and economical, the language colloquial though not ephemeral. This is artistry artfully concealed.

Is *Lazarillo* a true picture of contemporary Spain? Obviously the author will have selected his types for effect, but not all priests, pardoners, and so on, can have been alike. Besides, some of the incidents seem to derive from folk tales and other literary sources. Lázaro's own name is traditionally that of the poor boy. The unpleasant or hypocritical cleric (and the blind man is also a cleric in a sense, as his prayers were thought specially efficacious) was a well known figure in the literature of the time, and still is in the popular imagination. Anti-clericalism refuses to believe that a cleric can really live up to his vows. On the other hand, so popular a book must surely have accorded to some extent with fact, and history corroborates a lot of what the author says. We know that inflation caused by large imports of American silver was beginning to upset the economy, and that living without working was so easy that idlers and vagrants were legion. Local famine, as described in Chapter Three, was a common feature in a country frequently stricken by drought, and there is evidence that a great deal of free food was doled out by monasteries and convents. Formality and concern for social class and 'pure blood' (that is, no evidence of Moslem or Jewish ancestry) are illustrated in much of the literature of the time, as well as in the work of foreign commentators. Besides, that Spaniards are proud is a truism.

If *Lazarillo de Tormes* is the earliest picaresque novel, uncomplicatedly perfect but short, *La Vida del Buscón* represents the genre at its most amusing and stylistically sophisticated. There are others: *Guzmán de Alfarache*, which is something of a cautionary tale, *Marcos de Obregón*, and *La Pícara Justina*. None of them is as well known however, and of all of them *La Vida del Buscón* is the only one written by an already established author, worthy of individual introduction.

His full name was Francisco Gómez de Quevedo y Villegas. He was born in Madrid in 1580, and orphaned young. He was always connected with the court as his father had been secretary to the daughter of Charles V, later served the fourth wife of Philip II, and married a lady-in-waiting. He studied theology both at Valladolid and at Alcalá, not far from Madrid, where he obtained his degree. The scenes of student life in *El Buscón* are set at Alcalá. He was well versed in the classical languages, including Hebrew. He was a fecund writer and his poetical works, not to mention his prose, fill many volumes. He was both physically and mentally bellicose and by his early twenties had acquired a reputation for prickly humour. His waspishness made many enemies and in his lifetime many attacks on him were published. He attacked the imitators of the poet Góngora, scathingly criticizing their attempts to achieve his style, while only reproducing its difficulty without its poetic value. He carried on protracted lawsuits. In fact he was an aggressive man and not at all easy to get on with.

In 1606 when he was twenty-six, he returned to Madrid, where he had many powerful friends and enemies at court. Already in 1611, he had to move to Italy for a short time to escape the consequences of a duel in which he killed his opponent. He returned to the wars there in 1613. He was a close friend and colleague of the Duke of Osuna, Viceroy of Sicily, who sent him as personal ambassador to Madrid in 1615, where on behalf of the Duke, who had great political ambitions, he distributed vast bribes among influential courtiers. In 1618 he became a knight of the military order of Santiago. However, political intrigue eventually caught up with him in Venice, and he had to run for his life disguised as a beggar. His fortune came crashing down together with the Duke's, and in 1620, when he should have been at the height of his career, he was reduced to being governor of a provincial prison.

By this time, he had written a treatise on currency, several satirical poems, translations of Greek poets, an account of Stoic philosophy, and a translation of Epictetus. While he was prison governor he wrote a history of his times from 1613 to 1620, as well as comments on the death of Philip II in 1621. At the same time, he tried ceaselessly to ingratiate himself into court favour again. On the occasion of the attempt to marry the British Prince of Wales to a Spanish princess, in 1623, he circulated verses satirizing the official court poet, the Mexican born Juan Ruiz de Alarcón. He managed to accompany a royal party visiting Andalusian defences under threat of possible war with England, and in fact he lodged the king in his prison. In 1626 he went with the royal party on a tour of Aragón and Catalonia, and had his *Política de Dios, Los Sueños,* and *La Vida del Buscón* printed in Zaragoza.

But the enmity of powerful men caught up with him again, and he was exiled to his prison in 1648. It was there that he wrote his *Lince de Italia (Lynx of Italy)* in which he told much of what had happened in Italy. He thundered against the growing power of the King's favourites, especially the Count-duke of Olivares, and against unfair application of the law. One of his earliest poems had been 'Poderoso Caballero es Don Dinero' ('Mr Money is a very powerful gentleman'). In 1632, though, he was named royal secretary and offered the post of Ambassador to Genoa, which he refused. In 1634, at the age of fifty-four, he married. His wife was a widow named Esperanza de Mendoza, who was over fifty herself and had two children. They were not happy and soon separated, hardly seeing each other again before she died in 1642.

By 1639, when Quevedo was fifty-nine, Spain was reaching the depths of its much-discussed decline. Morally the court had reached its lowest point, though the outward forms were still kept up. Corruption was widespread among men in power, and Philip IV was either unable or unwilling to do anything about it. As a result of his writing, Quevedo was imprisoned in a monastery at León. He stayed until 1643, when one of the most determined of his enemies died. He was then sixty-three and prison life had greatly weakened him, but before he died he dictated the second part of a biography and composed some more poetry. He died at Villanueva de los Infantes in 1645.

Quevedo is famous mainly for his moral and satirical works, though he also wrote poetry in the style of his time, and translated from Greek, Latin, and Hebrew. His greatest achievements are his *Sueños* or *Visions*. They were published in 1627 although written much earlier. There are five: the *Vision of Judgement Day*, the *Bewitched Constable*, the *Vision of Hell*, the *World Inside*, and the *Vision of Death*. The *Visions* minutely analyse stupidity, ignorance, and evil, as these can be found in for instance bad poets, doctors, misers, innkeepers, corrupt officers of justice, bribable chaperones, immoral women, barbers, tailors, and bankers. The language is forceful, the wit caustic, the scenes macabre, and the images brilliant.

In these ways, *La Vida del Buscón* is similar to the *Visions*. Everything is just too real to be true. It was written in about 1608 when Quevedo was still young, though the first edition was not published until 1626. It was very successful and editions were published in Rouen (where there was a community of Castilian-speaking Jews), Brussels, and Lisbon, besides Spain itself. There were several translations of which the first in English appeared in 1657.

Like Lázaro, Pablos, the hero of *El Buscón*, comes from a criminal background, but unlike him, he is not sent away from home. On the contrary, his parents send him to school where he is taken up by a prosperous young nobleman. Like Lázaro, he has to learn to endure hunger, but when he goes to university in the company of his young master, he discovers that for him crime pays, though study probably does not. In due course he hears that a legacy from his father, who has been executed by his uncle, the public hangman, is waiting for him in Segovia, and he sets off on his own to claim it. He meets various people on the way. Most of them are very odd and Quevedo produces a series of amusing satires, some of them aimed at his personal enemies. Pablos, being a great snob and hypocrite, is ashamed of his uncle's profession and looks down on his drunken friends. He collects his money and quickly moves on, leaving an offensive letter and of course several debts behind him. He makes for Madrid, and on his way meets a character (very like the gentleman in *Lazarillo*) who devotes his life to seeming comfortably

13

rich without working. It is all make-believe, symptomatic of a Spanish preoccupation, *quedar bien*, reliance on past glory and bullion from Mexico and Peru, instead of expansion and work for future prosperity. Pablos learns from his new friend's companions how to impress by ingenuity and pretence, but when the whole group suddenly finds itself in jail, he buys his way out, deserts his friends and makes his way to the richest city in Spain at that time, and the centre of criminal activity: Seville, the only port allowed to trade with the Indies, and thus the city where all the treasure from America arrived. He travels with a company of actors, joins them, and makes quite a comfortable living as a playwright. But like Lázaro, he gives up work and goes looking for the easy life. The *pícaro* wants adventure, the spice of the forbidden, and he is quite happy to take a risk. Dullness and monotony are anathema to him.

The journey to Seville provides Quevedo with more fuel for scathing satire, but when Pablos finally arrives, he gets in with a crowd of cheating gamblers, takes up with a gambler's moll, and suddenly, as if to bring the book to a quick end, decides that sooner or later he will be caught. He plans to sail to South America with his girl-friend. So far, everything has gone well for him. Crime has paid, or at least, he has no cause to regret his criminal life. In a sense, therefore, the book would be immoral if Quevedo did not bring the story to an end, doubting whether his luck would last. No one's would, who thought he need only 'move his dwelling, without changing his life or ways'.

Unlike Lázaro, Pablos recognizes his faults, in fact he glories in his ability to cheat at cards, and deceive women into parting with their jewellery. But it strikes us quite strongly that while Lázaro, for most of the book, is quite an engaging character, Pablos is basically nasty. Even the author seems to have no sympathy for him.

La Vida del Buscón is better balanced than *Lazarillo de Tormes* and about three times as long. It shares of course the episodic construction of the earlier book (all picaresque novels are episodic), but the episodes run more smoothly. While *Lazarillo* begins when the hero is at most ten, ends when he is married, and at one point skips four years, *El Buscón* begins with Pablos about twelve and ends with him about eighteen, leaving no gaps. No chapter is disproportionately long or short, and time passes convincingly enough. *Lazarillo* has an almost classical starkness of description. *El Buscón* is much richer in content. There are striking character sketches, Dr Goat for example, but more striking still are the wealth of violent descriptive imagery, the puns, the conceits, and of course the scatological sordidness of the hero's misfortunes (he is always being thrown into ordure, or spat on, or treated as a chamber pot).

Translating these novels I was faced with several problems. Both books, though *Lazarillo* less so, are written in colloquial, racy language, interspersed with elegant literary mannerisms, and made up with considerable artifice. Previous translators I have read archaized the English to produce the impression that these early novels make on modern Spanish readers. I have tried to produce for English readers of today, the impression they will have made on Spanish readers of the time. For example, I have almost invariably used the contractions 'can't', 'shan't', 'wouldn't', 'haven't', etc. Actually, *Lazarillo* does not offer much difficulty and goes quite easily into colloquial English. *El Buscón*, on the other hand, bristles with problems. By Quevedo's time writers had abandoned Renaissance clarity, and made use instead of elaborate puns, conceits, obscure references, and similar literary artifice. The translator must reproduce these stylistic mannerisms in modern English, if he wants to convey the impression of the original. Present day English is normally much more concise than even modern Spanish, and the temptation is always to simplify. But I have fought against it, and if the translation is wordy in some places, so is the original. I have also tried hard to convey the sense of the puns, but what can one do for instance with a play on the words 'cardinal' and 'weal' which are the same in Spanish? Some parts of the novel are difficult for even Spanish commentators to interpret. I think the translator's responsibility is to provide an unbroken narrative for the reader, and not to make excuses. I hope that will placate, for instance, any specialist in seventeenth-century Spanish books on fencing, should he spot a mistake in the chapter where Pablos meets the fencing enthusiast. My consolation is that Quevedo was after all burlesquing these books' obscurity for the readers of his own day. Card games are also a difficult problem. In his fine translation of 1926, Charles Duff claims that the last chapter is virtually incomprehensible, but none the less he has done his best and not just left out – as previous translators had – what he did not understand. I have emulated Mr Duff and hope I have been able to produce as satisfactory a rendering. Proper names in *El Buscón* are sometimes meant to describe some characteristic of their owners: el Licenciado Cabra is an example. Cabra is not an uncommon surname in Spain, but it means goat, and that is rude in some contexts, so I think it better translated. Again, Pablos's uncle, the public executioner, is called Ramplón, which means rough, coarse, or crude, and fits Pablos's opinion of his uncle. So I have used the slang word yob, and made it look more like an English surname by adding an extra b. As a rule, I have tried to write modern colloquial English, but without being trendy. I have tried to avoid ephemeral vocabulary. Oaths and obscenities are a problem as Spanish uses them in profusion. I have tried to produce the same effect without being either crude or mealy-mouthed. I have certainly not been afraid to use four-letter words when I thought they were what the author intended. I have not been able to avoid the use of 'Jew' as a pejorative word but I think the modern reader will be aware that in seventeenth-century Spain the word was the ultimate insult, and that Judaism was very dangerous for anyone against whom it could be proved.

In the British Museum there are many translations of *Lazarillo*. The first, and most often published, was by David Rouland of Anglesey, which appeared in London in 1586 and was reprinted in 1596 and 1624. A translation of the spurious second part was made by Jean de Luna and published in London in 1631. The two parts were published together in translation in 1653, and between then and 1924 twelve editions of this or other versions appeared, an average of one every twenty years or so. Rouland's own version was edited in its turn by J. Crofts (Oxford, 1924).

La Vida del Buscón first appeared in English in a translation by 'a person of honour' in 1657 and 1670. The earliest in the British Museum is in a version of Quevedo's *Comical Works* by John Stevens produced in 1707. A further edition appeared two years later and another in 1742. In 1745 a version by Peter Pinneda was published, but it seems to me very like the one by Stevens. A *Complete Works* appeared in Edinburgh in 1798. The translation I have found most useful is the one by Charles Duff included in the 1926 revised edition of Stevens's *Humorous Works*. But in this edition archaic English is used and that is my excuse for offering a new version.

I should like to thank my wife for reading the proofs.

M.A.

Note on currency

The system in the sixteenth and seventeenth centuries was basically the following:

> Ducat=375 *maravedís* (this was about 9s. 8d. sterling)
> Escudo=330 *maravedís*
> Real=34 *maravedís*
> Cuarto=4 *maravedís*
> Blanca=½ *maravedí*

The *escudo* replaced the ducat in the sixteenth century and as it was gold it gradually increased in value until by Quevedo's time it was worth 440 *maravedís*. The doubloon was worth either two, four or eight (the famous 'piece of eight') *escudos* depending on a further description which we are not given where it is mentioned in the text.

(For the information in this note I am indebted to 'The Golden Century of Spain' by R. Trevor Davies, published by Macmillan, 1964.)

M.A.

Lazarillo de Tormes

‹‹–››

PROLOGUE

‹‹‹•›››

I THINK it's a good thing that important events which quite accidentally have never seen the light of day, should be made public and not buried in the grave of oblivion. It's possible that somebody may read them and find something he likes and others may find pleasure in just a casual glance; and as a matter of fact, Pliny says there is no book, however bad it may be, that doesn't have something good about it, especially as tastes vary and one man's meat is another man's poison. I say this because I think that nothing should be thrown away or given up completely so long as it's not really disgusting. I think everybody should have the chance to read it, especially if it's harmless and some benefit can be got from it. If we don't do this then we find very few authors who are prepared to write just for themselves. After all, it's not easy to write a book and if they go to the trouble they want to be rewarded, not financially but with the knowledge that their work is bought and read and praised if it deserves praise. And in connexion with this Cicero says: 'Honour encourages the arts.' Who thinks that the soldier who reaches the top of the scaling-ladder first hates life the most? No, of course he doesn't; it's desire for praise that makes him expose himself to danger and it's the same in the case of the arts and in literature. The new doctor of theology preaches very well and he's a man who only wants to help the immortal souls of his audience; but ask His Grace if it upsets him if people say to him: 'Oh, how well Your Reverence spoke!' So-and-so jousted very badly but gave the banner bearing his arms to the poet because he praised the way he used his lance. What would he have done if the praise had been justified?

Now it's the same in everything. In this childish little story I confess that I'm no better than my neighbour and it doesn't

23

worry me that anybody can read my story and enjoy it, if they do, even if it is written in a crude way. I think it's a good thing for them to know that there is a man alive who has seen so much disaster, danger and bad luck.

I beg Your Honour to receive this little gift from the author who would have written it better if his desire and skill had coincided. Your Honour has written to me to ask me to tell him my story in some detail so I think I'd better start at the beginning, not in the middle, so that you may know all about me. I'd also like people who are proud of being high born to realize how little this really means, as Fortune has smiled on them, and how much more worthy are those who have endured misfortune but have triumphed by dint of hard work and determination.

CHAPTER ONE

<<->>

W E L L, first of all Your Grace should know that my name is Lázaro de Tormes, son of Tomé Gonzáles and Antona Pérez, who lived in Tejares, a village near Salamanca. I was actually born on the River Tormes and that's why I took that surname and this is how it all happened. My father, God rest his soul, was in charge of a water mill on the bank of that river. He'd been there for fifteen years. My mother was there one night during her pregnancy, and her time came and she had me there, so I can say in fact that I was born on the river. Now when I was about eight years old they caught my father bleeding the sacks belonging to the people who came to have their crops milled there. So they arrested him, and he confessed, denied nothing and was punished by law. I hope to God he's in Heaven, because the Gospel says that people like him are blessed. About this time there was an expedition against the Moors and my father went with it. He was living away from home as part of his sentence, as a mule driver for a gentleman who went on the expedition, and he ended his life with his master like a loyal servant.

As my widowed mother saw that she had no husband and no protector she decided she would mix with respectable people so that she could become one of them. She came to live in the city, rented a house, and started to cook meals for students and to wash clothes for the stable-boys of the Comendador de la Magdalena. So she hung about the stables and she and a Negro, one of those who looked after the horses, got to know each other. He used to come to our house occasionally and leave in the morning. Sometimes he came to the door during the day, on the pretext of buying eggs, and came into the house. When he first started coming I was scared of him and didn't like him because of his colour and the way he looked, but as soon as I saw that when-

25

ever he came we ate better I began to take quite a liking to him, because he always brought bread, pieces of meat, and firewood to warm ourselves with in the winter. So he kept coming and staying with us and my mother gave me a baby brother, a very pretty little Negro, that I dandled and helped to keep warm. I remember my black stepfather was playing with the boy one day and the child saw that my mother and I were white and he wasn't. He was scared and ran to my mother and pointed to the black man and said:

'Mummy, bogeyman!'

He laughed and answered:

'Your mother's a whore!'

Although I was only a boy, I thought a lot about what my little brother had said and asked myself:

'How many people must there be in the world who run away from others in fright because they can't see themselves?'

It was just our bad luck that the relationship between my mother and Zaide (that was the Negro's name) came to the ears of his employer's steward who carried out an investigation. He found that Zaide was stealing about half the oats that he was given to feed the animals.

He 'lost' bran, firewood, curry combs, aprons and the horse-sheets and blankets; and when he didn't have anything else he removed the horseshoes. He brought everything to my mother for her to sell so that she could bring up my little brother. Seeing that love forces a poor slave to do this we ought not to be surprised that a priest robs his flock and a friar his convent for the benefit of his female devotees and others. The suspicions against him were proved and quite a bit more was found out because they threatened me to make me talk, and as I was only a boy, I was terrified and told them everything, even about some horseshoes which I had sold to the blacksmith on my mother's orders. My poor stepfather was whipped and basted with hot fat and the court sentenced my mother, not just to the usual hundred lashes, but never to go near the house of the said Comendador nor to have Zaide in her house after his flogging either.

In order not to make things worse than they already were, the poor woman made an effort and obeyed the court, and in order to avoid danger and get away from gossip, she went as a servant to the guests at the Solana inn; there she was put upon all the time but she managed to bring up my little brother until he was able to talk and me until I was a fine little boy who ran errands for the guests to get them wine and candles and anything else they cared to ask me for.

Round about then a blind man came to stay at the inn. Now he thought I would be the right kind of lad to set his feet straight on the road, and so he asked my mother to let him take me. She said that she would put me in his charge, and as I was the son of a good man, who had been killed for the greater glory of the Faith at the Battle of Las Gelves, I wouldn't turn out worse than my father. She begged him to treat me properly and care for me, as I was an orphan. He said he would and that he was taking me as his son, not just as his boy, and so I began to serve and guide my new master.

We stayed in Salamanca for a few days, but the takings didn't satisfy him, so he decided to go somewhere else. Just before we left, I went to my mother and we both cried. She gave me her blessing and said :

'I know I'll never see you again. Try and be good and may God guide you. I've raised you as best I know and I've put you with a good master. Now you must look after yourself.'

I went back to my master who was impatiently waiting for me. We left Salamanca and came to the bridge. As you get to it, there is a stone animal there which looks like a bull. The blind man told me to go up to it and then he said :

'Lázaro, put your ear close to the bull and you'll hear a loud noise inside it.'

I was so simple that I did just that, and when he felt that my head was against the stone, he straightened his arm and gave me such a blow that my head crashed against that blasted bull so hard that it hurt me for three days and more.

'You silly little nitwit ! You'll have to learn that a blind man's boy has got to be sharper than a needle !'

And he cackled with glee. At that moment I felt as if I had woken up and my eyes were opened. I said to myself : 'What he says is true; I must keep awake because I'm on my own and I've got to look after myself.'

We began travelling and in just a few days he taught me thieves' slang, and when he saw I was quite sharp, he looked very pleased. He kept on saying: 'I won't make you a rich man, but I can show you how to make a living.'

That was true because, after God, he gave me life, and though he was blind he revealed things to me and made me see what life was about.

I enjoy telling Your Lordship about these minor matters, because then I can show what a fine thing it is for a man of the people to rise in life and how awful it is to fall if you are highly placed.

Now, coming back to the blind man, I must tell Your Lordship that this world never saw anyone more astute or cunning. He was as sharp as a needle at his trade; he knew hundreds of prayers off by heart and he said them in a low, relaxed and sonorous voice which made the church vibrate; he put on a humble and devout expression and looked very respectable; he made no gesture nor faces, nor did he roll his eyes like the others do. Besides this, he had endless ways of getting money out of people. He knew prayers for lots of different things: prayers for women who couldn't have children, prayers for women who were pregnant, and prayers for women who were unhappily married, to make their husbands love them; he would also tell pregnant women if they were going to have a boy or a girl. In medical matters he said that Galen didn't know half as much as he did about toothache, fainting fits and morning sickness; and last of all, if anybody said he was suffering from anything at all, he said right away: 'Do this, do that, boil this herb, get that root.'

As a result everybody followed him around, especially women who believed everything he told them. He made a lot of money from these tricks and earned more in one month than a hundred blind men usually do in a whole year. But Your Lordship should also know that, even with all this money that he collected I never knew a meaner or closer-fisted man in my whole life; he almost starved me to death as he didn't give me even half what

I needed. It's a fact that if I hadn't used all my cunning and the tricks I knew, I would have died of hunger more than once: but for all his experience and craftiness, I caught him out so often that I always, or nearly always, got the most and best of what was going.

Of course, to do so I had to use all sorts of sharp practices. I shall tell you a few of them although I don't always come out of the story well.

He carried our bread and everything else in a canvas bag with a metal ring round its neck, which he kept padlocked. Whenever he put things in or took them out, he was so careful and counted everything so vigilantly that I doubt if anybody could steal a crumb from him; but I used to take the miserable scrap of food he gave me and gobble it up in two mouthfuls and when he had locked the bag and relaxed, thinking that I was doing something else, I used to unpick the bag, bleed it, and sew it up again, so I didn't get just my carefully measured-out piece of bread but good large pieces of bacon and sausage too: that's how I used to make him pay for the way he treated me.

Whatever I could filch or steal I carried in half *blancas* and, when people asked him to say prayers and gave him *blancas*, as soon as they offered the coin I grabbed it, popped it into my mouth and handed him a half *blanca*. However quickly he stretched out his hand I had already halved the value of the offering. Of course as soon as he touched the coin he knew it was not a whole *blanca* and he complained bitterly:

'What's going on? Ever since you've been with me I only get half *blancas* and before it was a *blanca* and often a *maravedí*! It must be your fault.'

He also shortened his prayer and only said half of it sometimes because I had instructions to tug his sleeve as soon as the person who had paid him had gone away. Then he would begin to shout again:

'Who wants this or that prayer?'

During our meals he used to put a jug of wine down next to him. I often used to take a couple of quick swigs and return it to its place without him hearing me. But that didn't last long because when he wanted to have a drink he soon noticed that some of it was missing and to keep his wine strictly for personal use he never let it go again but kept his hand round the handle all the time. But I had something even better than a magnet to attract the wine to my thirsty mouth and that was a long rye straw that I put into the mouth of the jug and sucked until he could say good-bye to his wine. But the old bastard was so sharp that I think he heard me and from then on he changed his plan and put the bag between his legs, covered it with his hand and drank his wine in peace. I had got used to the wine and was dying for a drink. I saw that the straw was of very little use in this new situation so I managed to make a little hole in the base of the jug which let out a thin jet of wine. I filled the hole very delicately with a wax plug. When we had our meals I used to pretend I was cold and crawl between the blind man's legs to get warm. We had a very small fire but gradually the wax melted in the warmth and the fountain began to spout into my mouth. You can be sure that what I missed wouldn't have satisfied an ant's thirst. When the poor old man wanted a drink there wasn't anything left in the jug. He jumped, cursed violently, swore at the jug and the wine and didn't have a clue about what had really happened.

'You're not going to say I've drunk it, are you, dad?' I said. 'You know you haven't let it out of your hand.'

He turned the jug over and over and round and round so many times that at last he discovered my little trick; but the crafty bugger didn't say a word and I thought I'd got away with it. The next day I was having a good swig at the jug as usual, without the slightest idea of the danger looming over me or that the blind man knew what I was doing. I was sitting in the usual position with my face turned heavenwards to receive those sweet drops. I had shut my eyes in order to heighten my pleasure. Then the pitiless old man saw that he had the chance to take his revenge and with all his strength he lifted the jug, which had been the source of pleasure and was now to be the instrument of pain, and from high over his head he let it fall straight on my mouth, helped with all the strength he could muster. Poor Lázaro wasn't expecting this; in fact he was relaxed and enjoying himself as before. I really felt as if the roof and everything on it had fallen right on me. The blind man's little tap was so hard that I was knocked right out and had bits of broken jug stuck in my face and was cut all over. My teeth were broken and that's why I haven't got any in my head today.

From that time on I had little time for the cruel old blind man. Although he made a fuss of me and treated me kindly, bandaging up my cuts, I could easily see that he had enjoyed his sadistic punishment. He washed the cuts from the jug with wine and said, smiling as he did it:

'What d'you know, Lázaro? The wine that caused all the damage is now making you healthy and well again!'

And he added a few other shafts of wit that didn't amuse me very much at all. When I had half recovered from the awful bashing I'd received and the marks were nearly gone I began to think that a few more 'taps' like that one and the cruel old blind man would get rid of me; so I decided to get rid of him first. But I didn't do it straight away as I wanted to be sure I'd come out of it all right. I really wanted to forget my anger and forgive him for hitting me so hard with the jug but he treated me so cruelly from then onward that I couldn't. He kept kicking me and pushing me away from him and hurting me for no reason at all. If anyone ever asked him why he treated me so badly up he'd come with the story of the wine-jug and say:

'Do you think this boy of mine is some innocent little angel? Well, listen to me and see if even the Devil could have thought out such a crafty trick.'

When they heard him tell the story they crossed themselves and said:

'Look, who'd ever think that such a little boy could be so bad?' And they laughed at the old man's revenge and said:

'That's right, you punish him. It's your duty and God will reward you.'

Of course when they said that, he didn't think of doing anything else. And so I always led him along the worst roads on purpose to make him footsore and to help him to fall down. I took him over stones if there were stones and, if there was mud, I took him through the worst and deepest part. Of course I had to lead him and got wet myself but to change a proverb, I enjoyed cutting off my nose to spite the eyes that he didn't have. He always kept the hook of his stick round my neck, which was bruised and skinned because of it. I swore I didn't lead him along the worst roads out of malice, but he was so sharp that he didn't believe me and my excuses weren't much use to me either.

Now, for Your Honour to realize just how crafty the blind man was, I'll tell you just one of the many things that happened to me in his company, and I think this will illustrate his sharpness well. When we left Salamanca, his plan was to go to Toledo, as he said that the people there were better-off, though not very generous. He relied on the proverb which says that a hard man will give more than a man who hasn't anything at all. On the road we travelled through the best towns. When he found a welcome and good takings he stayed. When he didn't, we cleared off on the third day. We came to a place called Almorox when they were harvesting the grapes and a picker gave him a bunch out of charity. As the baskets are often knocked about and the grapes are very ripe at that time of the year, the bunch began to fall to bits in his hands. If he put it into his bag it would turn to liquid and run over anything that came into contact with it. So he decided we should have a feast, not only because he couldn't carry the grapes but also to give me a treat as he'd been kicking me and poking me all day. We sat down in a little fenced-in field and he said:

'Now I want to be very fair to you and I suggest we share this bunch of grapes. You can have equal shares with me; we'll divide it like this: you take a grape and then I'll take one but you must promise that you won't take more than one grape at a time. I'll do the same until we finish them and so everything will be all fair.

We agreed to this and began. But on the second go the old bastard changed his ideas and began to take two grapes at a time thinking that I was probably doing the same. When I saw that he'd put on speed I wasn't satisfied just to follow him but drew ahead. From two at a time it became three. Soon I was cramming them into my mouth as fast as I could. When the bunch was stripped he sat there for a while holding the stalk; then he shook his head and said:

'Lázaro, you've been doing me. By God I swear you've been taking three grapes at a time.'

'I didn't, you know,' I said, 'but what makes you think I did?'

The crafty old man replied:

'You know how I spotted you were eating three grapes at a time? Because I was eating two at a time and you didn't say anything!'

I didn't reply. However I laughed to myself and marvelled at him.

We walked on and arrived at an inn. At the door there were lots of horns stuck in the wall for the mule-drivers to tie up their animals to. The blind man was feeling about to check that that was the inn where the innkeeper's wife paid him to recite the prayer of the walled-up nun every day, so he took hold of one of the horns and said with a great sigh:

'Oh, evil thing! You're even worse than you feel! How many men desire to put you on somebody else's head and how few want to have you or even hear of you at all!'

I heard him and said:

'What's that you're saying, dad?'

'Shut up, boy. One day this thing that I've got in my hand will give you an ill-deserved day's meals.'

'I won't eat it,' I said, 'and it won't give me anything.'

'It's the truth and you'll see what I mean if you live that long.'

So we went into the inn. I wish to God we'd never seen the place considering what happened to me there.

He said prayers for innkeeper's wives, wine-cellar women, nougat-sellers and prostitutes and all women of that type, but I never saw him say a prayer for a man.

But I don't want to go on and on so I'll miss out a lot of things which happened to me with this first master I had and which are quite funny when I look back on them. I'll tell you what made me decide to leave him, and finish with that.

We were still in Escalona, a town which belongs to the Duke of the same name, and he gave me a piece of sausage to fry for him. When I had basted the sausage and he had eaten the savoury grease, he took a *maravedí* out of his purse and told me to get some wine from the tavern. The Devil, who they say is often behind thieves, put temptation in front of my eyes. Lying next to the fire there was a long thin rotten turnip which must have been thrown away as not being good enough for the stewpot. We were alone and I was starving, and the savoury smell was about all I would get of that sausage, so I forgot about the consequences and drove out my fear of his anger. As the blind man groped for the money in his purse I took the sausage and swiftly put the turnip in its place in the pan. My master gave me the money for the wine and began to turn the pan around over the fire.

I went for the wine and wolfed the sausage in a flash. When I got back, I found him with the turnip in a fried bread sandwich. He had picked it up between the slices, so he did not know what it was yet. As soon as he bit into it, instead of biting into hot sausage, he got a shock and a mouthful of cold turnip. He started, and said:

'What's this, Lazarillo?'

'What are you starting on me for? You're not going to say it's my fault, are you? Haven't I been fetching you wine? Someone was here and pulled a fast one on you.'

'No, no!' he said, 'I didn't let go of the pan, it's impossible.'

I swore blind I had nothing to do with it, but it was no use. I couldn't hide anything from that evil old man. He stood up, seized me by the head, and bent down to smell me. He must have got the scent like a bloodhound, for to satisfy himself, and because he was so angry, he grasped me firmly, forced my mouth wide open, and thrust his nose down my throat. His nose was long and sharp and his rage had made it a lot longer so its tip touched my gullet. What with that, my terror and the brief space of time which had not let the sausage settle and most of all with the awful feeling of that enormous nose almost choking me, the deed and my greed were revealed and my master received his property back; for, before he could get his trunk out of my mouth my stomach was so upset that I brought it all up, and his nose and the half-digested sausage came out at the same time.

Oh God, I wished I'd been in my grave at that moment because I was certainly as good as dead! That perverse old blind man was so furious that he would have killed me for sure if the other people hadn't come running up at the noise. They got me out of his hands where I left most of the few hairs I had left on my head. His face was all scratched and so were my neck and throat. This he certainly deserved because of the cruel treatment that he'd meted out to me.

The cruel old man told everybody who came along how bad I was, and again and again he repeated the story of the jug of wine and the bunch of grapes as well as what had just happened. People laughed so loud that even passers-by came in to share in the festivities. The blind man recounted my tricks in such a funny way that although I was so badly knocked about and crying I thought it wouldn't be fair if I didn't laugh as well.

And during this period it occurred to me that I had been an awful coward and I was very ashamed of myself. Of course I should have bitten his nose off; after all I had plenty of opportunity as it was halfway down my throat already. All I had to do was clench my teeth and it'd have been all over. As it belonged to him my stomach might have been able to hold it better than the sausage. His nose wouldn't have had any say in the matter, that's for sure. I wish to God I had done it; it would have been a marvellous way of getting my own back.

The innkeeper's wife and the other guests treated me kindly and used the wine they had brought the blind man to wash the wounds on my face and throat. The blind man discharged a volley of funny remarks at this, saying:

'You know, this boy costs me more in washing in one year than I eat in two. I must say, Lazarillo, you ought to be more grateful to the wine than to your father because he only begot you once but wine's brought you back to life hundreds of times!'

And then he told them all the times he had knocked my head in and squashed my face and then cleaned up my wounds with wine.

'I tell you,' he said, 'that if anybody's going to be lucky with wine in this world, it'll be you!'

The people washing me thought this was very funny although I didn't share their sense of humour. But the old man was proved right and I've often thought of him since then. I'm sure he had the gift of foresight and I'm sorry for the way I played him up, although he was well-compensated in one sense considering that what he told me that day turned out absolutely true, as Your Honour will hear if he reads on.

When I thought about all this and the cruel way in which the blind man treated me, I made up my mind to leave him. I had already been thinking about it and this last episode made my mind up for me. This is what happened.

On the next day we went out begging. It had rained all the previous day and as it was raining again, he walked along under the arcades so as not to get wet; but night was coming on and the rain showed no sign of easing, so he said to me:

'Lázaro, it doesn't look as if it's going to stop and I think the darker it gets, the worse it will be; let's go back to the inn now.'

To do so, we had to cross an open sewer which was quite wide because of the rain. I said to him:

'Look, Dad, the water's wide but I can see a place further up where we can jump across without getting our feet wet, as it gets much narrower there.'

He thought that was a good idea and he said:

'You're bright, that's why I like you. Take me to where it's narrower because I don't like water much in the winter and I can't stand wet feet.'

Everything was just right, so I took him out from under the arcade and straight towards a pillar or stone post in the main square, on which the projecting roofs of the houses rested, and I said:

'Dad, this is the narrowest part of the ditch.'

As it was raining hard and the poor wretch was getting soaked, and because we were in such a hurry, and most of all because God (to grant me revenge) had blinded his good sense for that instant, he believed me and said:

'Put me straight and jump over first.'

I put him straight facing the pillar, took a leap and darted behind it like a bullfighter avoiding a charge, and cried:

'Now, jump as far as you can and you'll get over.'

I scarcely had time to say this before he reared up like a billy-goat and hurled himself as hard as he could, having taken one step back to give himself more impetus. He crashed head first into the post, which rang as if a pumpkin had hit it, and then fell back half dead with his head split open.

'What! You smelled the sausage and you couldn't smell the post? Olé! Olé! I jeered.

I left him in the care of a crowd of people who came out to help him and set off running to the town gates; before nightfall I was in Torrijos. I never found out what happened to him and I did not bother to inquire either.

CHAPTER TWO

—◄◄—►►—

I DIDN'T think I was very safe in that town, so the next day I went to a place called Maqueda, where for my sins I fell in with a priest. When I went up to him to beg for a few coppers he asked me if I knew how to serve at Mass. I said I did, which was true because the blind man had taught me hundreds of things, even though he did treat me badly, and this was one of them. So the priest took me on as his servant. Out of the frying-pan into the fire! I say this because, compared to this man the blind man was as generous as Alexander the Great, even though he was stinginess itself as I've already explained. All I can say is that all the money-grubbing meanness in the world had been collected into this single reverend gentleman. Mind you, I don't know if it was natural to him or whether he had assumed it when he first put on his clerical robes.

He had a very old chest which was securely locked; he kept the key tied to one of the laces of his cape. When he brought home the bread offerings from the church he used to open the chest, throw them in, lock it up again and fasten the key to his clothes. There wasn't a thing to eat anywhere in the house. After all there's usually something: a piece of bacon hanging up in the smoking room, a piece of cheese on a shelf in the pantry, or a basket with a few bits of bread left over from a meal. I felt that, even if I couldn't eat it, at least the sight of it would make me feel a bit happier. There was only a string of onions and that was under lock and key in a room at the very top of the house. My ration was one of them every four days. If I asked him for the key to go and get it, and if anyone was present, he used to put his hand into his inside pocket and untie the key very slowly and say as he gave it to me:

'Take it and bring it back straight away but don't indulge your greed too much.'

He said this as if the key could open the storehouse of all the fruit and vegetables in Valencia, although the room I've mentioned had damn all in it except the onions hanging on a nail, which he kept well-counted. If my sins had led me to take more than my ration it would have cost me dear. In the end, I was nearing my end from hunger. Actually, although he was very mean to me he was a lot more generous to himself. He spent five *blancas* on meat for his dinner and evening meal every single day. I must confess that he did share the gravy with me but as for the meat I had a hope! All I got was a piece of bread and I wished to God it'd satisfied half my hunger. In those parts, on Saturdays, they eat sheeps' heads and he used to send me to buy one for about three *maravedís*. He boiled it and ate the eyes, the tongue, the neck, the brains and the meat on the jawbones and then gave me all the bones he'd been gnawing on a plate and said:

'Take them, eat and be happy. The world's your oyster. You live better than the Pope himself!'

'I hope God gives you a life like mine one day,' I muttered to myself.

After I'd been with him for three weeks I was so weak that I couldn't stand on my two feet out of sheer hunger. I saw quite clearly that unless God and my common sense helped me, the next step would be the grave. I had no chance to use any of my tricks as there was no way I could attack him. And, even if I could, I couldn't take advantage of his blindness as I did with the other (may God pardon him if he died from the bang he gave himself against the post). He, though he was astute, didn't know what I was doing because he lacked that one precious faculty of sight. But this one! He was as sharp as a lynx. When we were at the offertory he noted every coin that fell into the collecting-box. He kept one eye on the people and the other on my hands. His eyes danced in his head like little balls of mercury. He knew exactly how many *blancas* had been collected and when the collection was finished, he took the box straight from me and put it on the altar. I didn't manage to nick a *blanca* all the time I lived, or rather died, in his company. I never brought him even a *blanca*'s worth of wine from the tavern but he made the little bit that had been left over from the offering and that he had put in his chest last so long that he didn't need any until the following week. To conceal his fantastic stinginess he used to say to me:

'Listen lad, priests have to be very temperate in their eating and drinking habits and so I don't make a pig of myself like others do.'

But the bastard lied in his teeth, because whenever we said prayers at brotherhood meetings or in houses of mourning he ate like a wolf at other people's expense and drank like a drayman. And, thinking of burials, God forgive me, I was never an enemy of the human race except then, and that was because we ate well and I stuffed myself at funeral feasts. I hoped and even prayed to God that each day should kill its man. And when we brought home the Sacraments to sick people, especially Extreme Unction, and the priest ordered those present to pray, you can be sure that I wasn't the last to begin, and that with all my heart and goodwill I prayed to the Lord not that He should do His will but that He should take the sick man from this world. If a sick man got better (God forgive me!) I cursed him over and over again, and I poured blessings over the head of anyone who died. In all the time I stayed with the priest, which would be about six months, only twenty people passed away and I'm sure that it was me who killed them, or rather that they died at my request. As the Lord could see my slow and painful death, I think He was glad to kill them to keep me alive. But still, even this wasn't much use to me because, if I lived on the day we buried someone, on the days when we didn't I suffered even more through having known what it was to have a full belly and having to go back to my daily hunger. So there was no solution except in death, which I prayed for sometimes for myself as well as for the others. But it did not come, although it hovered close.

I often thought of leaving that mean master, but I didn't for two reasons: one was that I didn't trust my legs because they were so weak with hunger. The other was that I thought it out and said to myself:

'I've had two masters. The first kept me half-dead with hunger and this one has almost got me into the grave with it. If I leave this one and find one who is worse, all I'll have left is to die!'

And so I didn't dare to move, as I was quite sure that every master would be worse than the one before, and if I went down one more step, the name of Lázaro wouldn't be heard in the world any more.

While I was in this awful plight, from which God deliver all good Christians, unable to take comfort from anything, and seeing myself going from bad to worse, one day when that stingy mean old bastard was out of town a tinker came to the door just on the off-chance. I think he was an angel sent by God in that guise. He asked me if there was anything to mend.

'There's plenty to mend in me and you'd have your work cut out if you repaired me,' I said quietly so that he didn't hear. But as I had little enough time to waste in making funny remarks, I said to him, enlightened as I was by the Holy Ghost:

'Look mate, I've lost a key that fits this chest and I'm afraid my master will give me a beating. Do me a favour, will you, and see if you can find one that fits in that bunch you're carrying. I'll pay you.'

The angelic tinker began to try one key after another from the huge ring that he carried around with him, and I helped him with my feeble prayers. When I was least expecting it I saw the bread in the box, and it was like the very face of God, as they say. I said to him:

'I've got no money to give you for the key. You'd better take your money in bread.'

He took one of the votive loaves, the one which looked freshest, gave me the key and went off very happy, leaving me even more so. But I didn't touch anything for the moment, as the priest would spot what was missing, and also because I saw I was such a rich man now that hunger wouldn't dare attack me. The priest arrived home and God was good enough to see that he didn't notice the votive loaf that the Angel had taken.

The next day as soon as he left the house, I opened my breadly paradise and took a loaf in my hands and then between my teeth and before you could say two credos I made it disappear. Of course

I didn't forget to shut the chest up again. Then I began to sweep the house out cheerfully thinking I knew the way to make my life easier from then onwards. But it wasn't in my stars for me to enjoy that short respite from hardship because after three days I was in trouble again as I saw my murderer at an unusual time bending over our chest turning the loaves over and over again and counting and recounting them.

I feigned innocence but secretly I prayed with all my heart:

'Saint John, blind him for me!'

After he'd spent a long time calculating, counting the days and loaves off on his fingers, he said:

'If I didn't have this chest so well protected, I'd swear that someone had taken some bread out of it; but just to set my mind at rest, from today onward I'll keep a very careful account of it. There are nine loaves and a bit left!'

'I hope God gives you the pox nine times!' I said to myself.

What he had said went through me like a hunter's knife and my stomach began to rumble with hunger as it saw that it was back on its old diet. He left and, to console myself, I opened the chest. When I saw the holy bread, I began to worship it, although I knew I could not receive it. I counted the loaves, just to see if by chance the bastard had made a mistake, but found his count far too exact for my liking. The most I could do to the bread was to kiss it over and over again and, as gently as I could, to scrape off a few crumbs from the loaf which had already been started on. I spent the day on that, not as happily as the day before.

But my hunger grew, even more so as my stomach had got used to having some bread those last two or three days, and I suffered horribly; so much so, that I couldn't think of anything to do but to open and close the chest and look at the face of God, as the children call it. But God Himself who succours the afflicted saw me in those straits and reminded me of a little trick. I thought for some time and then said to myself:

'This chest is big and old and broken here and there, though the holes are small. He might think that the mice have got in and eaten his bread. I can't take it all out as the miserable bugger'll see what's gone. He'll put up with this.'

So I began to crumble the bread on a few cheap cloths that were lying there. I took some and others I left so that I crumbled a bit off a few of them. Then I ate the crumbs like someone eating sweets and cheered up a little. When he came home, he opened the chest, saw the tragedy, and didn't doubt for a moment that it was mice that had done the damage, because I'd very carefully imitated the way they usually nibble. He examined the chest from top to bottom and saw a few holes which he suspected they had come through. He called me and said:

'Lázaro! Look what happened to our bread last night.'

I pretended to be very surprised and asked him what it could be.

'What can it be?' he said. 'Mice! They don't leave anything alone.'

We sat down to eat and, thank God, even this went well for me as I got more than my usual miserable bit. With his knife he scraped off all the bits that he thought the mice had gnawed and said:

'Eat this, the mouse is a clean animal.'

And so on that day I also ate by the work of my hands or rather of my nails and we finished eating. Mind you, I'd never really begun. But then I had another shock because I saw him searching around pulling nails out of the walls and looking for planks. Then he covered up and nailed down all the holes in the chest.

'Oh, my God,' I said then, 'how much misery and misfortune falls to the lot of your creatures and how short-lived are the pleasures of this vale of tears! Look at me! I thought I'd use this simple little remedy to cure my hunger and I was already cheerful and optimistic. But my bad luck wouldn't have it and it woke up my stingy bastard of an employer and made him even more sharp-eyed than he was already. In any case, misers never lack sharp minds. Now, as he closes up the holes in the chest, he's closing the door to my consolation and opening the one to my suffering.'

So I moaned to myself, while the dutiful carpenter finished his work with nails and pieces of wood.

'Now,' he said, 'my clever little rodent friends, you'll have to change your tactics because you won't do very well in this house.'

As soon as he went out I went to see what he had done and I found that he hadn't left a single hole in that miserable old chest even for a mosquito to get in. I opened it with my now useless key, without any hope of getting any benefit from it and I saw the two or three loaves I had started on, the ones that my master thought were gnawed by mice. I got a few crumbs off them, just touching them, like a skilled fencer. Still, necessity's a good teacher, so all the time, night and day, I thought of nothing but how to keep myself alive. I'm convinced that hunger was my guiding light in finding these solutions to my troubles. After all, they say it sharpens the wits, whereas a full belly does the opposite. Anyway it was certainly so in my case.

Well, one night I was lying awake thinking about this and how I could open the chest. I could hear that my employer was asleep because he snored and gasped when he was off. I got up very quietly. I'd already thought about my plan of attack during the day and left an old knife that I'd found knocking around in a place where I'd be able to find it again. I went to the chest and began working on it with the knife where it seemed to be weakest. I pushed the knife in like an auger. The chest was very, very old and had no real resistance in it; it was soft and worm-eaten and gave way at once, and allowed me to make a good hole in its side which would save my life. Having done this, I opened the wounded chest very quietly and felt around for the bread and scraped at it in the way I have already described. That cheered me up a bit. I closed the chest again and went back to my bale of straw, lay down and slept a bit, but very badly. I blamed this on my hunger. That must have been the reason because at that time even the worries of the King of France ought not to have stopped me sleeping.

The next day my master saw the damage that had been done to the chest and the bread as well. He began to curse the mice and say:

'I can't understand this at all. There've never been mice in this house before!'

I've no reason to believe he wasn't telling the truth because if there was any house in the kingdom that had the right to be free of mice, it was that one, because they don't usually go where there isn't a thing to eat. Again he looked for nails around the house and pulled bits of wood from the walls to stop up the hole. When night came and he was asleep I got up with my little knife and opened up every hole that he had stopped during the day. So it went on and we followed each other so quickly that we must have been the originators of the proverb which says, 'Where one hole is closed another opens.' In the end we seemed to be following the same plan as Penelope and her weaving because whatever he wove by day I tore at night. In a few days and nights we got the poor food-box into such a state that, if you wanted to describe it properly, you'd have to call it a suit of old-fashioned chain-mail rather than a chest, it had so many holes and repairs in it.

When he saw that his diligence was no use at all, he said:

'This chest is in such a bad state and the wood's so old and knocked about that any mouse can easily get through it. If things go on like this we won't have anywhere to put the bread at all. Then we'll really be in trouble, for although it's not much use now I'll have to spend three or four *reals* on a new one. None of my ideas up to now has worked, so I think the only thing is to fight these damn mice from inside.'

Then he got a mousetrap, borrowed, of course, and begged the neighbours for pieces of cheese-rind, and kept a trap baited all the time inside the chest. This was very helpful to me. Although I did not need anything to make the bread go down easier I still enjoyed the cheese-rind that I got out of the trap and apart from this the 'mice' still ate the bread.

When he found the bread gnawed and the cheese eaten, and yet the mouse that did it hadn't been trapped, he swore violently and asked the neighbours what it could be that could eat the cheese and get it out of the trap. The neighbours all agreed that it couldn't be a mouse because it would have fallen into the trap at least once.

'I remember,' said one neighbour, 'that there used to be a snake in your house, and that must be what's doing all the damage. It must be that because it's long and can get the bait, and even if the trap falls on it, it can easily get out as it's not completely under it.'

Everybody was quite convinced by what he said and my employer was very shaken. From then on he didn't sleep so soundly, and if he heard a worm moving in the night in the woodwork he thought it was the snake gnawing away at his precious chest. He got up at once and seized a big stick that he'd kept beside his bed ever since he'd been told about the snake and went to teach it a lesson. He woke the neighbours up with the noise he made and stopped me sleeping as well. He came up to my pile of straw and turned it over and over and me with it. He thought that the snake had come to me to wrap itself in the straw or in my coat, because he'd been told that those reptiles were cold at night and looked for warm places and often went into babies' cots and sometimes bit them and nearly killed them. Usually I pretended I was asleep and in the morning he'd say to me :

'Didn't you hear anything last night, boy? Well, I went after the snake, and I'm sure he goes to your bed to get warm as they say they're very cold animals.'

'Please God it doesn't bite me,' I said. 'I'm dead scared really.'

This matter kept him so agitated and sleepless that I must say the snake, or whatever it was, didn't dare gnaw at night or even go to the chest. But during the day, while the priest was at church or somewhere in town, I made my raid. He saw the damage and realized that he was quite helpless, so he kept walking around at night like a hobgoblin. I was afraid that one day his searching would reveal the key that I kept underneath the straw I slept on and I thought the safest thing would be to put it into my mouth before I went to sleep. Ever since I'd been with the blind man my mouth was as big as a bag because I often had fourteen or fifteen *maravedís* in it and all in half *blancas*. Even so, they didn't get in the way of my eating. I had no other way of keeping a *blanca* without that bloody old man getting hold of it, as I hadn't a pocket or patch in my clothes that he didn't search regularly. Well, as I said, I put the key into my mouth before going to sleep and slept without fear that my employer might find it in his nightly searches. Still, when disaster has to come there's nothing you can do about it.

My bad luck, or rather my sins, arranged that one night while I was asleep, my mouth fell open and the key worked itself into such a position that my breath passed over the hollow part of the key, which was like a small tube. I began to whistle very loudly, and of course my master, who was a bundle of nerves by now, heard me and was quite convinced that it was the snake hissing. It must have sounded very like it.

He got up very slowly with his stick in his hand and, following the hissing, he came up to me on tiptoe so as not to frighten away the snake. When he was close he was sure that the reptile was in the straw warming itself in the heat from my body. He lifted the stick high in the air, thinking that the snake was underneath and he'd be able to kill it with one mighty blow, and delivered such a crack on my undefended skull that he knocked me unconscious, bruised and bleeding.

Then he realized that it was me that he had hit because I gave a great yell at the unexpected blow: he told me later that he'd come up to me and shouted in my ear to try and bring me back to my senses. But when he touched me he saw I was bleeding badly and that he'd hit me pretty hard, so he ran off in a hurry to get a light. When he got back he found me groaning with the key still in my mouth, half hanging out, just as it might have been when I was whistling through it.

The snake-killer couldn't understand what the key was for. He pulled it out of my mouth and examined it carefully and soon saw what it was as the wards were exactly the same as the ones on his key. He went straight off to test it and proved his suspicions. The cruel hunter must have said to himself:

'Now I've found the mouse and the snake that persecuted me and stole my property.'

I can't say for certain what happened during the next two or three days because I was like Jonah in the belly of the whale; away from the world. But what I've just recounted I heard my master tell at length and often to anybody who cared to listen.

I recovered consciousness fully after three days. I was lying on the straw with my head all bandaged up and covered with creams and ointments. I was frightened and said:

'What's all this?'

The cruel priest replied:

'By God I've hunted down the mice and snakes that persecuted me!'

Then I looked at myself and realized what had happened to me.

Just then, an old woman who knew something about treating wounds came in and the neighbours began to remove the bandages and she dressed my wound. When they saw I had come to my senses they were very happy and said:

'As he's recovered consciousness, there's nothing wrong with him, thank God.'

Then they talked about my accident again and laughed like drains. I, sinner that I was, wept. Still, they gave me something to eat as I was half dead with hunger, but they could hardly satisfy me. So, little by little I got better and in a fortnight I was up and out of danger, but not out of hunger and so only half cured.

The day after I'd got up, my reverend master took me by the hand and put me outside the door and, once I was in the street, he said to me:

'Lázaro, from today on you're your own master. Look for a job and God be with you, for I don't want such a diligent servant anywhere near me. I can't find any way of combating your craftiness and I'm quite positive you couldn't have been anything else before you came to me than a blind man's boy.'

Then crossing himself as though I was bewitched by the Devil, he went into his house and shut the door.

CHAPTER THREE

<<->>

As a result, I had to bring forth strength from my weakness and, little by little, helped by generous people, I ended up in this noble city of Toledo. Here, thank God, after a fortnight my wound healed. While I was ill I could always rely on a hand-out, but when I got better everybody said:

'You, you're nothing but a scoundrel and a loafer. Go on, go and find somebody and get a job.'

'And where am I going to find somebody to work for,' I said silently, 'unless God creates somebody to work for as He created the world – out of nothing?'

As I was walking down the street, calling at every door and getting most of them shut in my face, because charity had not only begun at home but stayed there too, I chanced to meet a gentleman strolling along. He was quite well dressed, his hair was neat, and he looked pretty well-off. He looked at me, I looked at him, and he said:

'Boy, are you looking for a job?'

'Yes, I am, sir,' I said to him.

'Well, come along with me then,' he answered, 'and thank God for letting you come across me. You must have prayed very sincerely today.'

I followed him, thanking God for what I had heard the gentleman say. From this, and his clothes and bearing, I reckoned he was the sort of employer I needed.

It was in the morning when I met my third master and he took me around most of the city with him. We walked through the market where they sell bread and other food. I thought, in fact I even hoped, that he wanted to buy what was being sold and load me up with it. After all, that was the time when one usually bought what one needed for the day.

'Perhaps he doesn't like what they're selling here,' I said to myself, 'and he's going to do his shopping somewhere else.'

So we walked around until eleven o'clock. Then he went into the Cathedral and I followed him and I watched him attend Mass and the other divine services in a very devout way. He waited until everything was over and all the people had gone out. Then we left the church.

We began to walk down a street very slowly. I was as happy as could be when I saw that we hadn't bothered to buy anything to eat. I reckoned that this new master of mine probably bought his provisions in bulk and that dinner would be ready cooked just as I like and as, to tell the truth, I needed.

Then the clock struck one o'clock and we came to a house. My master stopped outside and so did I. He unslung his cloak from his left shoulder, took a key out of the sleeve pocket, opened his door and we entered my new home. The entrance was dark and so dim that it would frighten anybody entering it, although inside there was a little courtyard and quite large rooms.

When we were inside, he took off his cloak and after asking me if my hands were clean, we brushed and folded it. Then he blew the dust off a bench and laid the cloak on it. After this, he sat down by his cloak and asked me lengthy questions about where I was from and how I happened to be in that city. I didn't really want to tell him such a long tale because I reckoned it wasn't really the time for an interrogation but for ordering the table to be laid and the stew to be dished up. All the same, I satisfied him to the best of my lying ability about myself. I told him all the good things and didn't mention the rest, as I thought it wasn't very nice to mention them in a drawing-room.

When this was over he sat in silence for a while and then I saw something was wrong, as it was nearly two and he looked about as likely to be going to have a meal as a dead man. Next I thought about his keeping the door locked and about there not being a sign of anybody else living in the whole house. I hadn't seen anything but walls, not a chocolate grinder or a block for chopping meat or a bench or a table; not even a chest like the one the priest had. In fact the house seemed to me like a ghost's hideout. While I was working all this out, he said to me:

'Have you had lunch yet, boy?'

'No, sir,' I said; 'it wasn't eight yet when I met Your Honour.'

'Well, although it was quite early, I'd already eaten. If I eat early, you'd better know that I don't have anything else until nighttime. You'll have to make do as well as you can. We'll have supper later on.'

Your Honour can just imagine that, when I heard him say this, I almost fainted, not so much from hunger as from realizing that Fortune had its knife right into me. I thought of all my past suffering and wept over my hard life again. I remembered my thoughts when I was tempted to leave the priest. I'd said that, though he was a mean old bastard, I might meet someone worse. I cried bitterly over my wretched past life and the death that I felt was imminent. Yet this was all inside me and I hid my feelings as best I could and said:

'Sir, I'm a boy that doesn't worry overmuch about his belly, thank God. I've got the smallest stomach of all my friends and all the masters I've had up to now have thought very highly of me for that reason.'

'That's a great virtue,' he said, 'and I think more highly of you because of it. Stuffing oneself is natural for pigs but decent people eat with moderation.'

'Oh, I see,' I said to myself. 'To hell with the excellent virtues that all my masters have found in being hungry.'

I stood in the doorway and took a few pieces of bread from inside my doublet. I had them left over from what I had begged. When he saw me do that he said to me:

'Come here, boy. What are you eating?'

I walked up to him and showed him the bread. He took a piece of it from my hands. Actually it was the best and biggest of the three I had.

'I say,' he said. 'This bread looks pretty good.'

'I'll say it is. So you think it's good, do you?'

'Yes, very good. Where did you get it from? D'you think it's been kneaded by someone with clean hands?'

'That I can't tell you,' I said. 'But when I taste it it doesn't make me feel ill.'

'Well I hope not,' said my poor master.

51

He put it in his mouth and began to tear chunks out of it just as wolfishly as I did.

'It's very tasty bread, by God,' he said.

When I saw which way the wind was blowing, I got a move on because I saw that if he finished his piece before me he'd invite himself to help me out with what was left. So we both finished at more or less the same time. My master began to brush off a few little crumbs that had fallen on his clothes. He went into a little side room and picked up a jug that had a broken lip and looked very old. When he'd had a drink he invited me to do the same. I wanted him to think I was a teetotaller so I said:

'I don't drink wine, sir!'

'You can drink this,' he said. 'It's water.'

So I took the jug and drank some water, not much because thirst wasn't my main trouble. That's all we did until the evening. We talked about things he asked me and I replied as best I could. Then he led me into the room where the water jug was kept and said:

'Boy, just stand there and I'll show you how we're going to make the bed so you'll know how from now on.'

I stood on one side and he stood on the other and we made that terrible bed. Actually there wasn't much to make as there was only a framework stretched over some benches and on that he put the bedclothes. As they hadn't been washed very frequently, they didn't look much like a mattress, although that was what they were supposed to be. They had a lot less wool than any self-respecting mattress would have. We stretched the mattress out and pummelled it a bit to soften it, but that was near enough impossible because you can't make a silk purse out of a sow's ear. In fact it had damn all inside it because when we put it on the framework all the slats showed through and made the whole thing look like a side of very lean and skinny pork. On that pitifully thin mattress he put a blanket of the same family. I couldn't tell what its original colour had been. When we'd made the bed and night had come, he said to me:

'Lázaro, it's late and it's a long way from here to the market. And, besides, there are a lot of ruffians in the town who attack you and steal your cloak. Let's put up with being hungry tonight, and tomorrow God will provide. You see, as I live alone, I haven't laid in any provisions. Actually, lately I've been eating out, but of course we'll have to change all that now.'

'Don't bother yourself about me, sir,' I said. 'I know how to sleep one night and even more, if necessary, without any food in my stomach.'

'That's why you'll have a long and healthy life,' he replied. 'Because, as we were saying earlier today, there's only one way to a ripe old age and that's to eat little.'

'Well, if that's true,' I said to myself, 'I'll never die, because I've never been able to avoid following that rule and I expect I'll be unlucky enough to have to keep it all my life.'

He went to bed, using his breeches and his doublet as a pillow. He told me to lie down at the end of the bed, which I did. But I didn't get much sleep, as the wooden slats and my bones quarrelled violently all night long. That's not surprising because there wasn't an ounce of flesh on my body, what with the starvation and hardship I'd suffered. In any case I'd eaten hardly anything that day and hunger and sleep don't get on very well together. I cursed myself over and over again, God forgive me! I raged at my rotten luck most of the night. The worse thing was that I begged God to do away with me more than once. And all this I did without tossing about, as I was afraid to wake him.

When morning came we got up and he began to brush and dab away at his breeches, his doublet, his coat and his cloak. I acted as his valet. He dressed very slowly and solemnly. I poured water over his hands; he combed his hair and put his sword into his belt. As he did this he said to me:

'You don't realize, lad, what a fine weapon this is! I wouldn't sell it for its weight in gold. Of all the swords that the famous Antonio of Toledo made there isn't one as well-tempered as this one.'

And he took it out of the scabbard and tested it with his finger and said:

'See this? I bet I could cut straight through a ball of wool with it.'

'I could bite through a whole loaf,' I said to myself, 'and my teeth aren't made of steel.'

He sheathed his sword again and hung a ring of large rosary beads from his belt. He walked out of the door, dignified and erect. His demeanour and gait were proud and noble. He threw one end of his cloak over his shoulder and then under his arm. He rested his right hand on his hip with a swagger.

'Lázaro,' he said as he left, 'look after the house while I go and hear Mass. Make the bed and go and fill the water-jug at the river which is just down the slope at the back. And mind you lock the door when you go; I don't want to find anything missing when I come back. Put the key in the crack so that I can get in if I get back when you're out.'

And he walked up the road so proudly and with such a swagger that anybody who didn't know him would have thought for sure he was a near relative of the Count of Arcos, or at least his personal valet.

'Blessed art thou, O Lord,' I stood there saying, 'you send the illness and then the medicine. Who could meet my master and not think, seeing how pleased he looks, that he has had a good supper and slept in a comfortable bed and has had one good meal already today although it's early in the morning: you have great secrets, O Lord, unknown to common people. Who would not be deceived by his demeanour and his smart cloak and jacket, and who would think that that noble gentleman spent all day yesterday without taking a bite of food except that crumb of bread that his servant Lázaro had carried for a day and half under his shirt and where it couldn't have kept very clean, and today, when he washed his hands and face and didn't have a towel, he used his shirt-tail? Nobody would dream that was the case. And how many men like him must be scattered around the world, who suffer for the sake of their ridiculous honour what they certainly wouldn't suffer for Your sake?'

I stood there like that at the door, watching him and thinking about these things, until my master crossed the long, narrow street. Then I went back into the house and went right through it, upstairs and down, in a twinkling, without stopping or finding anything to stop for. I made that ghastly bed, took the jug and went down to the river where I saw my master in a field talking very animatedly to two veiled women. They looked as though they belonged to the profession that isn't in short supply round there. In fact many of those women have the habit of going down in the mornings to the riverside to relax and have an early lunch without taking provisions. The river bank is very cool and they're always sure of finding someone to give them lunch as the worthy gentlemen of the city are well aware of this custom.

Anyhow, as I said, he was acting like a real lover-boy, chatting them up better than Ovid. When they saw he was a soft touch they were brazen enough to ask him for the price of lunch on the usual terms. As his purse was as empty as his desires were full, he started to go hot and cold and went as white as a sheet. He began to stammer and make all sorts of excuses. They were pretty experienced and saw what was the matter with him, so they left him for what he was.

I was eating a few old cabbage stumps which was all I could find. Then, very diligently as a new servant should, I went back home intending to sweep the place. It certainly needed it but I couldn't even find a broom. I began to think of something to do. I thought I'd wait for him until midday to see if there was any chance of his coming and bringing something to eat but I waited in vain.

When I saw it was two o'clock and he hadn't come home and I was ravenous, I locked the door and put the key where he'd told me to and attended to my needs. I put on a quiet and weak-sounding voice, folded my hands over my breast, looked as if I were gazing at God and never let His name leave my lips and began to beg bread at the doors of the houses which looked the richest. I'd sucked this trade in with my mother's milk, I mean I'd learnt it with the blind man: I had learnt the art so well that, before four o'clock, I had four pounds of bread stored inside my body and more than two hidden in my sleeve and under my shirt; and this in a poor year and in a city where people don't give much away! I went back to the house and as I passed a tripe shop I asked one of the women to give me something and she let me have a piece of cow's foot and a few pieces of boiled tripe.

When I got back, my master was already there, with his cloak neatly folded and on the bench. He was walking up and down the yard. When I came in he came straight up to me. I thought he was going to tell me off for coming home so late but God punished me worse. He asked me where I had been and I said to him:

'I stayed here till two, sir, and when I saw that Your Honour wasn't coming I went into town to call on people and this is what they gave me.'

I showed him the bread and the tripe that I was carrying in the skirt of my coat. He brightened up at the sight of it and said:

'Well, I waited for you to come back for lunch and when I saw you weren't coming, I ate on my own. But you've behaved very decently I must say; after all, it's better to beg than to steal. I only hope God will help me through you as he sees fit. But there's one thing I want you to remember: nobody must know that you're living with me, it's a question of my honour you see. Mind you, I don't think anybody will find out as I'm hardly known in this town. I wish I'd never come here!'

'You can stop worrying about that, sir,' I said. 'If anybody asks me who I am I'll tell him to go to hell and I certainly shan't open my mouth about you.'

'All right then. Come on, eat, you wretch. This way, please God, we'll soon be out of trouble. Still, I can tell you that nothing's gone well for me ever since I came to live in this place. It must be cursed; there are unlucky houses, you know, which bring bad luck to anyone who comes to live in them. This must be one of them. I'll tell you something: when this month's over I wouldn't stay here even if they gave it to me rent free.'

I sat down on the edge of the bench. I didn't want him to think I was greedy, so I didn't tell him I'd already eaten quite a lot of what I'd been given. I began to bite into the tripe and the bread and watched my poor master out of the corner of my eye. He couldn't keep his eyes off the skirts of my coat which I was using as a plate. I hope God takes as much pity on me as I did on him, because I felt for his suffering as I had often endured it and still endured it most days. I wondered if I could go as far as inviting him to share. However, he'd said he'd already had his lunch, so I thought he'd probably refuse my invitation. In the end, I was wanting the poor devil to satisfy his hunger with the results of my begging. I wanted him to eat as he had the day before. After all, the food was better and I myself wasn't so hungry. God granted my wish and his own, I think, because when I began to eat and he began to walk up and down, he came up to me suddenly and said:

'You know, Lázaro, it's a real pleasure to watch the way you eat. Anybody watching you can't help feeling hungry even if he isn't really.'

'Why don't you come out straight with it?' I said to myself. 'You're starving.'

Still, I thought I ought to help him. He was helping me and showing me the way to invite him, so I said:

'Sir, they say that good tools make a good workman. This bread is really very tasty and the cow's foot is very well cooked and seasoned. Anybody's mouth would water at its smell.'

'Cow's foot, is it?'

'Yes, sir.'

'You know, that's the tastiest thing I know. I'd rather have that than pheasant any day.'

'Well, have a piece, sir, and you'll see how good it is.'

I put the cow's paw into his and three or four pieces of the whitest bread and he sat down beside me and began to eat as if he meant it, gnawing every little bone like a dog.

'This exquisite dish,' he said, 'has been made with garlic sauce.'

'You've got more sauce than the meat has,' I said to myself.

'God, it tastes so good that I feel I haven't eaten anything else today.'

'I hope I drop dead right here if you have,' I said to myself.

He asked me to get the water-jug and when I brought it it was as full as when I had come back from the river. That told me quite clearly that he hadn't eaten very much that day. We drank and went to bed very happily.

I don't want to go on too long so I'll tell you that we lived like that for about ten days. He, the old faker, used to go off pompously in the mornings to swagger down the road and poor Lázaro did his dirty work for him. I often thought about my life. I'd escaped from two previous cruel masters to try and find something better, and now I'd ended up with one who not only didn't feed me, but I had to feed both of us !

Even so, I was quite fond of him because I saw he owned nothing and couldn't do anything more. In fact I felt rather sorry for him. Quite often I myself went without to see he had a full belly. One morning he got up in his nightshirt and went to the top of the house to relieve himself. Just to make sure that he was as poor as he seemed, I shook out the doublet and breeches that lay folded at the head of the bed and found a little purse of smooth velvet folded over and over again. There wasn't a copper in it or any trace of one having been there for a very long time.

'This man,' I said, 'is poor and nobody can give what he hasn't got. But the stingy blind man and the evil priest, God gave them both plenty, one for his job and the other for his quick tongue; they nearly starved me to death and I was right to leave them, just as I'm right to take pity on this one here.'

As God is my witness, whenever I meet one of those gentlemen today, walking along as if he owns the place, I'm sorry for him and wonder if he's going through what my master suffered. Even though he was poor I enjoyed serving him more than any of the others for the reason I've given. There's only one thing I had against him; I wished he wasn't quite so vain and that he would come down to earth and face facts a little more. Still, as far as I can see; this sort of people have an old and well-kept rule. They may not have a penny in their pocket but they've got to keep up appearances. There's nothing anybody can do about it. They're like that until they die.

Well, that's how things were and I was living like that when my bad luck, which never seemed to leave me alone, put an end to that hard and shameful life. This is what happened: that year there had been a poor harvest and the Town Council decided that all poor people who weren't natives of the town should leave. The town crier announced that anybody who was found there would be whipped. The law took its course and, four days later, I saw a procession of poor devils being whipped around the main streets. That scared me so much that I didn't dare beg any more.

You can imagine, if you've any imagination at all, what we

went through and how miserable and silent we were. Sometimes we went two or three days without eating a thing or saying a word. I was fed by some women who worked at spinning cotton in their homes. They made hats and lived next door and I knew them quite well. They let me share the pittance they earned and I just about kept body and soul together.

Still, I wasn't half as sorry for myself as I was for my poor devil of a master who didn't eat as much as a piece of bread in a whole week. At least, I can assure you we didn't have anything to eat at home. I haven't the slightest idea what he did, where he went or what he ate, if anything. And what a sight it was to see him walking down the street at lunch time, walking with his head so high, and so skinny that he looked like a pedigree greyhound! And to satisfy that ridiculous honour of his he took a straw (there weren't even enough of them in the place) and went and stood in the doorway picking his teeth which had nothing stuck between them. He still complained about his mansion and said:

'It's quite clear there's a curse on this place that's bringing us all this bad luck. You can see how dark and miserable it is. So long as we stay here we'll suffer hardship. I'm only waiting for the end of the month to come so I'll be able to get out.'

Now one day when we were really starving and desperate, by some fantastic piece of luck my master got hold of one *real*, and he brought it home and showed it to me as proudly as if it had been the fabulous treasure of the Venetian republic. He gave it to me, smiling broadly, and said with a laugh:

'Go on Lázaro, take it; God's being kind to us at last. Go down to the market and buy bread and some wine and meat. We'll spit in the Devil's eye! I'll tell you something else that'll make you happy; I've rented another house and we don't have to stay in this bloody place after the month is up. I hate it and the first builder who put a slate on the roof. Things have gone badly for me ever since I've lived in it. By God, ever since I've been here, I haven't had a glass of wine or a piece of meat or any peace of mind and it's so miserable and dark and depressing and gloomy! Go on, and don't take too long about it. We'll eat tonight like royalty.'

So I took my *real* and the jug and got a move on and began to run up the street towards the market. I was really very happy. But what's the use? It's my fate that anything good that happens to me must always come together with trouble. And that's what happened this time.

I was walking up the street, thinking how to spend the *real* so as to get the best value, thanking God that in His infinite mercy He'd given me a master who had money. When I was least expecting it, I suddenly came face to face with a dead man being carried down the street on a stretcher with a lot of priests and people. I pressed myself against the wall to give them room to pass and as soon as the body had gone by, along came a woman behind the cortège who must have been the dead man's wife. She was accompanied by a lot of other women and she was crying and shrieking out:

'Oh my darling husband, where are they taking you? To the sad and accursed place, to the gloomy and dark dwelling, to the domain where there is no food or drink!'

When I heard that I nearly collapsed and said:

'Oh, Jesus Christ, they're taking the corpse to my house!'

I broke off my trip to the market and pushed through the procession. I ran down the street as fast as I could towards my house and when I got there, I shut the door violently and begged my master to protect me and defend the entrance. In my fear I clung to him.

He hadn't the slightest idea what I was making such a fuss about and said to me:

'What's the matter with you, lad? What are you shouting for? Why did you shut the door with such a bang?'

'Oh, sir,' I gasped. 'Come and help me. They're bringing a dead man to the house.'

'What are you talking about?'

'I saw it up the street. His wife was shouting: "Oh, my darling husband, where are they taking you? To the dark and gloomy house, to the gloomy dwelling of despair, to the abode where they neither eat nor drink!" They're bringing him right here, sir.'

I can tell you that, although he didn't have much reason to

laugh, when my master heard me say that, he went into such a fit that he couldn't speak for quite a long time. By this time I had shot the bolt and was leaning up against the door to make it more secure. The people passed on with their corpse but I was still afraid that they were going to bring it into our house. As soon as my master was tired of laughing and remembered that he was hungry, he said to me:

'Actually you were quite right, Lázaro, to think what you did when you heard the widow shouting that. But things haven't turned out so badly after all, so come on, open up and go and get something to eat.'

'Please, Sir,' I begged, 'let them turn the corner of the street.'

In the end my master came up to the street door. He pushed me out of the way and opened it. He had to push me because I was still terrified out of my wits. Off I went for food. We ate well that day but I didn't enjoy the food a bit and it was a good three days before I felt all right again. Every time my master remembered what I had imagined he roared with laughter.

So I lived with this my poor third master, the gentleman, for the next few days. All the time I was with him I was dying to know why he had come to that part of the country and what he was doing there, because, from the first day I met him, I knew he wasn't from those parts. He didn't know anybody and had no friends among the townspeople. At last my curiosity was satisfied and I found out what I wanted to know.

One day, after we had eaten quite well and he was feeling pleased, he told me about his affairs and said he came from Old Castile and that the only reason he had left his home was so as not to have to raise his hat to a gentleman who was his neighbour.

'But sir,' I said, 'if he was what you say and was higher than you, weren't you wrong in not taking your hat off first? After all, you said that he took his off as well.'

'Yes, he was a gentleman and he was higher than me socially and he did take his hat off to me. Still, I took mine off to him first so many times that it wouldn't have been a bad idea for him to take the initiative and beat me to the post just once.'

'I think that I wouldn't have bothered about that, especially with people who are more high-class than myself.'

'You're just a boy,' he replied, 'and you don't understand the point of honour. That's all that decent men have left today. I'll admit that I am, as you see, just a country squire. But, by God, if I meet a count in the street and he doesn't take his hat off to me, and properly too, then the next time he comes along, I'll duck into a house and pretend I have some business there, or I'll cross the road, if there is one. I'll do anything so as not to take my hat off to him. You see, a gentleman owes nothing to anybody except God and the King and it's not right for a gentleman to sacrifice any of his proper pride. I remember once at home I spoke sharply to a carpenter and nearly laid hands on him because every time he saw me he said: "God be with you, Your Honour" "You peasant scum," I said to him, "'God be with you,' you say to me, as if I were anybody?" and from then onwards he spoke to me properly and took off his hat as he ought.'

'But isn't it right for one man to greet another by saying "God be with you"?' I asked.

'You haven't got much idea,' he said. 'That's what you say to ordinary people, but high-class people, like me, we've got to be greeted by "I kiss Your Honour's hands" or at least, "I kiss your hand, sir," if the man who is speaking to me is a gentleman himself. So I wasn't going to put up any more with that peasant who wished God on me all the time and I wouldn't and I shan't put up with it from anybody at all from the King downward. Just let them try to say "God be with you".'

'So help me,' I said, 'that's why God doesn't care about you. You don't want anyone to ask Him to!'

'In any case,' he resumed, 'I'm not so poor that I haven't got a few houses at home. They're fallen down and are in a terrible state, but if they weren't they'd be worth more than two hundred thousand *maravedís*. They're twenty leagues away from where I was born, in the Main Street of Valladolid. They could be built up again and made to look absolutely magnificent. I've also got a dovecot which would give me more than two hundred pigeons every year if it weren't in ruins. I've got many other things that I won't bother to mention. I left them all because it was a question of my honour. I came down to this city, hoping to find a good position, but unfortunately things haven't gone as well as I ex-

pected them to. I can find plenty of canons and ecclesiastical
gentry, but they're very unimaginative and nobody can make
them change their ways. I'm often asked to be the right-hand man
of minor noblemen, but it's very hard working with them because you're no longer a man, just a thing they use. If you don't
do what they want then it's "Good-bye to you". And more often
than not your pay is in arrears. The worst thing of all is that you
have to be satisfied with your keep and forget about wages. When
they feel conscience-stricken and want to reward you for all the
work you have put in on their behalf, you are paid in the old
clothes' room with a sweaty doublet or a worn-out jacket or cloak.
And even if you get a job with a titled lord you still go through
the mill. Do you think I couldn't serve and satisfy one of them?
Well, by God, if I could find one I'd be indispensable to him and
he'd have to tell me all his secrets. I could tell him lies as well as
anyone else and flatter him all the time. I'd laugh at his jokes
and his little habits even if they weren't the best in the world.
I'd never say anything that might annoy him even though it
would be for his good. I'd be very diligent in whatever I said or
did regarding him. I wouldn't kill myself to do things well unless
he was going to see them and I'd tell the servants off, where he
could see me, so I'd seem to be very concerned about anything
to do with his comfort. If he was arguing with a servant, I'd
know how to slip in some malicious remarks to annoy my employer and show the servant up. I could speak pleasantly if he
liked that and make inquiries and find out about other people. I
could give him a full account of them, and of lots of other fine
things that go on in rich men's houses these days. Rich men
like this and they don't want honest men in their houses; in
fact they hate and despise them and call them stupid and say
they're not men of the world and that a gentleman can't relax
when he's in their company. So, as I've told you, clever men
these days make the best out of their employers and that's what
I would do if I could find somebody; but it's just my bad luck
that I can't.'

So my master grumbled about life because it was always against
him and told me what a fine fellow he was.

Now at this part of my story a man and an old woman walked

into the house. The man asked for the rent of the house and the woman for the hire of the bed. They counted up what he owed them at two months each and came to a sum that he didn't make in a year; I think it was a matter of twelve or thirteen *reals*. He gave them a very good answer; he said he'd just walk down to the market to change a doubloon and would they mind coming back in the evening? But he did a flit. They did come back later on, but it was too late. I told them he hadn't come back yet. Night came but he didn't and I was scared of staying in the house by myself. I went to our neighbours, told them what had happened and stayed the night there. The next day the creditors came back and asked for him at our door. The women replied:

'Look, here's his servant and the key of the door.'

They asked me where he was and I said I didn't know and that he hadn't come back after going out to get change for the doubloon. I said I thought he'd left all of us in the lurch and gone off with the change. When they heard this they went straight off for a constable and a clerk. Back they came with them, took the key, called me, got witnesses, opened the door and went into the house to put a lien on my master's property until he paid the debt. They went over all the house and found it quite bare, as I have said. They called me:

'Where's all your master's property? Where are his chests and the wall-hangings and his furniture?'

'I haven't the slightest idea,' I answered.

'There can't be any other explanation,' they said. 'They must have packed it all up last night and taken it somewhere else. Constable, arrest the boy, he knows where his master is.'

Up came the constable and grasped me by the collar of my doublet.

'Boy,' he said, 'it's the nick for you if you don't tell me where your master's hidden his property.'

I'd never seen myself in such a mess before. It's quite true I'd been grabbed by the collar many times, but gently, to show the blind man the way. This time I was very scared and began to cry. I promised to tell them what they wanted to know.

'Right,' they said, 'tell us everything you know and don't be afraid.'

The clerk sat down on the bench to make out the list and asked me what my master possessed.

'Sir,' I said, 'my master has, according to what he told me, a streetful of houses and a broken-down dovecot.'

'Very good,' they answered. 'However little it's worth, it's enough to pay off what he owes us. And whereabouts in the city are they?'

'In the place where he comes from,' I answered.

'Oh God, that's marvellous. And where does he come from?'

'He told me he comes from Old Castile,' I said.

The constable and the clerk laughed heartily at this and said:

'Oh, yes, that's quite enough information to get your debt. Mind you, we could do with more.'

My neighbours were there and said:

'Look, this boy is quite innocent. He's only been with the man for a few days and he doesn't know any more than Your Honours about him. In fact the poor little devil comes to our house for his food and we give him what we can out of charity's sake. At night he used to go back to the house to sleep, that's all.'

Then the clerk asked the man and the woman for their fees and over that there was a long argument and a great row; they claimed they weren't obliged to pay as there was nothing to pay with and there was no lien made. The others claimed that they had given up another important matter to attend to this one. In the end, after they had all shouted a great deal, a rag and bone man loaded himself up with the old woman's mattress although it was no great load as I knew from experience. They all went off shouting at the tops of their voices. I think the dirty old mattress paid off all the debts and it served it right. When it deserved to be at rest for all its past labours it was working hard again.

And that's how my poor third master left me. Now I was convinced of my tragic destiny and saw that everything was against me. All I did was upside-down, because masters are usually left by their servants but with me it was the opposite: he left me, in fact he deserted me.

CHAPTER FOUR

＊←→＊

I HAD to find a fourth employer and he turned out to be a friar of the Order of Mercy. The women I mentioned recommended me to him as they said he was a relative of theirs. He wasn't interested in singing in the choir and he wouldn't eat in the monastery. He loved going out and worldly affairs and visiting people. I think he wore more shoes out than the rest of his community put together. He gave me the first pair of shoes I ever went through in my life. They didn't even last me a week and I couldn't take the running around any more. I left him because of that and also because of one or two other things that I'd rather not mention.

CHAPTER FIVE

◄─►

THE fifth master that I chanced on was a man who sold papal
indulgences and I never saw anyone more adept or shameless in
my life. He sold more than I ever saw or think or hope I'll see
again. He had studied the salesman's art and he knew some really
clever tricks.

Whenever he came to the place where he wanted to sell his
indulgences, first of all he gave the priests and other clergy a few
little presents. They weren't worth very much: a Murcian lettuce,
if they were in season, or a couple of limes or oranges, a couple
of extra large peaches or a big green pear each. That is how he
used to make friends with them so that they would help his
business and summon their parishioners to buy the indulgences.

When they thanked him, he found out how well educated they
were. If they said they knew Latin then he never said a word in
that language so as not to put his foot in it. He used a Castilian
which was well-turned and elegant and spoke very fluently. If
he found out that the clergy were just reverends and, because
they had more money than education, had been ordained without following a proper course, then you'd think he was St Thomas
Aquinas. He would talk in Latin for two hours. Of course it
wasn't Latin but it did sound like it.

If people wouldn't buy the indulgences when he tried to sell
them honestly, then he tried dishonestly. He would make trouble
for everybody or else he would resort to some very crafty tricks.
It would take me a long time to tell you everything I saw him do
so I'll tell you about something very funny and also effective
which will show his abilities quite clearly.

He'd been preaching in a village near Toledo for two or three
days, trying as hard as he usually did and hadn't sold a single
indulgence and it didn't look as if anyone had any intention of

buying one. He was fed up with it and began to think of something to do. So he decided to summon the whole village the next day to try to place his goods.

That night, after supper, he and a constable began to gamble. They quarrelled over the game and abused each other. He called the constable a thief and the constable said he was a forger. At that accusation my master seized a small lance that was lying in the porch of the inn. The constable put his hand to the sword that was in his belt. We all shouted at the tops of our voices and all the guests and the neighbours ran up and separated the two. The combatants lost their tempers and tried to get away from the restraining hands as they wanted to kill each other. But as the noise grew louder, more and more people came and soon the house was full. The constable and the pardoner saw that they wouldn't be able to come to grips so they satisfied themselves with insulting words. Among other things the constable told my master that he was a forger and that the indulgences he was trying to sell were not genuine.

In the end the townspeople saw that they wouldn't be able to end the fight, so they decided to take the constable away from the inn. My master was left there fuming with rage. After the guests and the neighbours had asked him to calm down and go to bed, he went. Then we all turned in.

When the morning came my master went to the church and told the bell-ringer to ring the bell for Mass and his sermon. All the village came, muttering that the indulgences were forgeries and the constable himself had said so when he couldn't control his tongue in anger. In other words, they hadn't much inclination to take the indulgences before and now they were determined not to.

The pardoner climbed into the pulpit and began his sermon. He urged the people not to deprive themselves of the great benefit and advantages that the holy indulgences could bring to them. When he was in the full flow of his oratory, the constable walked in through the door of the church. He said his prayer and then got up and with a loud and carefully slow voice, began to say:

'Ladies and gentlemen, please hear me for a minute, then you can listen to anyone you like. I came here with this swindler who is now preaching to you. He tricked me and said that if I gave him some help in his business he'd give me a share in the profits. But now I see the harm it would do both to my conscience and your pockets and I have repented of what I did and I declare to you openly that the indulgences he is trying to sell are false. Do not believe him. Do not accept them. I have no part in them either directly or indirectly. Here and now I give up my staff of office and break it on the floor. If he is prosecuted for fraud at any time, you will be witnesses that I'm not with him and I'm not helping him. On the contrary I am trying to show him up in his true light as an evil man.'

That was all he said. A few public-spirited men who were there wanted to get up and throw the constable out of the church to avoid a public scandal. But my master stopped them and ordered everybody under pain of excommunication not to hinder him but to let him say anything he wanted to. And he also said nothing while the constable said everything as I have written it.

When he stopped, my master asked him, if he had anything else to say, to kindly say it, The constable said :

'There's a lot more I could say about your lying, but that's enough for the time being.'

Then the pardoner fell on his knees in the pulpit, clasped his hands, gazed heavenwards and said :

'Oh, God, from whom nothing is hidden but everything revealed; to whom nothing is impossible but all things possible. Thou knowest the truth and how unjustly I am accused. As for me, I pardon him, as Thou O Lord, pardonest me. Do not punish him who knows not what he says or does. But as for the sin he has committed against Thee, I beg, I entreat, for the sake of justice, do not ignore it. Perhaps someone here, who by chance intended to accept the indulgence, has believed the false words of this man and will not now take it. And, as this is hurtful to my fellow man I beg Thee, O Lord, not to look away, but to show a miracle here and now and let it be thus : if what he says is true and I bring evil and falsehood, may this pulpit sink with me forty feet into the earth and may neither it nor I be ever seen again. But if what I say is true and he has been won over by the

Devil to deprive and rob the people here of their reward, then may he also be punished and may everyone know how evil he is.'

Hardly had my devout master finished his prayer than the evil constable fell down with such a bump that the whole church shuddered with the impact. He began to howl and foam at the mouth and twist his face into horrible contortions. He struck and kicked. He rolled over and over from one side to the other. The shouting and the screaming of the people was so loud that they couldn't hear one another. Some were white with fear, others said :

'God help him !' others commented :

'It serves him right, perjuring himself like that.'

Finally a few of them, and pretty frightened they were too, I think, approached him and grasped his arms as he was punching anybody who came too near very hard. Others seized his legs and held them firmly because he kicked harder than a stubborn mule. They held them firmly like that for a long time. In the end there were more than fifteen men on him and everybody had his hands full and, if they didn't watch out, a kick in the face.

All this time my master was kneeling in the pulpit, his hands clasped and gazing up to heaven, transported into the Divine Essence. The noise and shouting in the church could not distract him from his holy contemplation.

The few good men came up to him and woke him up with a shout and implored him to come to the help of that poor man who was dying. They begged him to forget what had gone before and what the constable had slanderously said as he had been well punished for it. But if he could find some way of releasing him from his suffering and certain death, for the love of God would he do it? They saw quite clearly that the constable was guilty but *he* was true and good as God had brought down his wrath without delay when he had requested it.

Like someone waking up from a pleasant doze, my master looked at them and the delinquent and everybody who was standing around and said very calmly :

'Good people, you ought never to ask me to intercede for a

man in whom God has so obviously shown his will. But as He commands us to return good for evil and turn the other cheek, we may confidently implore Him to obey His own commandment. May the Almighty pardon the man who offended Him by putting a stumbling block in the way of the True Faith. Let us all kneel.'

So he came down from the pulpit and advised them to pray very sincerely that Our Lord should think fit to forgive that sinner and return him to health and sound mind, and cast the devil out from him, if the Almighty, for the constable's great sin, had allowed the Evil One to enter his body. They all knelt down and he and the priests began to sing a litany in front of the altar. Then he came up with the cross and the holy water and sang over the constable. My master clasped his hands, and turned his eyes up so far that you could see almost nothing but the whites, and began a prayer as long as it was devout, making all the people cry as they do at the Easter week sermons, with the special preachers. He begged Our Lord, as He did not desire the sinner's death but his life and repentance, to forgive that poor man who was inspired by the Devil and had surrendered to sin. He implored the Lord to give him life and health so that he might repent and confess his sins.

After that he asked for the indulgence to be brought and he put it on the constable's head. The sinner came to his senses little by little. When he was quite recovered, he threw himself at the pardoner's feet and entreated his pardon and confessed that he'd said what he had on orders of the Devil himself, first to revenge himself on the pardoner about the quarrel they had had and secondly and more important because the Devil was very hurt by the great good that was being done by everyone taking the indulgence. My master pardoned him and they became friends again. And there was such a rush to buy the indulgences that not a living soul in the village was left without one, husband and wife, sons and daughters, young men and women.

The news of what had happened spread through all the villages round about and when we arrived there, there wasn't any need for a sermon nor for a visit to the church. The people came to get the indulgences at the inn. You'd think we were giving something for nothing. So in ten or eleven places round about there which we visited my master sold ten or eleven thousand indulgences without preaching a single sermon.

When he performed his act, I must admit that it did frighten me as I think it would anybody else. But afterwards, when I saw my master and the constable laughing their heads off together I realized that it had all been planned by the clever, crafty pardoner.

Now in another town, that I will not name to save it embarrassment, something else took place. My master preached two or three sermons and did not sell a single indulgence. He saw how the land lay and that even though he had said astutely that the indulgences were valid for a year, they refused to take any. In other words they were obstinate and he was wasting his time. So he had the bells rung to let the town know he was leaving. He preached his farewell sermon from the pulpit. As he was about to come down, he called the clerk and me. I was carrying some heavy bags. We went up the first step and the pardoner took the indulgences that the clerk was holding. Then he went back into the pulpit and, smiling broadly, began to throw the indulgences down into the congregation ten and twenty at a time, shouting:

'Dear brethren, take, take the grace that God brings to you in your own houses. Rejoice, for the work of redeeming Christians in the hands of the Moors is holy. That they may not deny our holy faith and go into the flames of hell, at least help them to leave their prisons with your alms and with five Pater Nosters and five Ave Marias. And the indulgences will even help your parents and brothers and sisters and other relatives who are in Purgatory; it's all written down here by the Pope.'

When the people saw him throwing the indulgences around like something given for nothing, by the hand of God, as it were, they began to grab them, even for babes in arms and all their dead relations, counting from little children down to the lowest of the servants, and ticking them off on their fingers. There was such a rush that they almost tore my poor old coat right off me. I swear to Your Honour that in little more than an hour there wasn't a single indulgence in my bag and I had to go back to the inn where we were staying for more.

When they had all been taken, my master from the pulpit told his clerk and the town clerk to get up and write down the names of those people who were going to get the benefit of the holy indulgence so that he could give a clear account when he was asked to. So then everybody came forward openly to say how many they had, listing their children and servants and dead relatives. When he had made his list, he asked the mayor to be so kind as to certify the clerk's tally and the number of indulgences sold as he had to go elsewhere. After this, he said his farewell with his face wreathed in smiles and we left the town. You won't believe it, but before we left, he was even asked by the assistant priest and the town councillors if the indulgence was valid for children still in their mothers' wombs. The pardoner replied that, according to the books he had studied, the answer was no. He said they should go and ask theologians who were more learned than him, but that was his opinion for what it was worth.

So we left and everybody was happy at the way things had turned out. My master said to the clerk and the constable:

'Well, what do you think of them? These peasants think they've only got to say: "We're pure Christians" and they can go to heaven without good works and without it costing them anything at all. Well, I'll tell you something; they'll pay ransom for the release of at least ten Christian slaves in Algiers!'

Then we went to another village in Toledo, in the south, towards La Mancha, as it is called, and there we also found them very stubborn in refusing to buy indulgences. My master and the rest of us performed our usual act and after we'd been there on two holidays we found we still hadn't shifted more than thirty. The pardoner was furious and anxious about the money it was costing him, so that day he said High Mass. When he'd said his sermon and gone back to the altar, he took a tiny cross, hardly as big as his hand. On the altar was a little dish of hot coals that he'd brought to warm his hands over on that cold day. He put the dish behind his missal and quickly put the cross on the coals. Then, after he'd finished Mass and said the Benediction, he picked it up with his handkerchief, held it well wrapped up in his right hand and the indulgence in the left. He walked down to the last of the altar steps. Then he pretended to kiss the cross and signed to the congregation to do the same.

So first came the aldermen, by seniority one at a time, as the custom is. The first one was an old man and although the pardoner just brushed his face with the cross he was burned and stepped back smartly. My master saw this and shouted:

'Keep quiet, be still, sir, this is a miracle!'

The same thing happened with the next half dozen and he said to everyone:

'Still, quiet, it's a miracle!'

When he saw he had burned enough faces to have plenty of witnesses he stopped anybody else kissing the cross. He went up to the foot of the altar and from there proclaimed the miraculous event. Because they were so uncharitable God had allowed the miracle to take place; the cross would be taken to the cathedral church of the bishop's see; it had burned because the people were so mean. Then there was such a rush to take the indulgences that, even with two clerks and the clergy and the sacristans, they couldn't write all the names down. I'm pretty sure we placed more than three thousand indulgences, as I told Your Honour before. When we left, he went up very reverently and took the cross, saying that he would have to get it gilded, as was only right. He was begged by the town council and the local clergy to leave the holy cross there as a reminder of the miracle that had occurred, but he refused absolutely. But they pestered him so much that in the end he did leave it. In exchange they gave him an old silver cross that probably weighed two or three pounds, according to what they said.

So we left. We were happy with the exchange and the good business we had done. Nobody spotted anything he had done except me. I went up to the altar to see if there was anything left in the plates which could be turned into hard cash. That was my perk. When the pardoner saw me there, he put his finger to his lips to tell me to keep my mouth shut. I did so because it suited me. Mind you, after seeing the miracle, I wanted to tell everybody about it but I was scared of the crafty pardoner who forbade me to tell anybody. In fact I never did tell anybody be-

74

cause I swore never to reveal what had happened. I've kept my oath until now.

I was only a boy then, but his trick impressed me very much and I said to myself:

'I wonder how many others there are like him swindling innocent people.'

In all, I stayed with my fifth master more than four months and even with him I had some hard times. Mind you, he always gave me plenty to eat at the expense of the priests and the other clergy in the places where he went to preach.

CHAPTER SIX

AFTER this I lived with an artist who painted tambourines for a living. My job was to mix his colours for him and the life was very hard.

I was a well set-up young man by now and one day, when I was in the cathedral, one of the priests gave me a job. He provided me with a donkey, four jugs and a whip and I began to carry water around the city. That was my first step towards becoming a respectable citizen because now my hunger was satisfied. Every day I gave my employer thirty *maravedís* and on Saturdays I worked for myself. I kept whatever I earned every day if it was more than thirty *maravedís*.

I did so well at the job that after four years of careful saving, I had enough to dress myself very decently in second-hand clothes; I bought an old fustian jacket and a worn coat with braided sleeves and a vent. I also got a cloak which had had a fringe once, and an old sword made when they used to make them at Cuéllar.

As soon as I saw myself dressed up to the nines I told my employer to take his donkey as I did not want that job any longer.

CHAPTER SEVEN

AFTER I left the priest I went to work for a constable as it seemed a good idea to get in with the law. But I didn't stay long with him because my job was dangerous. In particular, one night my master and I were chased by some fugitives who threw stones at us and set about us with sticks. They didn't catch me but they gave my master a proper working-over. That decided me to break the contract.

I wondered how I could settle down to have an easy life and earn something for my old age. God was gracious enough to lighten my way and guide my steps along a fruitful path. I received a lot of favours from friends and gentlemen and found all the hardships and struggles till then well compensated for by getting the post I did. I got into the Civil Service ! I realized that you can't get on unless you are in a government job. I've still got it today and I live in the service of God and of Your Honour.

Now my job is to make public announcements of the wines that are to be sold in the town, and of the auctions and lost property. I also accompany criminals being punished for their misdeeds and shout out their crimes. In other words, or in simple English, I'm a town-crier.

Things have gone so luckily for me and I've been able to use my opportunities so well that almost everything passes through my hands. So if anybody anywhere in Toledo has wine to sell or anything else, he won't get very far in his business unless Lázaro de Tormes has a finger in the pie.

Soon after I got the job, the Archpriest of St Salvador's heard about me and saw how sharp and ready-witted I was, because I used to announce that his wines were for sale. So he arranged a marriage for me with a maid of his. I saw that only advantages and good could come from being associated with the reverend gentleman, my lord, and Your Honour's servant and friend, so I decided to marry the girl.

We got married and I've never been sorry because, besides her being a good and attentive girl, the priest is always very kind to me. Every year I get a whole load of corn; I get my meat at Christmas and Easter and now and again a couple of votive loaves or a pair of old stockings. He arranged for us to rent a house next to his. On Sundays and holy days we nearly always eat in his house. But evil tongues, that we're never short of and never will be, make life impossible for us, saying this and that and the other; that my wife goes and makes his bed and cooks his dinner. I hope God forgives their lies. Mind you, at the time I always had a nagging little suspicion and had a few bad suppers because some nights I waited for her until lauds or even later. I remembered what the blind man said to me in Escalona when he was holding the horn. Mind you, I think the Devil brought that to my mind deliberately to upset my marriage, but it didn't help him any because, besides the fact that she wasn't the sort of woman who thought that sort of thing was a joke, my lord Archpriest made me a promise one day and I know he will keep it. One day he spoke at length in her presence. This is what he said:

'Lázaro de Tormes, you'll never get on in life if you take any notice of what people say about you. I'm telling you this so you should not be surprised if someone says he sees your wife going into my house and leaving it. . . . Neither of you need be ashamed of what she does; this I can promise you. So, don't pay any attention to what anybody says; just think about your own affairs, I mean, what's best for you.'

'Sir,' I said to him, 'I made up my mind a long time ago to keep in with respectable people. It's quite true that my friends have said something to me about my wife. In fact they've proved to me that she had three children before she married me, speaking with reverence because she's here.'

Then my wife began to swear such fearful oaths that I was sure the house was about to fall down about our ears. She began to cry and curse the man responsible for bringing us together. I began to wish I were dead and had never said what I had. But between my Lord and me we talked her out of it and made her so many promises that she stopped crying. I had to swear that so long as I lived, I'd never again mention a word about it and that I was happy and satisfied that she went in and out of his house at any time of night or day as I was confident about her faithfulness. We were all happy about the arrangement. Nobody's ever heard us mention the subject again. In fact, when I sense that someone wants to say something to me about her, I cut him short and say:

'Look here, if you're my friend, don't say anything to upset me, because anybody who annoys me is no friend of mine, especially if he wants to make trouble between me and my wife. I love her more than anything else in the world, even more than myself. Thank God, life is marvellous for me with her, much better than I deserve. I swear on the Sacred Host itself that she is as good a woman as any in Toledo. If anyone says the opposite I'll kill him.'

As a result nobody says anything and there is peace at home.

That was the same year as our victorious Emperor entered this famous city of Toledo and held his Parliament here. There were great festivities, as Your Honour doubtless has heard. At that time I was at the height of my good fortune. I will inform Your Honour of my future in due course.

The Swindler

TO THE READER

━◄━►━

D E A R Reader or Listener (for the blind cannot read) I can just imagine how much you want to read about my delightful Don Pablos, Prince of the Roving Life.

Here you will find all the tricks of the low life or those which I think most people enjoy reading about: craftiness, deceit, subterfuge and swindles, born of laziness to enable you to live on lies; and if you attend to the lesson you will get quite a lot of benefit from it. And even if you don't, study the sermons, for I doubt if anyone buys a book as coarse as this in order to avoid the inclinations of his own depraved nature. Let it serve you as you like; praise it, for it certainly deserves applause, and praise the genius of its author who has enough common sense to know it is a lot more amusing to read about low life when the story is written with spirit, than about other more serious topics.

You already know who the author is.

You are well aware of the price of the book, as you already have it, unless you are looking through it in the bookshop, a practice which is very tiresome for the bookseller and ought to be suppressed with the utmost rigour of the law. You see, there are people who steal a free read as sparrows pick at a meal, and some who read books here and there and then piece the story together; and this is a great pity because they criticize the book even though it hasn't cost them anything; which is a mean swindle, as foul as anything I described in my *Knights of the Princess*. Dear Reader, may God protect you from bad books, police, and nagging, moon-faced, fair-haired women.

BOOK ONE

CHAPTER ONE

I COME from Segovia. My father was called Clemente Pablo; he came from the same place, may he rest in peace! He was, as everybody knows, a barber, although his head was so much in the clouds that it annoyed him to be so called and he said they ought to call him a 'reaper of cheeks and tailor of beards'. They say he came from very good stock and that's not hard to believe considering how much liquid he consumed! He married Aldonza Saturno de Rebollo, the daughter of Octavio de Rebollo Codillo and grand-daughter of Lépido Ziuraconte. The townspeople suspected that she had some Moorish or Jewish blood in her though she tried hard to show that her father's and grand-father's names indicated their descent from the Roman Triumvirs. She was very attractive and so well known that, during her life all the rhymesters in Spain composed things about her. Soon after she married she had a very hard time and later on as well, because evil tongues said that my father picked his customers' pockets. As he shaved them he lifted their heads to wash their faces and my little seven-year-old brother easily stripped their pockets of every farthing they had. He was caught in the act and the little angel died from a few lashes they gave him in prison. My father was very upset, because the child stole the heart of everybody who saw him. My father was gaoled for this and a few other trifles although to go by what people have told me since, he left prison in such a proud state that he went out with two hundred stripes on his body but not a single one gave him any rank. They say he always looked so handsome on foot or on horseback that the ladies came to their windows to see him. I'm not saying this just for the sake of boasting for everybody knows how unlike me that would be.

So my mother had no small share of trouble. The old woman

who brought me up told me one day that she was so charming that she bewitched anyone who had anything to do with her. The only thing was that there was some rumour about a billy-goat which brought her close to being tarred and feathered and having to try out her bewitching in public. She was rumoured to be able to repair girls' lost virginities, bring back hair and make white hair turn black again. Some people said she could arrange any pleasure; others called her a satisfier of unsatisfied desires and, on the bad side, a procuress and a hole in the pocket for everybody's money. But if you saw her laughing when she heard all this it would attract you even more to her. I shan't waste time describing the penances she underwent. Her room, which only she and sometimes I, being small, went into, was ringed with skulls, which she said were to remind her of death; but other people, always looking for the worst, said they were to put spells on the living. Her bed was hung on old hangman's ropes and she used to say to me:

'Why do you think I have them? I use the ropes to remind people who like to keep out of trouble to keep their wits about them so that nobody can have even a glimmer of what they're up to.'

My parents had great arguments as to which of their respective professions I should follow. But I had always fancied myself as a man of leisure so I didn't apply myself to either. My father used to tell me:

'Look, lad, being a thief isn't just a job, it's a liberal profession.' Then he would sigh and put his hands together as in church and say:

'If you don't thieve you won't eat. Why do you reckon the police and the mayor hate us so much? Sometimes they throw us out of town, and other times they whip us or hang us. I can't even talk about it without crying.' And the old man cried like a child, remembering how often his ribs had been well pounded. 'It's because they don't want there to be any thieves except themselves and their lot. But if you're crafty you can get away with anything. When I was young I used to hang around churches, and you can be sure it wasn't because I was a good Christian. And many's the time I would have taken my last ride on the donkey's back if I'd squealed on the rack. I never confessed except when Holy Mother Church commanded. And that's how I've looked after your mother as honourably as I could.'

'What do you mean looked after me?' shouted my mother, who was annoyed that I wasn't studying to be a male witch. 'I've looked after you and got you out of prison by hard work and kept you alive with money when you were inside. All right, you didn't confess. But was it because you had guts or because I gave you things to drink. It was all thanks to my little bottles and if I weren't afraid they might hear me in the street I'd tell you about the time when I got in through the chimney and got you out through the roof.'

She had got herself so worked up that she would have said more, but she banged her fist so hard that she broke a rosary of dead people's teeth that she always carried around with her. When the two of them calmed down I told them I wanted to learn to be an honest man and that they ought to send me to school, because you couldn't do anything without knowing how to read and write. They thought this was a good idea although they grumbled about it between themselves for a while. My mother got on with threading more teeth and my father went to scrape a customer (that's the word he used), maybe his face and maybe his wallet. I was left by myself thanking God for having given me parents who were so clever and concerned about my welfare.

CHAPTER TWO

⊷⊶

THE next day my books were brought and my education arranged for. I went to school and the master greeted me very cheerfully, saying that I looked a quick, bright lad. As I didn't want to disabuse him I did my lessons very well that day. The master used to make me sit down next to him. Most days I won the prize for arriving there first and I was the last to leave because I used to run some errands for Madame, which was the name we gave to the master's wife. I did favours for everybody and so they were all obliged to me. I was over-favoured and consequently the other boys began to feel jealous. I was taken up mostly by the sons of gentlemen and especially by the son of Don Alonso Coronel de Zúñiga, with whom I shared my lunch. On holidays I used to go to his house and I went around with him every day. Maybe because I did not speak to the others or because they thought I was too stuck up, they started calling me names after my father's job. Some of them called me Don Razor and others Don Swindler. As an excuse for their jealousy one of them said that my mother had sucked the blood of two little sisters of his one night. Another called my father a cat-thief and said his family had employed him to kill mice. Others called 'puss, puss' after me and others hissed. And yet another said:

'I threw two mouldy aubergines at your mother when she was being paraded in a cart as a witch.'

Well, even though they were always snapping at my heels I could always manage to show them a clean pair, thank God. And even though I was seething with rage, I hid it; I put up with everything until one day a boy dared to shout at me that my mother was a whore and a witch. And as he said it so clearly (if it had been quietly it wouldn't have annoyed me so much), I grabbed a stone and broke his head. I went running to my mother so that she might hide me and told her the whole story. She said to me:

'You did very well, you've shown your mettle. The only thing you did wrong was not asking who told him!'

When I heard this and, as my thoughts were always noble, I turned to her and said:

'Oh, mother! What upsets me is that some of the boys said that I shouldn't get annoyed because of that, and I didn't ask them if they meant that the boy who said it was very young and didn't know any better.'

I begged her to tell me if I could have honestly denied the insult, and if I really was my father's son, or if she had conceived me accidentally by one of lots of men. She laughed and said:

'Ah, so that's it. You understand, do you? You're no fool, in fact you're sharp. You did very well to knock his head in because nobody should say anything like that, even if it is true.'

When I realized the truth it was like a kick in the stomach. I made up my mind to get as much money together as I could in a few days and leave home, I was so embarrassed and ashamed. I hid my feelings. My father went and patched the boy up, calmed him down and took me back to school where the master was in a terrible rage. When he heard what the fight was about he calmed down and realized that I was justified.

During all this time Don Alonso's son Diego visited me regularly because he was a real friend. I used to swap him my spinning-tops if they were better than his. I shared my mid-morning snack with him and never asked him for any of his. I bought pictures for him, taught him how to fight, played leapfrog with him and generally kept him amused. So most days, since the young gentleman's parents saw how happy he was with me, they asked mine to let me have dinner, supper and even sleep there most days. It happened that, on one of the schooldays near the Christmas holiday, we saw a man called Pontius de Aguirre, a well-known magistrate, coming along the street. Don Diego said to me:

'Look, shout "Pontius Pilate" at him and run away.'

To please my friend, I called him 'Pontius Pilate'. But the man ran so fast that he came up behind me with an open knife. So

I had to run into the schoolmaster's house to save my life. He ran into the house after me, cursing me, but the master protected me from him by promising to punish me. And that is what happened, though Madame did speak up for me as I had done such a lot for her. He ordered me to take down my breeches and beat me, and at every stroke he said:

'Will you call him "Pontius Pilate" again?'

'No sir,' I answered, twice for every stroke.

I was so scared of saying 'Pontius Pilate' and learnt my lesson so well that when, the next day, he told me as usual to say the prayers to the other boys, when I got to the credo (notice my innocence) and reached the point where it says 'suffered at the hands of Pontius Pilate', I remembered 'no more Pilates' and said:

'He suffered at the hands of Pontius Aguirre.'

The master choked himself laughing at my simplicity and seeing how frightened I was of him, embraced me and promised me in writing to let me off the next two beatings I earned. This made me very happy.

Carnival time came round and the master wanted us boys to have a good time, so he said we should have a boy-king. He picked ten boys and made us draw lots and I won. I told my parents to buy me some fine clothes. The day came. Out I rode on a skinny old horse which kept nodding as it went by, more out of weariness than good manners. It had haunches like a monkey's, precious little tail and a neck longer than a camel's. It had only one eye in its head and that was all filmed over with white, like a hard-boiled egg. You could see the penances, fasts and cruel treatment that its master had imposed on it. Along I rode, nodding left and right like the people who take off Pharisees in the Holy Week processions, and all the other boys lined up behind me. We went through the square (I still get a fright when I think of it) and came up to the vegetable stalls. Heaven help me! The horse snatched up a white cabbage without anybody noticing. Down its throat it rolled and in a second it was in its guts. The vegetable women (they are all as hard as nails) began to shout. Up came some others and a few layabouts and began throwing big carrots, turnips, aubergines and other vegetables at the poor king. When I saw it was a turnip battle, not a cavalry charge, I got down; but they gave my poor horse such a clout that it reared up and fell down and brought me down with it into a pile of (excuse me) shit. You can imagine the state I was in. The boys had armed themselves with stones by then and threw them at the market women and brained two of them. After I had fallen into the muck I took the leading part in the fight. The police came, arrested the women and the boys, searched everybody for arms, and took them away because they had drawn the fancy-dress daggers they were wearing as well as short swords. They came to me and, finding no weapons on me because I had taken them off and left them in a house to dry with my cloak and hat, they asked me where they were. I answered that my weapon was a bad smell and that was the only one I had. And by the way I must confess that when they began to throw the aubergines at me, I thought that as I was wearing feathers in my hat, they had taken me for my tarred and feathered mother and were throwing things at her as they had done so many other times. I was just a silly boy and I began to say:

'I know I'm wearing feathers, girls, but I'm not Aldonza Saturno de Rebollo, my mother,' as if they didn't know. I can only plead fear and the speed with which it all happened. The policeman wanted to take me to gaol but he couldn't find anywhere to grab me because of the dung. Some went one way and some the other. I went home from the square, torturing all the noses I met on the way. When I got back I told my parents what had happened. They were so angry at the state I was in that I nearly got a good hiding. I blamed it all on the skinny, clapped-out old hack they'd given me. I tried to calm them down but, as I could not, I went out to see my friend Don Diego. He was at home with his head bandaged. His parents had decided not to send him to that school any more. There I found out that the horse in desperation had tried to kick a couple of times and because it was so thin it had dislocated its haunches and collapsed dying in the mud. So the holiday was spoilt, the town was up in arms, my parents were furious, my friend's head was knocked in, and my horse was dead. I made up my mind I wouldn't go back to school or to my home either but I'd stay on as Don Diego's servant, or rather, as his companion. His parents were delighted. I wrote home saying that I didn't need to go to school any more because, though I couldn't write very well, what I needed to satisfy my ambition to be a gentleman was actually bad handwriting. I was leaving school to save them money and leaving home to spare them worry. I told them where I was and what I was doing and that I wouldn't see them again until they forgave me.

CHAPTER THREE

So Don Alonso made up his mind to send his son to boarding-school, both to prevent him from being spoiled at home and to save himself worry. He found out that there was a certain Dr Goat in Segovia who tutored gentlemen's sons. So he sent his son there and me as well to be his companion and servant.

The first Sunday after Lent we fell into the power of Hunger incarnate. I could never exaggerate the sufferings he caused us. He was in holy orders, as skinny as a peashooter, generous only in height, with a small head and ginger hair. I need say no more, if you remember that Judas had red hair. His eyes were sunk so deep in his head that they were like lamps at the end of a cave; so sunken and dark that they looked like a draper's window. His nose was partly Roman and partly French, because it was poxy with cold sores (not the real pox of course; it costs money to catch that). His whiskers were pale, scared stiff of his starving mouth which was threatening to gnaw them. I don't know how many of his teeth he had missing: I suppose he had dismissed them as there was never any work for them to do. His neck was as long as an ostrich's and his Adam's apple looked as if it had been forced to go and look for food. His arms were withered and his hands were like dried-up vine shoots. His legs looked like the prongs of a fork or a pair of skinny dividers. He walked very slowly. If he rushed for any reason his bones rattled like the clappers that hospital charity collectors rattle in the streets; his voice was hollow and he had a long beard because he wouldn't spend money on shaving and, in any case, he said the barber's hands on his face made him feel sick and he'd rather die than feel them. One of the other boys used to cut his hair for him. When the weather was hot he wore a hat chewed all over by the cat and decorated with grease spots. It was made of something that had once been cloth and was well-lined with scurf. Some said his cassock was miraculous because nobody could tell its colour. As it had no nap left some said it was made of frog's skin; others said it was an optical illusion as it looked black from close up but bluish from a distance. He had no belt, collar or cuffs. With his long hair and short skimpy cassock he looked like the Angel of Death in person. Goliath's coffin could have fitted into each of his shoes. And his room! There weren't even any spiders there. He put a spell on the mice in case they nibbled the few crumbs he hoarded. He slept on the floor on one side so as not to wear out the sheets. In short he was the High Priest of Poverty and Avarice incarnate.

So I fell into his hands together with Don Diego. On the day we arrived he showed us our room and made us a little speech; little, to save time. He told us what we were to do and this took us until lunch time. The refectory was terribly small but it contained about five young gentlemen. First, I looked round to see if there were any cats and, as there were not, I asked an old servant why not.

He bore the mark of the place on his emaciated body. He softened and said:

'What do you mean, cats? Who told you cats like fasting and penance: it's not hard to see you're new; you won't stay fat for long!' When I heard that I began to get nervous and I got even more scared when I saw that the others looked as skinny as rakes with faces which looked as if they had been plastered with white lead. Dr Goat sat down and said grace. Then our masters ate an infinite meal, by which I mean it had no beginning and no end. They brought little wooden bowls of a soup so clear that if Narcissus had drunk it he would have fallen in quicker than into the pool. With a pain in my chest I saw the lean fingers paddling after one lone, orphaned chick pea at the bottom of the bowl. After each sip, Dr Goat said:

'Yes, they can say what they like, there's nothing like stew. All the rest is luxury and greed.' And as he said it he slopped his soup greedily, saying:

'It's all goodness and food!'

'I hope it chokes you,' I said under my breath when I saw a

94

listless servant with a plate of meat in his hands. He was so thin that it looked as if the meat had come off his own bones. Up came a brave pioneering turnip and Dr Goat said:

'Turnips today? Partridges have nothing on them. Eat up now, I love seeing how you enjoy your food!'

He shared out such a tiny piece of mutton that, between what got caught under the nails and between the teeth, there was nothing left and our masters' guts were not admitted to the sacrament. Dr Goat looked at them and said:

'Eat up! You're young lads and I like to see a healthy appetite.'

Marvellous encouragement if hunger is gnawing at you already, isn't it?

After the meal a few crumbs were left on the table and some skin and bones on a plate. Our tutor said:

'Leave that for the servants. They must eat too and we shouldn't be greedy.'

'I hope God makes you choke on your food, you mean old bastard,' I muttered. 'Fancy insulting my belly like that!'

He said grace and then:

'Right, let the servants sit down and you go and take some exercise until two o'clock to make sure you digest what you've eaten properly.'

At that I could not help laughing and I roared. He became very annoyed and told me I should learn to be humble, as well as two or three other old maxims. We sat down and I saw that this was a bad business and my guts were grumbling. Being craftier than the rest I grabbed the plate first and gobbled up two of the three crumbs as well as the single piece of skin. The others began to protest and, hearing the noise, in ran Goat saying:

'Eat like brothers! God has provided! Don't fight, there's enough for all.'

He went back into the sun and left us alone. I swear that one of us, Surre, a Basque, had so forgotten how to eat that he looked twice at a little sliver that he found and could not put it into his mouth. I asked for something to drink; the others did not because they ate almost nothing; and I was given a glass of water. Hardly had I put it to my mouth when the skinny youth

I mentioned snatched it away, as if it were a communion maundy. I got up very unhappily realizing that this was a house where one's appetite was whetted without being satisfied. I had the urge to relieve myself though I had not eaten and so I asked one of the older residents where the lav. was. He said:

'I don't know, we haven't got one. Do it anywhere just this once. I've been here two months and I haven't been since the day I came, and then, like you now, I dropped what I'd eaten at home the night before.'

How can I explain my feelings? I was so unhappy that, considering how little was going to go into my body, I did not dare let anything out, though I wanted to.

We whiled away the time until nightfall. Don Diego asked me what he could say to his belly to persuade it that it had eaten, because it would not believe him. Your guts were as full of air in that house as they were overstuffed in others. Suppertime came; tea-time had already come, but no tea. For supper we had less than for lunch, and not mutton either but a bit of our tutor's name, roast goat. I think it must be like that in Hell.

'It's very healthy and good for you,' said Dr Goat, 'to have a light supper. Then the stomach isn't overworked.' And he quoted a list of blasted doctors. He praised diets and said that they stopped you having bad dreams. He knew quite well that in his house the only thing we were likely to dream about was food. They had supper, we had supper, in fact nobody had supper. We went to bed but Don Diego and I couldn't sleep all night. He was thinking of a way of complaining to his father and asking him to take him away and I was advising him to do so, although I did say to him in the end:

'Sir, are you sure we're alive? I reckon we were killed fighting with the market women and we're souls in Purgatory. So it's not much good your asking your father to get us out unless someone prays for our souls and releases us with a Mass said at an altar with special indulgences.'

We talked and slept fitfully and it was soon time to get up. The clock struck six and Goat called us to class. We all attended it. My doublet was already hanging loosely on my shoulders and side, and seven other legs could have got into my breeches. My teeth were yellow, desperate fangs, rotten with tartar. I had to read out the first declension nominatives aloud to the others. I breakfasted on half of them, swallowing the words. I was ravenous. If you don't believe me, you will when you hear what Goat's servant told me. He once saw two draught-horses stabled by the house and two days later they'd lost so much weight that they flew off like race-horses. After a couple of hours he saw heavy mastiffs turn into racing greyhounds, and one Lent he found lots of people just outside the gate, some pushing their hands through, some their feet and some their whole body, all this for a long time; and a lot of people just waited outside. Goat hated him asking questions, so he asked them and one of them said that some had mange and others sores and the mange and sores died of starvation in that house and so didn't gnaw them any more. He swore blind that all this was true. I believed him as I knew the place. I've told this because I know it sounds as if I'm exaggerating. Anyhow, Goat gave the lesson and we said it in chorus and we carried on living like that. Once he did put a bit of bacon in the pot because they said something in the town about his having Jewish ancestry (Jews don't eat pigmeat). So he kept an iron box full of holes like the boxes which hold sand for blotting ink. He used to open it, put a piece of bacon in it, shut it again and hang it in the stew for some juice to come out through the holes without him losing the bacon. But later on he thought this was too extravagant and he just let the bacon look at the stew.

You can imagine what sort of life we led under these conditions. Don Diego and I were so near the end of our tether that, realizing there was nothing we could do about eating, we decided after a month to stay in bed and feign illness. We didn't say we had temperatures because the lie would be obvious. A headache or toothache wasn't much. In the end we said we had the belly-ache and had been constipated for three days, thinking he wouldn't take his hand out of his pocket to buy a laxative. But the Devil arranged things another way because Goat had inherited a prescription from his father who was a chemist. He found out what was wrong and made up the medicine. Then he sent for an old woman, an aunt of his of seventy who acted as nurse, and told her to give each of us an enema.

They began with Don Diego. The poor lad was trussed up and the old woman, instead of shooting it into him, shot it up between his shirt and his back and it hit his neck. So what ought to have been a stuffing inside ended up as a coating outside. The boy shouted for all he was worth and when Goat ran up and saw him he told them to give me the other enema and go back to Don Diego afterwards. I struggled, but it was no use, because Goat and the others held me while the old woman pushed it in. Still, I shot the result out right into her face. Goat lost his temper and told me he was going to throw me out and that it was plain I'd made everything up. But my luck didn't go as far as that. We complained to Don Alonso but Goat told him it was all because we didn't want to attend classes.

No amount of pleading helped. He brought in the old woman as housekeeper to cook and serve the students and sacked the servant because one Friday morning he found a few crumbs in his underwear. God knows what we endured under the old woman. She was so deaf she couldn't hear a thing. She understood by signs. She was blind and said such a lot of prayers that one day her rosary became unthreaded and she dropped all the beads into the pot. That day she served us the holiest smelling soup I ever ate. Some of the boys said:

'Black chick-peas? They must be Ethiopian!'

Others said:

'Chick peas in mourning? Who have they lost?'

My master got one bead in his spoon and cracked a tooth trying to chew it. On Fridays she usually served up eggs or tufts of venerable white hair (which presumably signified Goat's learning and status). It was quite common to find the fire-shovel for the soup ladle or a stone soup-bowl. I found insects, twigs and candlewicks hundreds of times in the stew. She put everything in so it could make a stand in our bellies and pad things out. We endured this hardship until the following Lent. At the beginning of the season one of the boys became ill and, to save money, Goat didn't call the doctor until the boy was asking to make his last confession more than for anything else. Then he called in a cheap doctor who took his pulse and said that hunger had killed the lad without giving *him* a chance to do so. They gave him the sacrament and when the poor lad saw it (he hadn't spoken for a day) he said :

'Sweet Jesus Christ. Seeing you in this house is the only thing that has convinced me I'm not in Hell.'

These words were written on his heart. The poor boy died. We buried him poorly as he was from another part of the country and we stood there stunned.

The dreadful story spread through the town. It came to the ears of Don Alonso Coronel and as he only had one son he realized just how cruel Goat was and began to believe the stories of the two wretched shadows to which we were reduced. He came and took us away and, standing us in front of him, asked us how we were. But he could see for himself and without more ado he violently abused Dr Starvation. He ordered us to be carried home in two litters. We said good-bye to our friends who followed us with their eyes and would have liked to do so with their feet, looking as unhappy as slaves in Algiers who see their ransomed companions leaving for home.

CHAPTER FOUR

※→

W E went back to Don Alonso's house and they laid us down in separate beds very carefully in case our hunger-rotted bones crumbled. They searched all over our faces with magnifying glasses, looking for our eyes, but it took them a long time to find mine as my sufferings had been greater and my hunger colossal (after all, I had been treated as a servant). Doctors came and ordered the dust to be wiped from our mouths with foxes' tails, like valuable pictures, and that's just what we were: pictures of misery. They also ordered us light chicken-broth and other liquids. Who can express the joy in our bellies at the first drink of almond-milk and the first poultry we had? After all, everything was new to them. The doctors ordered that nobody should speak in a loud voice in our room for nine days, because every word echoed in our hollow stomachs. So with all this care and other treatment we began to feel ourselves again slowly. But we couldn't release our jaws which were black and twisted. So they told us to prise them open gently once a day with the handle of a kitchen-mortar. We began to take a few tottering steps after four days but we still looked like shadows of other men and as yellow and thin as the descendants of desert hermits. We did nothing all day but thank God for rescuing us from the clutch of that beast Goat, and we begged Him not to let any Christian ever fall into his hands again. Sometimes during meals we remembered his 'meals' and we grew so hungry that we upset the kitchen accounts that day.

We used to tell Don Alonso stories of how Goat would tell us about illnesses caused by greediness, just as we were sitting down to eat. Not that he'd ever suffered one in his life. Don Alonso laughed heartily when we told him that Goat included partridge and capons and anything he didn't want to give us in the commandment 'Thou shalt not kill.' One of the things he didn't want to give us was appetite; he seemed to consider it a sin not only to satisfy it but even to encourage it.

So we whiled away three months and then Don Alonso made arrangements to send his son to Alcalá to learn what he needed of grammar. He asked me if I wanted to go. I wanted nothing more than to get as far away as I could from the name of that goddamed stomach torturer so I offered to go as his son's servant. He gave him another servant as a steward to control his household and keep an account of his expenses. He sent us cash in drafts on a certain Julian Hake. We loaded our baggage into a cart belonging to a Diego Monk. There was one small bed and a truckle bed to go under it for me and the steward, whose name was Aranda; five mattresses, eight sheets, eight pillows, four wall-tapestries, a chest of white linen and the other household odds and ends. We ourselves left in a coach about an hour before dusk and before midnight we arrived at the Viveros Inn, blast it to hell! The host was a dog of a Moor and I can honestly say I never saw a dog and a thief get on so well together. We were received well as he had a fifty per cent agreement with the carter's men who had arrived earlier with our luggage. He came out to the coach, helped me down and asked me if I was a student. I told him I was and went inside where there were a couple of roughs with some whores, a priest saying his prayers to protect himself from their stink, a stingy old tradesman trying to forget to have supper and two working students, the sort who wear short gowns and always have their eyes on free scraps of food to swallow. As my master was the most recent arrival and just a boy, he said:

'Landlord, please serve whatever you have for me and my two servants.'

'We're all your servants,' said the two roughs in unison, 'and we'll look after you. Landlord! He'll be very grateful for anything you do; empty your pantry!'

As they said that one of them came and slipped my master's cloak off.

'Have a rest, sir,' he said, putting it on a bench.

This made me feel very important and I thought the place belonged to me. One of the young ladies said :

'What a fine young gent ! So you're going to the University ! Are you his servant ?'

I thought they meant everything they said so I said that I was, and so was the other lad. They asked me what my master's name was and I scarcely had time to say it before one of the students ran up to him weeping, flung his arms around him and said :

'Oh, Don Diego, sir, who could have told me ten years ago that I should be in this state when you saw me again? I bet you can't even recognize me.'

My master and I both stood there with our mouths open and swore we'd never seen him in our lives before, either of us. The other student was walking around, staring at Don Diego from all angles, and he said to his friend :

'Is this the gentleman whose father you told me such a lot about? We're very lucky to have met him, he's grown so tall, God bless him.' He began to cross himself. Anybody would have thought he had grown up with us. Don Diego was very polite and asked his name. Just then the landlord came in to lay the table. He smelled what was in the air and said :

'Leave that now; you can talk later or your supper will get cold.'

One of the roughs came and put benches around for us all and a proper chair for Don Diego, and the other one brought a plate. The student said :

'You eat your supper and we'll wait on you while they cook whatever there is.'

'Oh, good heavens no,' said Don Diego, 'please sit down.'

Then the roughs said :

'Later sir, it's not ready yet,' though Don Diego hadn't even spoken to them.

When I saw that the students had been invited and the others had invited themselves I began to worry and I was right, because the students took the salad, which didn't look bad at all, glanced at my master, and said :

'It's not right for such a fine gentleman to eat when these ladies go without; ask them to help themselves to some.'

They sat down and between them and the students they finished the lot except for a tiny lettuce-heart which Don Diego ate. As he handed it to him that scum of a student said:

'Your grandad, who was my father's uncle, was so odd that he fainted when he saw a lettuce.'

As he said this he gobbled a roll and so did the other. Then the young ladies finished a loaf, and the priest's eyes were so big that they ate more than any of the others' mouths. The roughs sat down with half a roast kid, two sides of bacon and a couple of boiled pigeons and said:

'Now, Father, here you are! Come and eat up, because young Don Diego is treating us all.'

He was at the table before they had finished speaking. When my master saw that they had all latched on to him he began to worry. They shared all the food out and gave Don Diego a few odd bones and a couple of wings. The priest and the others wolfed the rest.

'Don't eat too much before you go to bed,' said the roughs, 'it doesn't do you any good,' and the student, blast him, chimed in:

'And in any case you'll have to get used to not eating much when you get to Alcalá.'

The other servant and I were praying that they might not eat everything. When they had eaten the lot and the priest was picking the bones, one of the roughs turned round and said:

'God, we haven't left anything for the servants. Come up here, gentlemen. Landlord! Give them all you have, here's a doubloon.'

Straight away up jumped that confounded relative of my master (I mean the student) and said:

'I'm sure you'll excuse me, sir, but you really don't know much about gentlemen; you obviously don't know my cousin. He will feed his own servants himself, and would feed ours too if we had any, just like he treated us. Don't be annoyed, you just don't know him.'

I thought I'd never finish cursing him when I saw his hypocrisy.

The tables were removed and they all told Don Diego to go to bed; he offered to pay for supper but they said there would be plenty of time next day. They talked for a while. He asked the student his name and he said it was Don So-and-So Coronel. Wherever the liar is I hope he roasts in Hell. He saw that the stingy merchant was asleep and said:

'Fancy a laugh? Let's play a trick on the old man. He's only had a pear all day and he's rolling in money.'

'Right, good for the student,' said the roughs.

So he went to the old man and took his saddle-bags from under his feet. He untied them and took out a box like a drum. Everybody flocked round as if it were beating for war, and when it was opened they found it was full of sweets. He took them all out and put sticks and stones and anything else he could find in their place. Then he shat on it and on top of that he put a dozen little shining stones. He shut the box and said:

'No, that's not enough: he has a wine skin, too.'

He poured out the wine and, pulling the cover off one of the cushions from our coach, he poured some wine back and filled the skin up with wool and tow. Then he stoppered it, put everything back into the saddle-bags, and finally left a large stone in the hood of the old man's greatcoat. After that, we went to sleep for the hour or so left of the night.

When it was time to leave everyone got up except the old man. They called him but when he tried to get up he couldn't lift the hood of his coat. He looked to see what it was and the landlord told him off on purpose, saying:

'God Almighty, couldn't you find something else to pinch, dad? What if I hadn't seen you? That's worth more than a hundred ducats to me, it's wonderful for the belly-ache.'

The old man swore blind he hadn't put the stone in his hood. The roughs counted up the bill and it came to sixty *reals*, though I guarantee even a professor of mathematics couldn't have followed their calculations. The students said:

'We'll make it up to you by acting as your servants in Alcalá.'

We had a bit of breakfast and the old man picked up his saddle-bags. Since he didn't want us to see what he was taking out or share it with anyone, he undid them under his coat. He took a well-coated bit of plaster out and, biting into it with the tooth and a half he had left in his head, he nearly lost them. He started to spit and make faces as if he was in pain and was going to be sick. We all rushed up, the priest first, and asked him what the matter was. He began to swear blue murder and dropped the saddle-bags. Up came the student and said:

'Back, Satan, behold the Cross!'

The other opened his breviary and they made him think he was possessed, until he himself said what was wrong with him and asked them to let him wash his mouth out with a little wine he had in his leather bottle. They did and he took it out and opened it. When he tried to pour some wine into a glass, out with the tow and wool came some foul wine, so hairy and furry that it wasn't drinkable and it couldn't be filtered either. Then the old man really lost his temper, but when he saw that we were killing ourselves laughing at him he thought he'd do better to keep quiet and get into the cart with the roughs and the women. The students and the priest got on donkeys and we got into the coach. We were just leaving when they began to laugh and sneer and boast about the way they had swindled us.

'Young man,' said the innkeeper, 'a few more first times like this and you'll soon grow up.'

'I'm a priest,' said the ecclesiastic, 'and all my colleagues will tell the story as often as they say Mass.'

The student yelled:

'Scratch when it itches, not after.'

The others called out:

'Pox on you, Señor Don Diego.'

We pretended not to take any notice but we felt like something the cat brought in.

And so, after a few other adventures, we arrived and put up at an inn. All day long, for we arrived at nine, we talked over the supper, but we couldn't get straight what it had cost us.

CHAPTER FIVE

―‹‹·››―

BEFORE night came we left the inn and went to the house which had been rented for us. It was outside the Santiago gate. It's a students' district, full of them, but our house only had three. The owner and landlord was one of those who believe in God out of good manners and not sincerely; half-Moors they're called by the people. There's no shortage of those people or the ones who have long noses and only need them to smell out bacon. Of course I'm not hinting at any impure blood among the aristocracy, oh no! Well, the landlord welcomed us in a more unfriendly way than if I were the Blessed Host itself. I don't know if this was so we should respect him or whether it was natural to him; after all, if their religion is odd then their characters are likely to be odd as well, aren't they? We put down our luggage, made the bed and got everything else ready, and went to sleep. Day came and in came all the students who were living there, in their nightshirts, to ask my master for his entrance fee. He didn't know what this was, so he asked me what they meant. I had already dived between the sheets in case anything happened, and only half my head was showing, like a tortoise. They asked for a couple of dozen *reals*! They got them and set up a terrible noise, singing:

'Long live our comrade, admit him to our circle! Let him enjoy the privileges of an old student! Let him have the pox, go unwashed, and get hungry like the rest of us!'

Some privileges! They charged down the stairs, and we dressed straight away and went off to lectures. My master was looked after by some college men, friends of his father, and began his course. But I began to tremble as I had to go somewhere else and was alone. I went into the courtyard and at once they blocked my way and began saying:

106

'New! New!'

To pretend I didn't care, I began to laugh as if I wasn't taking any notice, but it was no use. Seven or eight of them came up close and began to laugh. I went red – oh God, if only I hadn't – and at once one of them put his hand to his nose, turned away and said:

'It's about time Lazarus here was brought to life again, he stinks.'

So all of them turned away, holding their noses. I thought I could get away, so I also held my nose and said:

'You're quite right, it does stink here.'

They laughed uproariously, and by then there were about a hundred of them. They began to hawk and prepare for a volley and, seeing their mouths opening and closing and hearing the coughing, I saw they were getting gobs of phlegm ready for me. Then a student from La Mancha with a cold let go a mighty one, saying:

'That's for me.'

Then I saw what I was in for and said:

'By God, I'll...'

That was as far as I got, for the barrage and shower that came down on me was so heavy that I couldn't finish the sentence. I covered my face with my cloak. I was an easy target and their aim was accurate. By this time I was slimy from my head to toe but one crafty bastard, seeing that my face was protected, ran up and shouted angrily:

'That's enough, don't kill him.'

I thought that was just what they were trying to do so I uncovered my face to see who it was. And that's when he got me with a gob right between the eyes! You can imagine the state I was in. Those devils shouted so loud they deafened me. From what they threw up at me from their stomachs I thought they were trying to save on doctors and chemists by giving themselves a good clean-out on the new students. After this they tried rabbit-punches, but they couldn't do so without picking up half the muck on my black cloak, now unfortunately white with spit. They left me like an old man's spittoon. I went home. I only just managed to find it and luckily it was morning and I only met two or three boys. They must have been in a good temper as they only threw a few dirty rags at me and went away. I went in. When the half-Moor saw me, he began to laugh and pretend to spit at me. I was afraid he was going to do so and said:

'Please don't, I'm not Christ on the Cross, you know.'

I wish I hadn't, because he was a bit sensitive and lost his temper and knocked me about with a pair of scales he was carrying, as if I hadn't been crippled enough already. So I went upstairs, where it took me a long time to find somewhere to hang my cassock and my gown. At last I took them off and hung them out on the roof. When my master came back and found me asleep he was very angry as he knew nothing about the disgusting thing that had happened to me. He began to pull my hair so hard that I nearly woke up bald. I got up yelling and groaning, and he said in a very angry voice:

'Is this what you call being my servant, Pablos? You haven't got the slightest idea.'

When I heard him say this I lost control completely and said:

'You're not helping me very much with what I've got to put up with. Look at my cassock and gown. They've been used as handkerchiefs by the biggest noses you've ever seen outside a Passion Week procession,' and then I began to cry. He believed me when he saw me crying and went and had a look at the cassock. He felt sorry for me and said:

'Pablos, you've got to wake up. Watch out for yourself. You know your father and mother can't do it for you.'

I told him everything that had happened and he ordered me to undress and go to my room where four other servants of the lodgers slept. I went to bed and fell asleep and by the time night came, and after a good dinner and supper, I felt a new man. But when trouble starts you think it's never going to end, because it's one damn thing after another. The other servants came to bed. They all nodded and asked me if I was ill and whether I was comfortable in bed. I told them what had happened and right then, as if butter wouldn't melt in their mouths, they began to cross themselves and say:

'Even savages wouldn't behave like that; how could they do that sort of thing?'

Another said:

'It's the Rector's fault. He ought to do something about it. Do you know who they are?'

I said I didn't and I thanked them for their kind intention. Then they undressed, went to bed, put out the light and I went to sleep. I pretended I was with my father and my brothers. It must have been about midnight when one of them woke me up, howling:

'They're killing me! Burglars!'

From his bed I could hear blows and shouts. I sat up and said: 'What's all this?'

Hardly had I done so when they laid about me with a thick rope like a cat o' nine tails. I began to scream and tried to get up. The other servant was also groaning but it was me they were hitting. I began to scream: 'Jesus, help me!' but as they pulled the blanket off and the blows were coming down fast, all I could do was to hide under the bed. I did this and then the three who were asleep began to shout also. As I could hear the blows I thought that someone else was beating all of us. Meanwhile, the bastard who slept next to me got into my bed, crapped in it and covered the mess up; when he went back to his own bed, the beating stopped and all four got up, shouting:

'This is intolerable, we're not going to put up with it.'

I was still under the bed, groaning like a dog caught in a door. I was so curled up I looked like a greyhound with cramp. The others pretended to shut the door so I came out from my hiding-place and asked if anybody was hurt; they all complained terribly. I went to bed, covered myself up, and fell asleep again. I twisted and turned while I was dreaming, so when I woke up I was smothered in shit. They all got up and I used the beating as an excuse for not getting dressed. I wouldn't get up for all the devils in Hell. I wondered if I had fouled myself without realizing it, out of fear, or if it happened while I was dreaming. So I felt both that it was my fault and that it wasn't, and I couldn't think of a good excuse. The others came up to me grumbling, and like the hypocrites they were asked me how I felt. I said I felt very ill as I had been badly beaten. I asked them who it could have been, and they said:

'Don't you worry, he won't get away, we have an informer who'll tell us where he is. But never mind about that; let's see if you're injured, because you yelled your head off.'

As they said this they lifted the bedclothes to try and embarrass me. Just then in came my master and said:

'What's all this, Pablos? Haven't I any control over you at all? It's eight o'clock and you're still in bed? Get up or you'll be sorry.'

So as to keep the joke going the others told Don Diego what had happened and asked him to let me sleep, and one of them said:

'If you don't believe us, lift his bedclothes,' and he pulled at the covers. I was holding them in my teeth so nobody should see the shit, and when they saw they couldn't get them off me, one of them said:

'God, doesn't he stink!'

Don Diego said the same, because it was true enough. Then they all began to look around to see if there was a chamber pot where the smell was coming from.

'A fine place this is to study,' said one.

They looked at the beds and moved them to look underneath and said:

'There must be something under Pablos's bed. Let's move him to one of ours and look underneath his.'

I saw that I'd had it and that they were going to grab me, so I pretended to have a fit. I grabbed hold of the bed-head and made faces. They knew what I was doing, so they held me down saying:

'Poor fellow.'

Don Diego held on to my middle finger and five of them managed to pick me up. They lifted the sheets and bellowed with laughter at what was there – not bird droppings, but great turds.

'Poor fellow,' the bastards said. I pretended to have fainted.

'Pull that middle finger good and hard,' they said, and my master, thinking it would do me good, pulled it so hard that he disjointed it. The others tried to tie my thighs together and said:

'Poor boy, he must have soiled himself when he had the fit.'

Who can realize how I felt, what with shame, a disjointed finger and the fear that they would cramp my legs? They had the ropes round me already so I pretended to come round. But they were trying to hurt me and before I could open my eyes they had already twisted the cords deep into me. Then they left me, saying:

'God, aren't you skinny?'

I was crying with rage and they said on purpose:

'Your health is more important than the fact that you soiled yourself, shut up!' And they washed me, put me to bed and went away.

When I was alone all I could think of was that in one day in Alcalá I had suffered more than in all the time with Dr Goat. At midday I dressed, cleaned my cassock with a horsecloth as well as I could and waited for my master who asked how I was as soon as he arrived. Everybody in the house had dinner. I ate a little but without much appetite and then, when we all gathered to talk in the corridor, the other servants told me what they had done to me. But first they jeered a little and all laughed. I felt doubly insulted and said to myself:

'Now watch out, Pablos.'

I determined to change my outlook. We made it up and from then on we all lived like brothers and nobody bothered me any more in the schools or the courtyards.

CHAPTER SIX

❖

'WHEN in Rome, do as the Romans do,' says the proverb, and how right it is. After thinking about it I decided to be as much a tearaway as the others and worse than them if I could. I don't know if I succeeded but I certainly tried hard enough. First I sentenced to death any pigs that might wander into the house and any of the housekeeper's chickens that found their way from the yard into my room. One day two of the finest-looking swine I'd seen came in. I was playing about with the other servants when I heard the pigs grunting, so I said to one of them:

'Go and see who's grunting in our house.'

He went and said there were two pigs. I got very annoyed and said it was disgusting and a real cheek to come and grunt in other people's houses, and I shoved my sword right into them behind closed doors and then slit their throats. They died at our hands and we pretended to sing at the tops of our voices as we did the job. We took out the guts, collected the blood, and half singed them in the yard over a burning straw palliasse. So when their owners came it was all over except for the guts. We hadn't made the black sausages, though not out of slowness but because in our haste we left half the innards inside. Don Diego and the steward heard about it and were so angry that the other boarders, though they were roaring with laughter, had to stand by me. Don Diego asked me what he could say if I was arrested and prosecuted and I answered that I would claim hunger, the students' stand-by, and that if that didn't help me I would say:

'As they came in without knocking I assumed they were ours.'

They all laughed at my defence.

'I say, Pablos,' said Don Diego, 'You really are beginning to learn.'

The strange thing was to see my master so quiet and religious

112

and me so rough, that each of us showed up the other's virtue or vice.

The housekeeper was very pleased because she and I were allies; we had cornered the food supply. I did the issuing, and a right Judas I was, and ever since then I've loved petty thieving. The meat always went from greater to less, the opposite of the laws of rhetoric, and if she could serve goat or ewe-meat she never gave mutton. If she had doves, there was never any flesh on them; so she made stews so weak they looked consumptive. If you'd frozen her soul you could have made glass beads out of it.

At Christmas and Easter she used to throw some ends of animal-fat candles in her cooking, just for some fat to make a change. When I was present she used to say to my master:

'You know, you'll never find a servant like young Pablos. If only he weren't such a tearaway! Keep him, though, his loyalty is worth the trouble he gives. He always brings home the best from the market.'

I used to say the same about her, so we managed to deceive them all. If we bought oil, coal or bacon for all of them, we hid half of it and, when we judged the time right, the housekeeper and I used to say:

'Keep your expenses down. If you go on like that the King's treasury won't be enough. There isn't any more oil or coal, you've used it up so quickly. We'll have to buy some more and we'd better be more careful; give your Pablos the cash.'

They gave me the money and we sold them the half we had pinched and half of what we bought, and that's how we went on with everything. And if I ever bought anything in the market at its proper price, the housekeeper and I pretended to have a row. She shouted:

'Don't tell me, Pablos, that this is two *cuartos*' worth of salad.'

I pretended to cry. I shouted and went and complained to my master, and begged him to send the steward to check the price so as to shut the old woman up, as she was telling me off on purpose. He went and checked, and so we got my master and the steward on our side. They were grateful for my honesty and to the housekeeper for her zeal in their interest. Don Diego used to say to her that he was very satisfied with me, and added:

'I wish Pablos was as well-behaved as he is trustworthy. He is all loyalty. What do you think of him?'

And so we bled them like leeches. I bet you'd be surprised at what it came to in a year. It must have been a lot but we didn't feel obliged to give it back because the housekeeper made confession and took Holy Communion regularly every week and I never saw in her any hint of giving back anything nor having anything on her conscience, because you see, she was a saint. The rosary round her neck was so large that it would have been easier for her to carry a load of firewood on her back. From this rosary hung bundles of images, crosses and beads and she said that she prayed to all of them every night for her benefactors. She had a hundred or so saints on her side in Heaven and believe me, she needed all their help to shift her load of sin. She slept in a room above my master's and said more prayers than a blind man. She began with the Just Judge and finished, so she said, with the *Conquibus* (or *Con Quibus*) and the *Salve Retina* (or *Regina*). She said the prayers in Latin just to pretend she was simple and we all nearly died laughing. She was clever in other ways; she could overcome people's will and bring lovers together. In other words she was a procuress but her excuse to me was that she inherited the talent just like the King of France had the touch to cure scrofula.

I suppose, sir, you think we two were always in agreement, but everyone knows that two friends, especially if they are greedy, always try and trick each other. Now the housekeeper kept hens in the yard. I fancied one of them. She had ten or eleven quite big chickens, and one day, while she was feeding them, she began to call out:

'Pio, pio, pio . . .' This went on for quite a time.

When I heard how she called them I began to shout and say:

'Oh my God, woman, if you'd done a murder or clipped the King's coin I could have kept quiet about it, but I can't keep what you've just done to myself. Heaven help me and you!'

When she saw how excited I was she began to worry a bit and said:

'But what have I done, Pablos? If this is all a joke please don't make me suffer any more.'

'What do you mean, a joke? The hell with that! I've got no alternative but to notify the Inquisition or else I'll be excommunicated.'

'Inquisition?' she said, beginning to tremble. 'Have I done anything against the Faith?'

'That's the worse thing you could do,' I said. 'Don't try to be clever with the inquisitors. Say you were silly and you didn't mean it, but don't deny you blasphemed and weren't respectful.'

She was very scared and asked:

'Pablos, if I say I didn't mean it, will I be punished?'

'No,' I answered, 'they'll absolve you.'

'Well I didn't mean it then,' she said. 'But tell me what I did. I don't know, and I want my dead family to rest in peace.'

'Do you mean you didn't realize? I don't even like to say it, it's so bad. Don't you remember you called "Pio, pio," to the chickens? Well, isn't that the name of popes, vicars of Christ and heads of the Church? Now you see your sin.'

She was dumbfounded and said:

'Pablos, I admit I did say it, but God knows it wasn't with any bad intention. I was wrong. Look, can't you see your way not to denounce me, because I'll die if I end up in the Inquisition.'

'If you swear on a Holy Altar that you didn't mean any harm then I can certainly see my way not to denounce you. But those two chickens who ate their food after you called them with the sacred name of the Holy Father – well, you'll have to give them to me to take to an agent of the Inquisition to be burnt, as they are unclean and then you must swear never to do anything like that again.'

She was overjoyed and said:

'Take them away now, Pablos, and I'll swear tomorrow.'

In order to trick her even more, I said:

'The trouble is, Cipriana,' – that was her name – 'that I'm taking a risk in going, because the inquisitor may ask me if I'm the guilty one and bring trouble down on me. You take them, I'm scared to.'

'Please Pablos,' she said, 'For God's sake have some pity and take them; nothing can happen to you.'

I let her beg for a long time and at last, as I had planned, I said 'yes', took the chickens, hid them in my room, pretended to go out, but came back and said:

'It went better than I thought; that inquisitor chap wanted to come with me and see the woman but I tricked him and settled his hash neatly.'

She flung her arms round me and gave me another chicken for myself; and I went off with it to where I'd left its companions. I had them roasted in a pastry-shop and ate them with the other servants.

Don Diego and the housekeeper heard the trick I'd played and the whole house talked of nothing else. The housekeeper was so upset that she nearly died, and was so enraged that she would have revealed all my thieving, if only she hadn't been so deeply in it as well.

Now that I saw I was no longer in with the housekeeper and couldn't play any more tricks on her I looked for other ways to enjoy myself. I started on the students' game of snatching and running. And some very funny things happened to me. One night at nine o'clock, when there were very few people about, I was walking across the main square and I saw a confectioner's with a basket of raisins on the counter. I got up speed, arrived, grabbed it and made off with the confectioner and his assistants and some locals running after me. I realized that they would catch me up as the load was heavy, so as I went round a corner I sat down on the basket and quickly arranged my cloak over my legs and holding one leg I began saying:

'Oh, blast him, he kicked me.'

They heard me say this, and as soon as they came up I began:

'By our most Holy Lady' and the usual rigmarole about bad luck and infected air that beggars use to blame their misfortunes on. They came up shouting and said:

'Have you seen a man, lad?'

'Further on. He trod on me, God be praised.'

So they went off again. I was left alone and took the basket home and told them all about my exploit. They wouldn't believe what I said, although the trick was praised, so I invited them to come and watch me perform the next night. They came and saw that the boxes were inside the shop and couldn't be snatched easily, and so they considered it impossible – even more so because the confectioner was wide awake this time and determined not to lose anything in the same way as he had lost the raisins. I went up and, twelve steps before I got there, I unsheathed my sword, which was a good firm weapon. I charged up and as I arrived I lunged at the shopkeeper, saying:

'Say your prayers!'

He collapsed, begging for confession, and I thrust the sword through the box and carried it out. They were astounded at the trick and roared with laughter when the confectioner asked them to look at him as he must have been wounded and I was a man he had had words with already. But when he looked around and saw the boxes disarranged because one was missing, he saw what I had done and started to cross himself as though he'd never stop.

I must confess I never felt better in my life. My comrades said that I could keep the whole house by myself with what I nicked (that's thieves' slang for stole). Every day I came home with my belt loaded with nuns' cups which I asked them to lend me for a drink and then ran away with. Because of me they refused to lend them any more without a deposit. Then I promised Don Diego and all the others to come home with the swords of the police patrol itself. We decided which one to pick on and went together with me in front. When we spotted the police I ran up with one of the servants and said, very excitedly:

'Police?'

They answered:

'Yes!'

'Is this the Magistrate?'

They said he was. I fell on my knees and said:

'Sir, you must help me and revenge me, and it's for the public good as well. Let me speak to you privately for a couple of minutes if you want to make an important arrest.'

He stepped to one side while his men began unsheathing their swords and the sergeants brandishing their truncheons. I said to him:

'Sir, I've come from Seville following six of the most evil men in the world, all thieves and murderers. One of them killed my mother and one of my brothers to rob them. This has been proved and I've also heard they're with a French spy, and I suspect, from what I heard, that it is' – and I lowered my voice – 'Antonio Pérez.'*

At this the Magistrate jumped back and said:

'Where are they?'

'Sir, in the brothel. Don't be put off. My mother's and my brother's soul will intercede for you in Heaven and the King will reward you.'

'Come on, follow me, all of you, give me protection,' said the Magistrate.

I took him aside again and said:

'Sir, it'll all go wrong like that. What you should do is go in unarmed one by one. You see, the murderers have pistols and they'll fire as they know it can only be the police if you go in with swords. You're better off with daggers, securing them from behind. There are enough of us to do it.'

The idea of getting a jail sentence for somebody suited the Magistrate down to the ground. By now we were quite near the place. The Magistrate craftily ordered everybody to hide their swords under the grass in a field almost opposite and we went forward. I had already told my companion that as soon as they put their swords down he had to pick them up and make for home. I brought up the rear after he had done so. As they went into the house and mingled with the other people leaving, I nipped off sharply through an alley-way that comes out near La Vitoria. They went in and couldn't find anything except students and good-for-nothings (all the same thing); so they started to look for me and suspected something when they couldn't find me. When they looked for their swords – not a clue. You can imagine the hours the Magistrate and the Rector put in that night looking at all the beds in the dormitories. They came to our house and I concealed myself by lying with a nightcap on, a candle in one hand and a picture of Christ in the other, with a 'priest', one of the others, giving me the last rites. The Rector and the Magistrate came, but when they saw the performance they left, convinced that nothing like what had happened could have origi-

* Ex-secretary of Philip II. Accused of treachery, he fled to France.

nated there. They didn't look at anything; in fact the Rector said a prayer for me. He asked if I could still speak and he was told I couldn't, so they went away having given up all hope of finding a lead. The Rector swore he would give him up if he found who it was and the Magistrate that he would hang him, even if he was a grandee's son. I got up and they still tell the story in Alcalá today.

I don't want to go on too long, so I won't tell how I used the main square as a firewood shop. I never forgot how they treated me when I was boy king so I stocked the woodshed all year round with chopped-up clothshearers' and jewellers' tables – and fruiterers' of course. I shan't say anything about my raids on beanpatches, vineyards and orchards round about. With these and other exploits I began to be known as a crafty tearaway. The gentlemen treated me well and hardly gave me time to attend to Don Diego, whom I always respected as I should because he treated me very well.

CHAPTER SEVEN

A B O U T this time Don Diego had a letter from his father and in the same envelope one from an uncle of mine named Alonso Yobb, a very virtuous man and well known in Segovia for his passion for justice, especially final justice, because he'd been responsible for all those who had experienced it in the last four years. In other words, he was a hangman, and a very able one too. Seeing him at work made you feel like being hanged yourself. Anyhow he wrote me a letter from Segovia as follows:

'Dear Pablos' – he really did love me – 'the onerous duties of this post to which His Majesty has appointed me have prevented me writing to you before. The only thing wrong with serving the King is the work, although that is much relieved (or supposed to be) by the honour of being his servant. I am sorry to have to give you bad news. Your father died a week ago as bravely as any man ever did. That I can guarantee as I topped him myself. He got on the donkey without using the stirrup. The condemned man's uniform looked tailor-made on him, and with the holy images of Christ in front of him and his dignity, nobody would have thought he was going to be hanged. He was very much at his ease and looked up at the windows and bowed to people who left their business to look at him. He curled his moustache twice, ordered his confessors to rest, and praised them for their ability. He came to the gallows and climbed up, neither on his hands and feet nor slowly, and when he saw that one step was broken he told them to repair it for the next hanging because not everybody was as brave as he was. I cannot exaggerate the impression he made on everyone. He sat down on top and pulled the neck of his shirt open; he put the rope round his neck and when the monk was about to preach to him, he turned and said:

' "Father, take it as said already. Let's have a bit of Creed and finish it all quickly. I shouldn't want people to feel I'm drawing it out." '

'That is what happened. He asked me to take the hood off and wipe his saliva, which I did. He dropped, keeping his legs straight and without making faces. One could not have asked for a more dignified death. I quartered him and buried his remains along the roads. God knows I can't bear to see the crows getting a free meal from him. Still, I reckon the pastry-cooks will cheer us up by putting his bits in their four-*real* cakes.

'Your mother is still alive, but she might just as well not be, because the Toledo Inquisition has got her for digging up the dead and, as you know, only evil-tongued old women are allowed to do that. They say she kissed a billy-goat's arse every night in her house. They found more legs, arms and heads than in a miraculous shrine, and the least she did was to fake virgins. She appeared in an *auto-de-fé* on Trinity day, together with four hundred people condemned to death. I'm very upset because it dishonours all of us, especially me as an officer of the King who should not be related to that kind of person. There is some money hidden here belonging to your parents. It is about four hundred ducats altogether. I am your uncle and what I have will go to you. Now you can come here and with what you know of Latin and rhetoric you will be a first class executioner. Answer this letter at once. God bless you, etc.'

I can't say I wasn't upset at this new disgrace but I was also rather relieved; parents' vices can console their children for their misfortunes, however great they may be. I went running off to Don Diego, who was reading the letter from his father telling him to leave Alcalá and not to take me with him. He had been disturbed by the news of my exploits. Don Diego told me that he planned to go and do everything else that his father had ordered him, and that he was sorry he couldn't take me (I was, too). He told me he would fix me up as servant to another gentleman friend of his. I laughed at this and said :

'I'm not the same boy, sir, and my plans have changed. I want to make something of myself and get a position. Up to now I've had my foot on the rung like anyone else, but now I've got my father's reputation to live up to.'

I told him how he had died as honourably as the greatest aristocrat, how he was carved up into quarters, and how my uncle the hangman had written to me about this and my mum's little stay in gaol. Since Don Diego knew all about me I could tell him everything without being ashamed. He was very sorry for me and asked me what I planned to do.

I told him what I had in mind. The next day he went to Segovia in a very sad mood and I stayed in the house hiding my bad luck. I burnt the letter in case I lost it and somebody saw it. Then I began getting ready to leave for Segovia to collect my money and find out who my relations were and steer clear of them.

CHAPTER EIGHT

<+>

T H E day came for me to leave the best life I had ever had. God alone knows how I felt at having to leave so many friends and all my acquaintances. I sold the little I had, secretly, to get some money for the journey, and with a bit of trickery I collected about six hundred *reals*. I hired a mule and left my lodgings. I had no right to take anything more out of the house than my shadow. You can't imagine how angry the shoemaker was about the shoes I had on tick, how worried the housekeeper was about her salary, and how furious the owner was about the rent of his house. Some said:

'I always knew it,' and others:

'They were right when they told me he was no good.'

In other words, so well-loved was I that when I left half the town were in tears because I had gone and the other half were laughing at their bad luck.

I was whiling time away along the road thinking of all this when, just after crossing the river Verote, I came up with a man on a pack-mule who was talking away to himself nineteen to the dozen and so absorbed that he didn't see me even though I was riding alongside him. I said 'hullo' to him and he said 'hullo' to me; I asked him where he was going and, after a few pleasantries, we began to talk about whether the Turks would attack and about the King's army. He began to tell me how the Holy Land could be taken and how Algiers would be won. From the way he talked I could see he was one of those cranks who could run the country all on their own if anyone let them. We carried on talking in this way, which was just about right for layabouts, and the conversation led us to Flanders. Then it happened: he began to sigh and say:

'That part of the world has cost me more than it has cost the

King, because I've got a project which if it weren't impossible (as it is) would pacify the place entirely.'

'What can it be?' I asked. 'If it's so right, how can it be impossible to carry out?'

'Who told you it can't be carried out,' he said. 'It can be done; being impossible is quite another kettle of fish. I'd tell you all about it if it wouldn't bore you. But you'll see it later, as I'm thinking of publishing it with two or three other little things, among which I show the King how to capture Ostend in two ways.'

I begged him to tell me, so he took his plan out of the skirt of his coat and showed me a picture of the enemy fort and our own and said:

'You can easily see that the major difficulty is this bit of sea; well, I'd order it to be sucked up with sponges and taken away.'

At this nonsense I roared with laughter, and he looked me straight in the face and said:

'Everybody I tell it to does the same thing. They all seem to find it very funny.'

'I'll bet they do,' I said. 'It's certainly a new idea. But, look, if you suck up all the water, the sea will only flow in again.'

'It won't do anything of the sort, I'm positive about that,' he replied. 'In any case, I've thought of an invention to lower the sea by about twelve fathoms there.'

I didn't dare answer him in case he said he had a plan to pull the sky down! I never saw anybody as mad as that in my life. He told me that what the engineer Juanito Turriano had done was nothing. He was making a plan to pipe all the water of the River Tagus up to Toledo in an easier way. Then he told me what it was – a magic spell, no less! Can you believe it? And after that he said:

'I'm not going to get it going unless the King gives me an estate first. I could look after one properly and I've had no Moors or Jews among my ancestors.'

With these exchanges and other nonsense we reached Torrejón, where he stopped to see a relative of his.

I went on, killing myself laughing at the plans on which he wasted his time when, God help me, I saw in the distance a single mule and a man standing next to it who was looking at a book and drawing lines which he then measured with a pair of dividers. He ran backwards and forwards, from this side to that, and every now and again he put one finger over another and jumped around again. I confess that I watched him from a distance for a long time and thought he was a magician and was afraid to go on. At last I got up my courage. He heard me as I came near, shut the book, put his foot in the stirrup, slipped and fell. I lifted him off the ground. He said:

'I didn't measure the proportion properly to make the circumference to mount.'

I couldn't make head or tail of this and was very afraid of him because nobody as mad as that could be an ordinary human being. He asked me if I was going to Madrid by the straight or the circumflex route. I didn't understand what he meant but I said 'circumflex' all the same. He asked whose was the sword I wore by my side and when I said it was mine he said:

'Those quillons ought to be longer to guard against the cuts in the middle of the thrusts.'

Then he began such a long rigmarole that I had to ask him what he was professor of. He told me he was a genuine fencer and could prove it anywhere. I began to laugh and said:

'Well, when I saw the circles you were drawing in the field there, I reckoned you were a magician.'

'Oh that! you see, there was an opening in quart with the larger arm of the dividers, so I could trap my opponent's sword and finish him off there and then, so that he wouldn't be able to say who did it.'

And he started explaining it, using mathematics.

'Do you mean to say there's maths in this?' I asked.

'Not just maths, but theology, philosophy, music and medicine too.'

'I'm not questioning the last subject, since it's a matter of killing.'

'Don't joke about it,' he said; 'now you're going to learn a first-class guard: how to make the major thrusts which themselves include all the spirals of the sword.'

'I don't understand any of the words you use, big or small.'

'Well they're all in this book,' he answered; 'it's called *The Greatness of the Sword* and it's first-class, quite marvellous. Now I want you to believe me, so when we get to Rejas, where we're going to spend the night, you'll see me perform miracles with a couple of meat-spits. And believe me when I tell you that anybody who has read this book will be able to kill whoever he likes.'

'Either this book was written to turn men into food for worms, or some doctor wrote it,' I replied.

'What do you mean, a doctor? He understands everything, he's a very wise man.' *

So we came to Rejas. We rode up to an inn and, as I dismounted, he shouted at me to make an obtuse angle with my legs, then make them parallel and put myself perpendicular to the ground. The landlord saw me laughing and laughed also. He asked me if the gentleman spoke like that because he was an American Indian. I thought I'd die laughing. Then my companion went up to the landlord and said:

'Landlord, please give me a couple of spits to do a few angles. I'll give them back straight after.'

'Eh?' said the landlord. 'You give me the angles and my wife will roast them, though I must say I've never heard of any birds called that.'

'They're not birds,' he said, turning to me. 'See? That's ignorance for you. Give me the spits – I only want them to fence with. I dare say what you see me do here now will do you more good than all the money you've earned in your whole life.'

After all that, it turned out that the spits were being used and we had to be satisfied with two soup-ladles. You've never seen anything funnier in your life. He gave a little skip and said:

'With this move my reach is longer and I have you from the side. Now I take the advantage of the remiss movement to kill you with a straight thrust; this should be a cut and this a thrust.'

He was miles away from me, running around with the soup-ladle, and as I didn't stand still he looked as if he was stabbing at a pot boiling over.

'This is the real thing,' he said, 'not the cavortings that those

* This is a deliberate sneer at a work on the theory of fencing composed by an enemy of Quevedo.

126

quack fencing-masters teach. All they know is how to drink!'

Before he had stopped speaking, out from one of the rooms came a huge mulatto with his teeth bared, a hat as big as an umbrella, and a buff jacket made of suède under a loose coat bedecked with ribbons. He was as bandy-legged as the imperial eagle, his face was covered in scars, his beard turned up sharply and he had a handlebar moustache. He wore a dagger with more wrought iron on it than the windows of a nunnery parlour. He stared at the floor and said :

'I've been examined and I've got my diploma and so help me I'll make mincemeat out of anyone who doesn't show proper respect to any of the lads who profess the art of fencing.'

I saw what was about to happen so I got between them and said that nobody meant him and he had no cause to take offence.

'Put your hand to your sword, if you've got one, and we'll see where the real skill is; you can forget your soup-ladles,' shouted the mulatto.

My poor friend opened his book and said in a loud voice :

'It's in the book, it has the King's permission to be printed and I'll maintain it's true, with the ladle or without the ladle. If you say no, we'll measure it.'

And he pulled out his dividers and began to say :

'This is an obtuse angle.'

Then the swordsman took his dagger out and said :

'I don't know Angle and I don't know Obtuse and I never heard of anybody called that in my life, but I'll carve you up with what I've got in my hand.' He attacked the poor devil, who began to retreat through the house, jumping up and down and shouting :

'He can't wound me, I've got past his guard.' The landlord, myself and some of the other guests pacified them, but I couldn't stop laughing. They put the fellow into a room and me with him. We all had our supper and went to bed. At about two o'clock in the morning he got up and started running around the bedroom in the dark, jumping about and gabbling mathematical rubbish. He woke me up and, not satisfied with this, went down to the landlord and asked him for a lamp, saying he had found a fixed object for the thrust for the segment on the arc. The landlord cursed violently at being woken up and said he was off his head. He came upstairs then and said that if I got up I would see the most famous feints that he had invented for use with the Samaritans against the Turks. He wanted to demonstrate them there and then to the King because it would help the Christians. By now it was light so we dressed and paid for our room. He made up his quarrel with the swordsman, who said that my companion's ideas were good but that his theories would produce more madmen than swordsmen because most people couldn't understand a word he said.

CHAPTER NINE

I took the road to Madrid and he said good-bye to me and went by another road. He had already gone some way when he started running back and in the middle of the country, where nobody could hear us, he whispered in my ear:

'Whatever you do you mustn't breathe a word of all the solemn secrets I've confided to you on the subject of fencing. Keep it all to yourself; I can see you're an intelligent man.'

I promised I would do so and he left me again and I began to laugh at that funny sort of secret.

Then I travelled for more than three miles without meeting a soul. I thought about how difficult it was for me to be honourable and virtuous, because first I would have to hide the fact that my parents were neither, then I would have to be so honourable and virtuous that nobody would know me. I thought these ideas were most praiseworthy and complimented myself for having them.

'People should think better of me,' I said to myself, 'than of somebody who learnt to be good from his grandparents, because I didn't have anyone to teach me.'

I was thinking about all this when I met a very old priest on a mule on his way to Madrid. We started to talk and first he asked me where I had come from – I told him I had come from Alcalá.

'Damn them, awful people,' he said; 'there's not one intelligent man there.'

I asked him how on earth he could say that of a town where so many brilliant men lived. He got very angry and said:

'Brilliant? I'll have you know they're so brilliant that in the fourteen years I've been in Majadalonda * where I'm the sacris-

* A town proverbial for the ignorance of its inhabitants.

tan and have composed carols for Corpus Christi and Christmas they've never given me a prize for my verses. Now I want you to see how unjust they've been, so I'll read them to you.'

He began:

> 'Shepherds, isn't it very funny,
> Today is Saint Corpus Christi?
> It's the day of the dances
> When the Lamb Immaculate
> Does Himself humiliate
> And visits all our paunches,
> And mid all these lucky chances
> Comes into the human gut,
> Sound the merry sackbut,
> It makes us all very happy,
> Shepherds, isn't it very funny,' etc.

'Even the original inventor of puns couldn't do better than that, I'll bet. Look at the deep significance of that word "shepherds". It took me more than a month to work that one out.'

By now I couldn't control myself and the laughter was coming out of my eyes and nose. I roared and said:

'It's marvellous. The only thing I can criticize is that you say Saint Corpus Christi and Corpus Christi isn't a saint but the day when the Holy Sacrament was instituted!'

'Isn't that clever of you,' he sneered. 'I'll show you the name on the calendar. He's been canonized and I'll bet my life on it.'

I couldn't go on because I was choked with laughter at his abysmal ignorance: in fact I told him his rhymes deserved all the prizes and I'd never read anything so well put together in all my life.

'No?' he said at once. 'Well, just you listen to a little piece from a book I've written about the eleven thousand virgins. I've given each one fifty octaves, it's good stuff.'

I wanted to escape listening to so many million octaves, and I begged him not to recite anything in the religious style to me. Then he began to drone away a play that had more acts than it takes days to get to Jerusalem.

'I finished it in two days,' he said, 'and this is the rough draft.'

I reckon there were about a hundred and twenty sheets of paper there. Its title was *Noah's Ark*. It was full of cocks, mice, donkeys, vixens and wild boar, just like Aesop's fables. I praised its plan and the language and he replied:

'It's all my own work. Nobody else in the world has done anything like it, and novelty is the most important thing. If I can get it acted, it'll be famous.'

'How can it be put on,' I asked, 'if the parts are all animals and they can't speak?'

'That's the trouble. If it weren't for that it would be a marvellous thing. But I think I'll do it all with parrots, thrushes, and talking magpies, and I'll put monkeys in to do the funny turns between the acts.'

'Oh, yes, it's great,' I said.

'I've done better,' he said, 'for a woman I'm in love with. Look, here are nine hundred and one sonnets and twelve other poems' – he counted them like cash – 'that I've dedicated to my beloved's legs.' I asked him if he had ever seen them and he said he had done nothing of the kind because of his vocation and orders, but her statements were like those of the prophets, a question of faith. I must admit that although I found it quite amusing to listen to him, I was scared of so many bad verses and so I began to steer the conversation on to other subjects. I told him I could see some hares.

'Right, I'll begin with one where I compare her legs to that animal,' and away he went.

To lead him off the subject I said:

'Can you see that star, shining even during the day?'

He said in answer to this:

'As soon as I finish this one I'll give you sonnet number thirty where I compare her to a star. You seem to know all my subjects without my telling you.'

I was so irritated when I realized that there was nothing I could bring up which he hadn't written some rubbish about, that when I saw we were getting near Madrid I was overjoyed, thinking he'd be modest enough to stop. But it was the exact opposite, because as we went into the town he began to shout louder to let everyone know. I begged him to stop, trying to make him see that if the children smelled a poet every cabbage stump in the town would fly around our heads. Poets had been declared mad in a proclamation issued by a man who had been one before and decided to live a better life. He was very concerned and asked me to read it if I had it on me. I promised I would do so at the inn. We went to one where he usually stayed and found more than twelve blind beggars around the door. Some recognized him by his smell, others by his voice. They welcomed him, all talking at the same time. He embraced all of them. Then some began to ask him to write them a prayer to the Just Judge, in a solemn and ponderous tone that could obtain results. Others asked for a prayer for dead souls and so on. He took eight *reals* as a deposit from each one. When he had got rid of the beggars he said to me:

'I'll get over three hundred *reals* from the blind men so, with your permission, I'll go to my room for a time to do some of the prayers and we'll hear the proclamation about poets after supper.'

What an awful life! Nobody has a worse time than madmen who earn their living from other madmen.

CHAPTER TEN

◄‹–›►

H E took himself off for a while to make up heresies and nonsense
for the blind men. While he was away the meal arrived. We ate
and then the others asked me to read the proclamation against
poets. Having nothing else to do, I took it out and read it. I
include it here, because it seems very well put for what it is
meant to condemn. It went like this:

'A Proclamation Against All Idiot, Useless and Rubbishy
Poets.'

The sacristan roared with laughter and said:

'You should have said so before! Christ! I thought you meant
me before, but this only applies to useless poets.'

I thought this was really funny; he talked as if he were really
first-class. I left off reading the prologue and began the first
chapter, as follows:

'Whereas that species of vermin called poets are our fellow
men and Christians, though bad ones; whereas they continually
worship eyebrows, teeth, ribbons and slippers as well as committing other graver sins, we order that in Holy Week all poets and
idlers, as well as loose women, be collected and advised of the
error of their ways, and that an attempt be made to convert them.
And for this purpose we have established houses for the penitent.

'Article one

'Considering the heatwaves caused by the torrid and eternally
sunny verses of the poets of the sun, who are shrivelled up like
raisins because of the suns and stars they use to construct their
works, we impose perpetual silence on them regarding the sky and
establish close seasons for the Muses, just as for hunting and fishing,
so that they may not exhaust their energies.

133

'Considering that this infernal sect condemned to perpetual pun-
ning, chewers up of words and upsetters of phrases, have infected
women with the said disease of poetry, we declare ourselves quit of
any wrong we have done them in return for what they did to us at
the Creation. And as the World is now poor and in need, we order
that all verses be burned, like old rags, to remove the gold, silver
and pearls, because most verses make their beloveds of all metals.'

The sacristan couldn't stand any more and he stood up and
said:

'No more! Take our living away, that's all! Don't read any
more, I'm going to appeal against it! Not in the High Civil Court
of course, but to my ecclesiastical superiors, otherwise I'll bring my
cloth into disrepute. And I'll spend all I've got on it. It would be
a fine thing if a clergyman like me had to put up with such treatment. I'll prove that verses by poets in Holy Orders are not subject
to that proclamation. I'm going straight off now to the law.'

I thought this was very funny but, as it was getting late and
I didn't want to hang around, I said:

'Sir, this proclamation is all a joke, it's got no force and no
authority behind it.'

'Oh, my God!' he said, very distressed. 'You should have told
me before, you would have saved me an awful lot of aggravation.
Can you imagine what it's like for a man with eight hundred
thousand verses in hand to hear this? Go on, and I hope God
forgives you for giving me such a scare.'

I went on:

'Article three

'Considering that after they ceased to be Moors, though they still
follow some Moorish customs, they became shepherds, and that is
why the sheep are so thin because they drink their tears and are
scorched by their burning souls and so bewitched by the music of
the poetry that they forget to graze, we order them to leave that
profession and we establish hermitages for those who love solitude.
The others will have to be mule-drivers as that is a cheerful job with
much occasion for obscene remarks.'

'Some queer sod of a Jewish bastard must have ordered that,
and if I knew who it was I would do a satire on him that would

flatten him and anybody else who read it. What's the use of a hermitage to a young chap like me? And a mature sacristan like me a mule-boy? Oh this is terrible!'

'I've already told you,' I retorted, 'that it's all a joke and that's how you should take it.'

I went on:

'To prevent major theft, we order that no verses should go from Aragon to Castile, nor from Italy to Spain, and any poet who tries to pass them should be sentenced to wear decent clothes and, on committing a second offence, to keep himself clean for one hour.'

This he found very funny because he wore a cassock so old that it had white hairs and covered in so much mud that to bury himself he'd only have had to pull it slowly over his body. With the muck on the coat you could have manured two plots of earth.

And so, with my tongue in my cheek I told him that the decree also ordered that:

'All women who fall in love with poets only should be considered equal to suicides who hang themselves or throw themselves over cliffs and, like them, should not be buried in consecrated ground. And considering the large harvest of quartets, songs and sonnets in these recent fertile years we order that any bundles of them not considered good enough for grocers' wrapping-paper should go straight to the lavatory without right of appeal.'

And to finish I went on to the last article which went as follows:

'But realizing with sympathy that there are three kinds of people in the State who are sunk so low that they cannot do without the said poets, that is, cheap actors, blind beggars and sacristans, we order that there may exist practitioners of the art, provided they have a certificate of examination from their local chief poet and provided that actors do not finish their sketches with gallows or devils, nor their plays with weddings, that blind men do not set their ballads in Morocco, and that the words "brotherly" and "point of honour" be forbidden. And we decree they do not say "tragedy" for "play" and that sacristans in their nativity plays do not call their peasants Giles or Pasqual, do not pun and do not write in such a style that they may change the words around and use them at the next festival. And finally we order all poets to lay aside Jupiter,

Venus, Apollo and other gods, under pain of having them for advocates at the hour of death.'

Everybody who had heard me read out the decree thought it just perfect and they all asked me for a copy of it. Only that twit of a sacristan began to swear by the Holy Vespers, the Introit and the Kyrie that it was a satire against him (because of the references to blind beggars) and that he knew his job better than anyone else. And last of all he said :

'I once stayed at an inn with Liñán and I've had dinner more than twice with Espinel.'

And in Madrid he'd once been as close to Lope de Vega as he was to me, and he'd seen Alonso de Ercilla dozens of times, and at his house he had a picture of the incomparable Figueroa, and he'd bought Padella's * breeches when the latter went into a monastery, and he still wore them even if they were falling to pieces. He showed them to us and we all laughed so much that nobody wanted to leave the inn.

By now it was two o'clock and we had to be on our way, so we left Madrid. I said good-bye to him much against my will and made my way towards the city gate. So that I shouldn't think of things I ought not to, God had me meet a soldier. We started up a conversation straight away. He asked me if I had come from Madrid. I said I had passed through the town on my way.

'That's the best thing you could have done, pass through it,' he said; 'it's a lousy place. By God, I'd rather be somewhere in snow up to my waist, doing a manly job and chewing wood, than put up with the way they fleece an honest man.'

I retorted that you could find all types of people in Madrid and that any man of spirit was always well thought of there.

'Well thought of !' he exclaimed furiously. 'I've been after a command for six months after twenty years' service and shedding my blood for the King as these wounds show.'

He showed me a scar from a 'knife wound' six inches long in his groin. Actually it was as plain as a pikestaff that it was a plague-scar. He also showed me two marks on his heels that he said were from bullets, but I had two the same so I reckoned they were old chilblain scars. He took off his hat and showed me his

* Poets and playwrights. Lope de Vega is the most famous.

full face. He had had sixteen stitches in his face and the same number in a wound which had slit his nose. Another three slashes made his face look like a much-folded map.

'These,' he said, 'I got in Paris in the King's service, for which I have had my features altered. All I've received are smooth words which are what they use now for dirty deeds. Read these papers. God Almighty, there's never been a man so distinguished, with distinguishing marks on his face.'

He began to drag out tins and show me papers which must have belonged to someone else whose name he had taken. I read them and told him they were really impressive and that he'd obviously done more than either the Cid or Bernardo del Carpio.* He jumped at this and said:

'What are you talking about, God Almighty! More than García de Paredes or Julián Romero† or any of them, by God! In the old days there wasn't any artillery, God Almighty! Bernardo wouldn't have lasted an hour in these days. You ask them to tell you about what Old Toothless did in Flanders and you see what they say.'

'Are you Toothless by any chance?' I said to him.

'Well, who else could I be?' he replied. 'Can't you see the holes in my mouth? Anyhow that's enough of that, it's not right to boast about oneself too much!'

While we were talking we met a hermit riding on a donkey. His beard was so long that it trailed in the mud; he was gaunt and thin and dressed in a coarse, brown robe. We greeted him with the usual 'Deo Gratias' and he began to go on about how marvellous the harvest had been and how great were the mercies of God. The soldier jumped at this and said:

'Oh, father, I've had pikes flying at me thicker than wheat and, by God, I was in the front at the sacking of Antwerp‡, by God I was!'

The hermit told him off for swearing so much and the soldier answered:

'It's easy enough to see, father, that you've never been a soldier; you're telling me not to do my own job.'

* Heroes of medieval epics.
† Military men of the Spanish Golden Age.   ‡ 1576.

I thought his way of looking at soldiering was very funny and I realized he was probably a bad lot because among soldiers, especially the higher ranks, blaspheming like that is not approved of.

We reached the top of the pass. The hermit was telling his beads with a load of old firewood made into balls so heavy that each Hail Mary sounded like two woods hitting each other in a game of bowls. The soldier compared the cliffs to the castles he had seen and pointed out the natural fortresses and where he would put his artillery.

And I watched the two of them, feeling uncomfortable at both the giant beads of the hermit and the soldier's lies.

'Wouldn't I just fancy blowing up this pass,' I said to myself. 'I'd certainly be doing something to help travellers in the future.'

And so we reached Cercedilla. It was already night when all three of us went into the inn. We ordered supper and, while they were getting it ready, the hermit said:

'Let's amuse ourselves a bit. You know idleness is the root of evil. Let's play, and the loser will have to say a "Hail Mary".' And he slipped a deck of cards out of his sleeve. Considering the beads, I thought this was very funny.

'No,' said the soldier. 'Let's play to a limit of the hundred *reals* I've got on me, just a friendly game.'

I was greedy and put up another hundred and the hermit agreed, so as not to be awkward, and said he had the money for the church oil-lamps on him, almost two hundred *reals*. I must admit I thought I'd easily take him for that – I wish my luck on the Turks! We played Lansquenet* and his trick was to say he didn't know the game and pretend to make us teach it to him. He let us win two hands and then set to work and cleaned us out. He inherited all our money while we were still alive. He scooped it up in the palm of his hand; it broke my heart. He lost with small stakes and won with big ones. At every hand the soldier cursed twelve 'Gods' and an equal number of 'sod its'

* A card game where one card is given to each of the players and another to the dealer. One version of the game allows the player who draws two cards of the same suit to win; another makes him lose. It originated among mercenaries in the Middle Ages.

wrapped up in 'buggers'. I chewed my nails while the friar used his to scrabble for money. He called on every saint in the calendar; he skinned us; we wanted to gamble our clothes and other things but he said it was just a game and we were fellow men and he didn't want to strip us of everything – this after taking all my six hundred *reals* and the soldier's hundred!

'And don't swear,' he said, 'because things went well for me; it's because I put myself in God's hands.'

We believed him because we did not know how quickly the cards could move between his fingers and his sleeve. The soldier swore he'd never gamble again and so did I.

'Goddam it,' exclaimed the poor ensign (he told me his rank), 'I've been with Protestants and Moors but I've never been cleaned out like that.'

But the friar just laughed and took out his rosary again to pray. I hadn't a penny on me, so I asked him to pay for my supper and lodging for both of us until we got to Segovia, as we were broke. He promised he would do so. I've never seen an appetite like his; he stuffed himself with a good sixty eggs! He said he was going to bed. We all slept in one room with some other people who were there, because the rooms were already taken. I went to bed feeling very low and the soldier called the landlord and asked him to look after his papers in their tin boxes, and a bundle of pensioned-off old shirts. We lay down. The father crossed himself and we did so also, to protect ourselves against him. He went to sleep but I lay awake planning how to take the money off him again. In his sleep the soldier kept on about the hundred *reals* as if they weren't past all hope already.

Then it was time to get up. He shouted for a candle. They brought one and the landlord brought the soldier his shirts but forgot his papers. The poor ensign shouted the house down asking for his papers. He pestered the landlord, and all of us told him to bring them, so he ran off and came back with three chamber-pots.

'Here's one for each of you,' he said, 'do you need more paper?'

He thought we had the diarrhoea. That was all the soldier needed. Dressed in his nightshirt, he chased after the landlord, waving his sword and swearing he would kill him because he was trying to make fun of a man who had been at Lepanto and St Quentin and other battles, by bringing him chamber-pots instead of the papers he had asked for. All our combined strength wasn't enough to hold him back.

'You did ask for papers, sir,' said the landlord. 'How was I supposed to know that you meant your service record?'

We smoothed matters over and went back to our room. The hermit was wary and stayed in bed saying that the fright wouldn't do his health any good. He paid for us and we left the inn for the mountain pass.

From the attitude of the hermit we could see we weren't going to get our money back, and we were in a very bad mood indeed.

We fell in with a Genoese – you know, one of those bankers who've ruined Spain – who was crossing the pass with his page behind him and his parasol over his head, very prosperous-looking indeed. We got into conversation and all he talked about was money; the Genoese are people who are born with financial acumen. He began talking about Besançon and whether it was worth investing money in, and went on until the soldier and I asked him who Señor Besançon might be. He laughed and replied:

'It's a town in Italy where business-men meet. The ones we call legal robbers. They fix the discount rates.'

We gathered from this that he was mixed up with money-lenders. He spent the journey telling us how he was ruined because a banker who held over sixty thousand *escudos* of his had gone broke; he swore it all on his conscience though I think that conscience in business men is a bit like virginity in whores – they sell it when they haven't got it any more. Hardly anybody in business has a conscience, because they've heard it's likely to get in your way, so they leave it behind with their umbilical cords when they're born.

And so we saw the houses of Segovia, which made me feel very happy, in spite of the memory of Dr Goat which might have had some effect. I reached the town and, at the gate, I saw my father waiting for me by the road – in quarters of course. I lost some of my cockiness and went in, looking rather different from when I left the place, with only the beginnings of a beard and wearing decent clothes. I left the others and tried to think who would know my uncle best in the town, besides the gallows; I couldn't find anyone. I went up to many people and asked them if they knew Alonso Yobb but nobody had a clue. It cheered me up to think there were so many honest men in my native town, but then I heard the town crier followed by my uncle. Along came a group of half-naked men, walking in front of my uncle, who was brandishing a whip, playing a pizzicato on the backs of five human violins, who wore ropes instead of strings. I was watching all this with a man whom I had asked about my uncle, saying I was a very important person. I saw my uncle and as he came by he saw me and rushed up to embrace me and called me 'nephew'. I thought I'd die of embarrassment, and I didn't say good-bye to the man I'd been talking to. I went off with my uncle and he said to me:

'You can come with me while I finish with this lot, as we're on the way back already. You're going to have dinner with me today.' As I was on horseback and in line, it would have looked as if I were being whipped with the others; I said I would wait for him there. So I got away from him feeling so ashamed that if I hadn't depended on him to get my legacy I would never have spoken to him nor gone anywhere near him in my life.

He finished going over his prisoners' shoulders, came back and took me to his house, where I dismounted and we went in to have dinner.

CHAPTER ELEVEN

MY uncle lived near the abattoir in a water-seller's house; we went in and he said to me:

'It's no palace, my place, but I can assure you it's just right for my business.'

We went up a flight of stairs, with me waiting to see what would happen when we reached the top, as it was just like the steps of the gallows. We went into a room with such a low ceiling that we walked about as if we were being blessed all the time, with our heads bowed. He hung his whip on a hook next to some others from which there dangled ropes, nooses, knives, meat-hooks and other tools of the public executioner's trade. He asked me why I didn't take my coat off and sit down; I replied that I wasn't used to doing so. I was paralysed with shame at my uncle's profession. He told me I was lucky to have found him on such a good day as there was a good meal coming and he'd invited some friends. At that moment in walked one of those beggars who ask for money to pay for Masses for souls in Purgatory, with his purple robe trailing down to his feet. He rattled his collecting box and said:

'I've made as much out of my souls today as you have out of your criminals; let's shake on it.'

They chucked each other under the chin and the soulless collector for souls tucked up his robe and showed a pair of bandy legs wrapped in linen leggings and started jigging around. He asked if Clemente had come. My uncle said he hadn't. Just then, wrapped up in a hood and wearing clogs, in walked an acorn-collector, I mean a pig-keeper. I knew he was a pig-keeper because of the horn he held in his hand which – if you'll excuse me – should really have been on his head. He said hullo in his crude way and behind him came a loutish, cross-eyed mulatto, wearing a hat with a brim as broad as an umbrella and a crown higher than a tree. His sword had more ornament on it than a courtier's. He wore a buff-coloured doublet and his face was seamed with razor-slashes. He came in and sat down with a nod to everyone there, and my uncle said to him:

'Well, Alonso, Pugface and Snatcher certainly got it today.'

The beggar butted in:

'I gave four ducats to the Ocaña executioner Flechilla, to push the donkey on quickly and not use the three-tailed whip when I had my back slapped there.'

'Christ!' said the Mulatto. 'I overpaid Lobrezno in Murcia, the donkey crept along like a tortoise, and the bastard laid on so hard that I was covered in welts.'

The pigman, shrugging his shoulders, said:

'I've never been caught yet.'

'Your turn will come,' said the beggar.

'I can be prouder,' said my uncle, 'than anybody else in my profession, because I do what I'm paid to do. The ones today gave me sixty and they only had a few friendly strokes with the single-thong whip.'

When I saw what sort of people my uncle mixed with, I must admit I blushed and couldn't hide my shame. The mulatto spotted this and said:

'Is this the priest who was punished the other day with a few whacks on the behind?'

I replied that I was not the type of person who was punished in that way. Then my uncle stood up and said:

'This is my nephew, an Alcalá University graduate and an important man.'

They begged my pardon and were very friendly to me. I was dying to eat, collect my legacy and get away from my uncle. They laid the tables and lowered a hat on the end of a cord, just like convicts do to collect charity, and pulled up their food from a wine-shop just behind the house. Up came the food on a few chipped old plates and in broken jugs and pots. You can't imagine how disgusted I was. They sat down to eat, with the beggar at the head of the table and the others all over the place. I shan't describe what we ate, except that it was all things to drink. The mulatto noisily slurped down three full glasses of red wine and the pig-keeper snatched the jug from me and drank more than all of us. We had no thought of water and less taste for it. Five four-*real* pies came up. They took off the pastry and, holy-water sprinkler in hand, they all said a prayer and a *Requiem Aeternam* for the soul of the person to whom the meat in the pies had belonged originally.

'You remember, my boy,' said my uncle, 'what I wrote to you about your father.'

I remembered.

They ate, but I was satisfied with the base of the pastry and that's the only part I eat now. In fact, whenever I eat pies I say a Hail Mary for the soul which once belonged to the meat in it.

They refilled two jugs time and time again and the mulatto and the beggar drank so much that when a plate of sausages like black men's fingers was brought up they asked why they were having stewed tubes of gunpowder. My uncle was so drunk that he stretched his arm out, took one, and said in a hoarse, cracked voice, with one eye half shut and the other swimming in wine:

'My boy, by the Host that God created in his likeness and image, I've never had better red meat in my life.'

Then I saw the mulatto stretch out his arm, take the salt, and say:

'This soup is very hot.'

And the pig-keeper took a fistful of salt, shoved the lot in his mouth, and said:

'This'll give me a thirst.'

I began to laugh through my shame and anger. Then came soup, and the beggar picked up a bowl of it in both hands, saying:

'Cleanliness is next to Godliness.'

Then he put the bowl to his cheek, poured it out, scalded himself and got himself into a filthy state from head to toe. When he saw the state he was in he stood up and, as his head was whirling, he steadied himself against the table, which was on wheels, overturned it, and messed up the others. Then he said that the pig-keeper had pushed him. When the pigman saw the beggar coming for him, he stood up and cracked him on the head with his bone horn. They came to blows and in a clinch the beggar bit him on the cheek. What with his excitement and rage, the pig-keeper vomited everything he had eaten into the beggar's face. My uncle, who was more sober, asked why there were so many priests in his house. Seeing that things were getting noisier, I calmed them down, separated them and picked up the mulatto, who was weeping noisily. I laid my uncle down on his bed, but not before he had bowed to a wooden candlestick, thinking it was one of the guests. I took the horn away from the pig-keeper but, although the others were asleep, I couldn't shut him up. He kept asking for his horn because he could play more tunes than anybody else on it, and he wanted to give us a go on the organ. To cut a long story short, I didn't go until they were all asleep. I left the house and spent the afternoon walking round my native town. I went to Goat's house and was told he had died. I didn't bother to ask what of as I knew all about hunger.

Four hours later, in the evening, I went back and found one of them crawling round the room on all fours, looking for the door and saying that they'd lost the house. I got him on his feet and let the others sleep until eleven o'clock. Then they woke up and yawned, and one of them asked what time it was. The pig-keeper, who hadn't slept it off yet, said it was early, still siesta-time and very hot. The beggar asked for his cloak as well as he could, saying:

'The souls have had a day off; after all, they're my bread-ticket.'

He went, but to the window, not the door. He saw the stars of course, so he began to call the others, shouting that there were stars at midday and there was a big eclipse. They all crossed themselves and kissed the ground. When I saw how deceitful he was I was very shocked and made up my mind to have nothing to do with people like him. After all that dirt and coarseness I couldn't wait to get among better-class people. I got rid of them as best I could, one by one, and put my uncle to bed. He wasn't dead-drunk, just sozzled. I made myself comfortable on my own clothes and a few that belonged to people by then in God's hands.

That's how we spent the night. Next morning I had a talk

with my uncle about getting my legacy settled and collecting it, as I felt ill and thought I'd better have myself attended to properly. He showed a leg, got up, and we had a long talk about my affairs, but it was very difficult talking to an ill-educated character such as him. At last I got him to tell me the whereabouts of part of my estate – not all of it though – and he told me about three hundred ducats or so that my father had earned with his nimble fingers and left with a trustworthy lady who acted as a receiver for a good forty miles around. To cut things short, I collected and pocketed my money, at least the cash which my uncle hadn't drunk or spent, which was quite a lot for such a stupid man. He thought it would be enough to see me through college and that I could easily be a cardinal with a red hat. He made red marks on everybody so easily that he thought I wouldn't have any difficulty. As soon as he saw I had the money, he said:

'Pablos, my boy, if you don't get on and make something of yourself, it'll be all your own fault; you've got a model to follow. You've got money and I'll be behind you. Everything I've got and anything I can do is for you.'

I thanked him very much for his offer. We spent the day talking pointlessly and visiting all those people I've mentioned before. My uncle, the beggar and the pig-keeper spent the evening playing a game called Taba.* The beggar gambled away the money he'd collected for Masses as if it were water. They handled the stones very cleverly, catching them in the air and flipping them with their wrists. Five-stones, like cards, was an excuse for drinking, and the jug was there between them all the time. Night came and off they went. My uncle and I went to bed, each one in his own place, as I had already provided myself with a mattress. In the morning I got up before he was awake and went off to an inn. I shut my uncle's door, locked it and threw the key down a hole used to let the cat in and out. As I said, I went to an inn to hide and wait for a suitable time to go to Madrid. In the room I left him a sealed letter in which I told him why I had gone and that he shouldn't try and find me as I had made up my mind I never wanted to see him again.

* A game played by throwing a knuckle-bone of a sheep. The score depends on which side of the bone is left uppermost when it falls.

CHAPTER TWELVE

◄◄►►

THAT morning a carter was leaving the inn with a load for Madrid. As he had a donkey I hired it and went to wait for him outside the town gate. He came out and I got on the donkey and began my ride. I said to myself as I rode along:

'Good riddance, you bugger, you're a disgrace to decent people, making a living out of wringing people's necks.'

I told myself I was going to Madrid where nobody knew me (that was what cheered me up) and I would get on through my own merits. I reckoned on hanging up my student's gown as soon as I got there and buying the short clothes more in style. But to get back to my uncle and what he did, he was offended by my letter which went like this:

'Mr Alfonso Yobb,
'As God was so good to me as to deprive me of my beloved father and imprison my mother in Toledo (where I know she will make sparks fly) all I need is to see you get what you give others. I want to be one more worthy scion of my family. I can't be two unless I fall into your hands and you cut me up like you do others. Don't make inquiries about me as I want to forget we are even related. Serve God and the King.'

I've no need to detail the blaspheming and cursing that that letter must have given rise to. But to get back to my journey: I was riding on a grey donkey like Sancho Panza and the last thing I wanted was to meet anybody when, in the distance, I saw a gentleman walking along with his cloak on and his sword by his side, wearing light breeches and high boots. He looked pretty smart with his shirt open and his hat perched on the side of his head. I thought he was a gentleman who had left his carriage behind him, and as we came up I greeted him. Looking at me he said:

'I dare say, professor, you're a lot more comfortable on your donkey than me with all my things.'

By 'things' I gathered he meant his coach and servants that he had left behind, so I said:

'Yes, sir, as a matter of fact I do find it more comfortable to travel this way than in a coach, though you must be very much at ease in the one you've left behind. The jolting gets on my nerves.'

'What coach have I left behind?' he said, very surprised, and as he turned round too sharply, the only strap that held his breeches broke and they fell down. He saw I was killing myself with laughter at the sight of him and asked me to lend him one of my straps. I saw he only had a scrap of shirt which barely covered his backside, so I said:

'I'm sorry sir, but you'll have to wait for your servants. I can't help you; my breeches are only held up by one hook as well.'

'If you're trying to be funny,' he said, holding his trousers up with one hand, 'it's not very nice. I don't know what servants you're on about.'

It didn't take me long to realize that he was as poor as a church mouse because only a few miles on he admitted that if I didn't let him ride a while on the donkey, he'd never get to Madrid as he was fed up with holding his trousers up by keeping his hands in his pockets. I felt sorry for him, so I got off, but as he couldn't let go of his trousers I had to help him up. I was shocked at what I found when I got hold of him. His slashed breeches were interweaved with buttock pure and simple, just covered by his cloak. When he realized I must have seen the state he was in he cleverly got his word in first.

'Professor, all that glistens isn't gold. When you saw me walking along so proudly with my shirt open you must have thought I was Lord Somebody or other. Well, plenty of fake fronts cover backsides like the one you've just touched.'

I admitted I'd thought at first that he was in quite a different position.

'Well you haven't seen anything yet,' he retorted, 'because you can see everything I've got. I can't hide anything. I'm a gentleman, genuine and honest, with my house and estate in the North. If I could look after myself as well as I look after my honour I'd be all right. But you can't look after noble blood if you've got nothing to eat, professor. There's no such thing as blue blood, and you can't be somebody if you haven't got anything. I know just what letters of nobility are worth, because one day I hadn't anything to eat and they wouldn't take my letters for a couple of slices off the joint in a chop-house. Fancy the waiter telling me they weren't written in gold! Well, the gold in doctors' pills, though it's pretty useless, is worth more than the gold in letters and does you more good. Letters of nobility aren't worth the paper they're written on. I didn't even have anywhere to crawl away and die, so I sold my grave. My father's estate (he was Toribio Rodríguez Valligo Gómez de Ampuero – yes, all those names) was lost after he gave it as security for a loan. The only thing I've got left to sell is my "don" but my luck's so bad I can't find anyone to buy it. If they haven't got it in front of their names they've got "esquire" after them.'

I must admit that the poor fellow's bad luck intrigued me, even though he spoke about it very humorously. I asked him his name, where he was going and what he was planning to do. He said he used all his father's names: Don Toribio Rodríguez Valligo Gómez de Ampuero y Jordán. I never heard such a resounding name. It began with 'Don' and ended in 'dan' like a clanging bell. Then he said he was going to Madrid, because a down-at-heel eldest son like him began to go stale after a couple of days in a village and couldn't keep himself alive. So he was going to everybody's home from home, 'where there's a room for everyone and the eating's free if you want to risk your stomach, and whenever I myself go there I've always got a hundred *reals* in my pocket, a bed, food and a good tumble in the hay. If you've got your wits about you in the city it's like having a licence to print money.' The sun began to shine brightly for me and to while away the journey I asked him to tell me how people like him lived in Madrid without money and who they lived with, as it looked to me to be a bit tricky. Everybody seemed to want things from other people there.

'You can find all sorts there, son; flattery's the way to get round people in places like that. And, in case it's hard for you to believe me, listen and I'll tell you some of the ways I've found and you'll soon learn.'

CHAPTER THIRTEEN

+‹--›+

'THE first thing you've got to know is that in Madrid you can find all types, half-wits and very sharp minds, the very rich and the very poor! The city hides criminals and a good man's qualities are not appreciated, and there are some people there, me for example, that you don't know anything about, where they came from or who they are. We've all got different names. Some of us are gentlemen without funds, others empty-bellied, half-baked, scabby, skinny and wolfish. We live by our wits: more often than not our bellies are empty as it's very hard to get other people to feed you. We're the terror of feasts, the mice in eating-houses, and we always invite ourselves. So we live on air and we're happy. We can eat a leek and imagine it's a capon. A person can come to our rooms and visit us and he'll find the place full of mutton and poultry bones and fruit peelings, and the door can't be opened because of all the feathers and rabbit skins behind it. Most of this we scrounge from the city dustbins at night and use it to show off the next day. If a visitor comes we get very annoyed and say:

' "Doesn't that girl take any notice of me when I tell her to sweep up? You must excuse me; I had some friends in to dinner and these servants, you know . . ."

'Anyone who doesn't know us swallows it and thinks the mess is the result of a party. Now what can I tell you about having your meals in other people's houses? You've only got to have half a minute's talk with someone and you know where his house is and at meal-times, so long as you know he's going to eat at home, you say that he is a fascinating conversationalist (he can't resist that). If he asks you if you've eaten, you say "no" if they haven't begun yet. If they invite you, don't wait for a second invitation; sometimes we've starved waiting for one. If they've begun you say you have eaten already. Now even if he serves the bird or cuts the bread or carves the meat or whatever it is, very well, if you want to get a nibble, you say :

' "Now, let me be your butler – because So-and-so, God rest his soul (and you drop the name of some dead gentleman, a duke or a count), used to enjoy seeing me carve more than he loved eating."

'While you are saying this, you take the knife and you slice off a few pieces, and then you say :

' "Oh, what a marvellous smell! It would be an insult to the cook not to have a taste."

'The turnip goes, because it's a wonderful turnip, and so does the bacon and everything else.

'When you can't do this there's always the monastery soup-kitchen in reserve. We don't eat the food in front of everybody; we do it secretly and make the friars think we take it not because we're hungry but because we're religious.

'You should see one of us in a gambling joint. He's very attentive, bringing candles and snuffing them, fetching chamber-pots, preparing the cards and solemnly nodding at everything the winner says, just for a miserable little one-*real* tip.

'We know all our stock of old clothes by heart and, just as in some places there are fixed times for saying your prayers, we have special times for our repairs. You should see the selection we bring out. Our sworn enemy is the sun because it shows up all the darns, stitches and rags. So in the morning we stand in its full glare with our legs open and see the shadows of the tears and tatters between our legs and we give our breeches a trim with a pair of scissors. As it's always the crotch that wears badly we take bits off the back to fill up the front and sometimes our arses are so cut about that they're left bare : our cloaks cover them but we have to watch ourselves carefully on windy days, or on a lighted staircase, or when riding. We have to stand in special ways when the light is on us and on a bright day we keep our legs close together and bow just from our ankles. If our knees come apart you can see air-holes. There's nothing on our backs that wasn't once something else and hasn't a story to tell. For example, you see this waistcoat? Well, first it was a pair of wide breeches, the grand-daughter of a cape and great grand-daughter of a long cloak and now it can look forward to a future as footrags and many other things. Our linen socks are handkerchieves and before that they were towels and before that, shirts, descended from sheets, and afterwards we make them into paper. We write on the paper and then we make it into shoe polish and rub it in hard. I've seen shoes as good as dead brought back to life with the powder. And then again, we avoid the street lights at night in case people see our bare backsides and ragged jackets. Our clothes are rubbed as flat as a pebble and God puts more hair on our faces than there is on what we wear.

'We can't afford to spend money on barbers so we wait till a friend needs a haircut and then we do each other, obeying the Gospel which says we should help each other like good brothers. And we're very careful not to go into houses which our friends regard as their own manors, if we find we're trying it on the same people. Empty stomachs are very punctilious, you know. We have to ride a horse once a month, even if it's only a little donkey, and it's got to be in full view of everybody in the street. And once a year we've got to ride in a coach, even if it's only on the boot or the back. But if we ever ride inside the coach, it's in the corner seat, mind you, sticking our heads out and nodding to everybody and talking to our friends and acquaintances even though they look somewhere else.

'If we feel itchy in ladies' company we've got all sorts of tricks to scratch ourselves in public without being seen. If it's our thighs, we say we once saw a soldier run through the leg and we rub the itchy part instead of just pointing to it. If we're in church and our chests itch, we cross ourselves even if the Mass is just beginning; we stand up and lean against a pillar to pretend to be looking for something, and then we have a good scratch.

'And what about the way we lie? We lie all the time. We drag dukes and counts into our conversation. Some we say are our friends and others our relatives, but we're always careful to mention only people who are dead or a long way away. And the most important thing: we never fall in love unless we can get something out of it. The rules of our order forbid us high-class ladies, however pretty they may be. So we always butter up the eating-house woman for our food, the landlady for our room and the washer-woman for our collars. Even though with so little food and drink we can't satisfy all their desires we favour them in rota and they're happy enough.

'Look at these boots of mine: would you ever think I was wearing them over my bare legs, without hose or anything else underneath? Look at this collar; would you ever think I wasn't wearing a shirt? Well, a gentleman can do without most things, professor, but not his open starched collar; first because a man looks good in one, and then because, once you've turned it, it can feed you, because the starch can keep you going for some time if you suck it carefully. In other words, professor, a gentleman like me has to go without more than a pregnant woman does, and that's how he lives in Madrid. Sometimes he lives well with plenty of money and other times in the workhouse. But he lives, and if he knows how to manage he can live like a king, even if he hasn't got a penny.'

The gentleman's strange way of life interested me so much that I forgot I was walking and carried on on foot, fascinated, until we reached Rozas where we spent the night. The gentleman shared my meal as he hadn't a copper. I felt very obliged to him for his warnings which opened my eyes to a lot of things and let me into the criminal life. Before we went to bed I told him what I intended to do. He embraced me warmly, saying that he'd always expected that a man of my intelligence would see he was right. He offered to introduce me in Madrid to his comrades in crime and find me somewhere to stay with them. I accepted his offer, but I didn't tell him about all the money I had on me and said I only had a hundred *reals*. This, together with the fact that I had paid for him and was still paying, bought me his sincere friendship.

I bought three straps from the landlord for him and he fixed his trousers. We went to bed, got up early and soon found ourselves in Madrid.

BOOK TWO

CHAPTER ONE

-‹‹-››-

W E reached Madrid at ten o'clock in the morning and, as we had decided, we went first to Don Toribio's friends. We went up to the door and he knocked. The door was opened by a ragged, ancient crone. He asked for his friends and she said they were out seeing what they could find. So we waited alone there until noon. We passed the time with him urging me to take up his profession of cheap living and me all ears, not missing a word he said. At half past twelve in through the door came a sight dressed from head to foot in a baize robe, more threadbare than his conscience. He spoke to Don Toribio in thieves' slang and the result of the conversation was that he embraced me and placed himself at my service. We talked for a while and then he took out a glove with seventeen *reals* and a letter. He said it was a licence to beg on behalf of a poor woman which he had used to collect money. He emptied the glove and took out another and folded the pair carefully like a doctor. I asked him why he didn't put them on and he said they were both for the same hand and that gloves were only an elegant accessory. All this time I saw he didn't take off his cloak and hood and I asked him why this was so. He answered :

'Son, I've got a hole in the back of my coat and a patch and a grease-stain. It's all covered by this bit of cape and that's how I carry on.'

He took off his cape and hood and I saw that under his robe he had something rather bulky. I thought it was his breeches because that's what it looked like. But then he got ready to delouse himself so he hoisted up his clothes and I saw he had two cylinder-shaped pieces of cardboard tied to his waist and fixed round his thighs so as to stick out under his cloak, because he didn't have any leggings or a shirt. In fact, he really had very little to delouse. He was almost bare. He went into his delousing room and put up a placard, just as they do outside the sacristy, saying 'engaged', so that nobody else would go in. I gave heartfelt thanks to God, seeing that, though He might not give wealth, at least He was generous in providing labour.

'I,' said my good friend, 'have come back with my breeches torn so I'll have to go away and mend them.'

He asked if there were any odd pieces, and the old woman, who collected rags two days a week like the women who sell pieces of magic paper to cure incurable diseases in gentlemen, said there weren't and that Don Lorenzo Iñíguez del Pedroso had had to stay in bed for the last fortnight because he had no jacket and there were no rags.

Just then one of them came in wearing travelling boots and a dun-coloured coat, together with a hat with both brims caught up. He was told all about me by the others and spoke to me very kindly. He took off his cloak and – would you believe it? – his jacket was dun-coloured in front and made of white linen at the back and the bottom all sweaty. I couldn't help laughing and he said, without any shame:

'You'll soon get used to it and won't laugh. I bet you don't know why I'm wearing my hat with the brims folded up.'

I said it was because it looked smarter and so that he could see more easily.

'On the contrary,' he said, 'it's because it hasn't got a ribbon and you can't see that with the brim turned up.'

As he said that he took out more than twenty letters and twenty *reals* and said he hadn't been able to deliver the letters he had left to anybody. Each one had to be paid for by the addressee at the rate of one *real* and he had written them himself. He signed any name that came into his head. He invented news about the smartest people and wrote it in the letters and collected the postage due. He did this every month. I was amazed at what life was revealing to me at every turn.

Then two more came in, one with a thick jacket hanging halfway down his thighs and a cape just as thick. He had his collar turned up so that his neckband, which was torn, couldn't be seen. His Walloon-style breeches were made of goatskin but only the part you could see, and the rest of his clothes were made of red baize. He was shouting at his companion as they came in. The latter wore a muffler for lack of a collar, a short coat for lack of a cloak, and a crutch, with his leg bound up in rags and skins, because he only had one stocking. He acted like a soldier and had in fact been one, but a bad one and in quiet places. He talked about his strange adventures in the services and claimed the right to go anywhere uninvited and without paying. The one with the short coat and only half his breeches said:

'You owe me half, or at least a good share. If you don't give them to me, by God . . .'

'Don't "by God" me,' said the other, 'because once we're home I'm not lame any more and you'll get a good thumping with my crutch.'

'Give them to me! . . .' 'I want them! . . .' 'You're a liar!' And so it went on until they came to blows and tore away bits of their clothes as they clutched at one another. We calmed them down and asked what the cause of the quarrel was.

'Try it on me, would you?' said the soldier. 'You haven't a chance. Now listen, everyone. We were at San Salvador's and a child came up to this poor specimen and asked him if I was Ensign Juan de Lorenzana. He said I was as he saw that the child had something in his hand. He brought him up to me and said:

' "Ensign, the boy wants something. See what it is."

'I saw what the game was and said I was the Ensign. I took the message and with it were a dozen handkerchiefs, so I sent a proper answer to his mother who had obviously sent them to somebody called Juan de Lorenzana. Now he's asking me for half the handkerchiefs, but I'll see him in Hell first. My nose will blow every one of them to pieces.'

The case was judged in his favour; the only thing was that he wasn't allowed to blow his nose on them but had to give them to the old woman for the benefit of the community, to make cuffs so that people might think they were wearing shirts. In any case, making rude noises with their noses or otherwise was forbidden.

Night came; we were as close together in bed as tools in a box. Supper was not included. Most of them didn't even undress. In many cases going to bed dressed as they went around all day was as good as being in their birthday suits.

CHAPTER TWO

✦✦➤

DAY came and we all stood to arms. By now I was as well in with them as if we were brothers; you can always find life easy and friendly in criminal circles. It was quite a sight to see one of them put his shirt on in ten operations, as it was in ten different pieces, and saying a prayer each time like a priest robing himself. Another one lost track of a leg in the alleyways of his trousers and found it sticking out in the most awkward place. Another asked for help in putting on his doublet and couldn't get it straight even after half an hour's work.

After this was finished – and it was pretty impressive – they all got needles and thread and put a few stitches into the tears in their clothes. One of them got himself into an L shape to darn under his arm. Another on his knees looked like a figure 5 : he was giving first aid to his stockings. Another stuck his head between his legs and doubled himself up to repair a hole in his crotch. Even Bosch's twisted postures can't compare with what I saw. They sewed and the old woman gave them the materials: rags and patches of various colours which she had brought in on the Saturday. Mending time, as they called it, came to an end and then they inspected each other to see if anything was wrong. They decided to go out and I said I wanted a suit ordered because I wanted to spend my hundred *reals* on one and get rid of my student's gown.

'Oh, no,' they said, 'the money goes into our fund. For now, let's dress him out of stock and tell him his beat in town where he can see what he can pick up for himself.'

This seemed a good idea to me. I banked the money with them and in a second they converted my gown into a short black jacket just by cutting the skirts off. They made the left-over cloth into an old refurbished hat. For a ribbon they fixed some cotton soaked in ink on to it. They took away my collar and my wide Walloon breeches and instead gave me some others slashed only in front; the sides and seat were just chamois-leather. My silk half-stockings weren't even halves because they only reached just below my knee and the rest, red socks, were just covered by my boots. They put it on me and said:

'It's a bit worn at the sides and behind so if anybody looks at you, you'll have to follow his eyes like a sunflower as they move round. If there's two people, move off, and for those behind you pull your hat down over your neck so that its brim covers your collar but leaves your face exposed. If anyone asks why you're acting like that, say it's because you've got nothing to be ashamed of and can go and show your face anywhere you like.'

They gave me a box which had black and white thread, string, a needle, a thimble, cloth, canvas, satin and other bits and pieces as well as a knife. They put pieces of notepaper in my belt, tinder and steel in a leather pouch, and said:

'You can go anywhere you like with this box and you won't need any friends or relations. All our comforts are contained in it. Take it and look after it carefully.'

They gave me the Parish of San Luis as the beat to earn my living in, and I went out to work, leaving the house with the others. Still, as I was new they gave me a guide, the same one who had brought me in and converted me. This was just to make sure I knew the tricks, like a priest saying his first Mass.

Walking sedately and holding our rosaries, we left the house and went towards the district which had been allotted to me. We greeted everybody we met. We took off our hats to the men and wished we could take off *their* cloaks. We bowed to the women because they love that and if you're fatherly with them, it's even better. My instructor said to one man:

'I've got some money coming tomorrow!' and to another:

'Just one day more; the bank's causing trouble.'

One person asked him to pay for his cloak; another dunned him about his belt. All this showed me that he had so many friends that he had no possessions of his own. We zigzagged from one pavement to the other so as not to pass by his creditors' houses. But even so, one asked him for the rent, another for the hire of the sword, and another for the hire of sheets and shirts. So I realized that he was a gentleman who was all rented, like a mule. Well, he saw a man some way off who was really sucking him dry, so he said, for a debt, but he just didn't have the money. In order not to be recognized he undid his hair which he wore tied behind his head and let it fall over his ears. That way he looked like a Holy Week penitent, halfway between Jesus Christ and a long-haired fop. He stuck a patch on his eye and started jabbering away at me in Italian. He had time to do all this before we came up close to the other man. The latter hadn't seen him as he was nattering away to an old woman. I swear I saw him stop and turn round like a dog getting ready to jump at you. He crossed himself more than a sorcerer and walked away saying:

'Christ! I could have sworn it was him. If you lose cows you're always hearing bells!'

Looking at my friend, I was killing myself laughing. He went into a doorway to pull his hair back and take off the patch, and said:

'That's the way to repudiate debts. You'll learn, son; you'll see this sort of thing over and over again here!'

We went on and as it was morning we got a couple of pieces of preserved fruit and some brandy from some old scrubber, who gave it to us for free after saying hullo to my instructor.

'Well, that's the food question settled for today,' he said; 'at least we're sure of that.'

My heart sank as I saw that we weren't really sure of eating. My stomach was grumbling so I answered him back, and he replied:

'You haven't much faith in our religion and way of life. God provides for crows and ravens and even public notaries, so do you think He'll let skinny devils like us down? You haven't got much guts.'

'That's true,' I said, 'but I'm scared I'll have less and less in them.'

While we were talking, the clock struck twelve, and as I was new to the game the preserves in my belly weren't very satisfying. I was so hungry that I might just as well have eaten nothing.

Now my mind was on food again and I turned to my friend and said:

'Look here, mate, keeping an apprentice hungry is pretty hard training. A man's got to eat more than a flea and you've made me go without anything. If you're not hungry that's not surprising, as you've been brought up like that, just like Mithridates was raised on poison, and you're all right. I can't see you putting yourself to any great trouble for your belly so I'm going to do what I can for myself!'

'Christ! Listen to him! It's only twelve o'clock and he can't wait. Your belly's very much on time, isn't it? I'm afraid you'll have to accept some of your pay in arrears. You'd like to eat all day, would you? Well, that's just being like an animal. I've never heard of any of our boys having to have a lavatory in his house. We don't provide for them as we don't provide for our bodily needs in any case. I've already told you that God doesn't let anybody down, and if you really can't hold out I'm off to the free soup-kitchen at San Jerónimo's, where the friars are as fat as capons, to stuff myself there. If you want to come, you're welcome and if you don't, you can do what you bloody well like!'

'Good-bye,' I said, 'I'm not so desperate as to have to go and get somebody else's leftovers. I'll go my own way.'

My friend pranced off looking at his feet. He took some breadcrumbs out of a box which he kept specially for this purpose and brushed them over his chin and clothes to make out he'd eaten a meal.

I walked off coughing and hawking so as not to look so skinny. I brushed up my whiskers, muffled up my face and threw my cloak over my left shoulder, playing with the ten beads that were all I had left on my rosary. Everybody who saw me thought I'd had a good meal. Actually the fleas on me had never had it so good.

I wasn't too unhappy as I had a few *escudos* left, although my conscience bothered me as I knew that people of our sort who scrounged meals ought never to use their own cash. I'd made up my mind to get something to eat. I got to the corner of the Calle de San Luis where there was a pastry shop. There was a big baked pie right there in the window, and the savoury smell from the oven knocked me back. I felt like a game-dog that knows it mustn't eat the partridge. My eyes were riveted on the pie and I stared so hard that it seemed to shrivel up as if I'd put the Evil Eye on it. I can't explain how many ways I thought of to steal it. In fact I even made up my mind to pay for it. While I was standing there the clock struck one o'clock. I felt so hungry that I decided to nip into a chop-shop. I had one just in my sights when – life is funny ! – I met a college friend of mine called Sharp, his gown flying in the wind. He had more pimples on his face than someone who has just been bled by a leech, and he was as filthy as a street-cart. When he saw me he ran up to me. (I'm surprised he knew me, considering what I looked like). I embraced him. He asked me how I was getting along, so I said :

'I've so many things to tell you, sir ! But I'm awfully sorry as I'm leaving tonight.'

'I'm sorry as well,' he said, 'and I'd stop, but it's late and I'm due for lunch with my sister and her husband.'

'You mean Señora Ana's here? Well, let's go. I mustn't leave without seeing her.'

When I heard that he hadn't eaten yet, I pricked up my ears. I went off with him and began telling him about a tart that he'd fancied a lot at Alcalá. I knew where she lived and could get him into her house. This really interested him and I deliberately tried to work him up a bit. We talked about the whore all the way to the house. We went in and I was politeness itself to his sister and his brother-in-law. They thought, of course, that I was embarrassed at turning up at lunch-time, so they began to say that they'd have got something special ready if they'd known such an important guest was coming. I grabbed the chance and invited myself and said I was an old friend of the family and would be annoyed if they went to any special trouble for me. We all sat down. To cheer Sharp up a bit (he hadn't invited me or even thought of it) I brought the girl up every now and then, saying she'd been asking me about him and that he'd got under her skin and other lies of the same kind, so he didn't feel so bad watching me stuff myself. 'Stuff' is the word, because I made a bigger hole in the gherkins than a bullet does in a jerkin ! Up came the stew which I bolted down in a couple of mouthfuls. I didn't have anything against it but I was in such a hurry that I didn't feel sure of it even when I had it in my mouth. I swear by God that the old cemetery in Valladolid that can break down a body in twenty-four hours couldn't have got rid of a whole family's food for a day as fast as I did. It went as quick as an express letter. Of course they must have seen me gulping the gravy, wiping my plate, harrying the bones and tearing the meat to pieces. To tell the truth, every time I moved my hands I tipped bits of bread into my pockets as well. We finished the meal and Sharp and I went into a corner to talk about how he could get into that woman's house. I showed him how easy it was.

We were standing by the window and I made out that somebody was calling up to me from the street.

'Do you want me?' I called down. 'I'll be down in a minute.'

I excused myself and said I'd be back straightaway. For all I knew he waited there for hours. I disappeared because I'd eaten so much and probably made them quarrel. We often met afterwards and I made my excuses with one lie after the other that I shan't bother to repeat here.

I went off, wandering along the streets, and when I got to the Guadalajara gate I sat down on one of the benches that the shopkeepers put outside their premises. It just so happened that two women who had 'can you let me have ...?' written all over their lovely faces, muffled up to the eyebrows and accompanied by the usual old woman and young lad, came to the shop outside which I was sitting. They enquired about some very elaborately embroidered velvet. I wanted to get into the conversation so to attract their attention I began to jabber nonsense about 'vel' and 'vet' and 'velly' and 'marvel' and so on and so forth until I had them standing there with their mouths open. I reckoned that, being so familiar with them, they thought they could rely on me as surety for something in the shop. I couldn't lose anything so I said they could have anything they fancied. They made a a bit of a fuss of course, and said they couldn't accept presents from a man they didn't know. I seized this opportunity and admitted I had been a bit cheeky but that I would be honoured if they accepted some Milanese cloth. A page would take it that night to where they lived. I said 'a page' and pointed to one who was opposite waiting for his master who was in another shop, because he was bareheaded and looked as though he was attending me. As I wanted them to think I was an important and well-known man, I took off my hat to all the legal and other gentlemen who passed by. I didn't know a single one but I bowed to all of them in a familiar way. When the girls saw this, and a gold *escudo* that I took from my savings to give a beggar who asked me for alms, they thought I was a very great man. As it was late, they decided they'd better go, and they excused themselves, warning me not to let anybody find out about my servant's visit. As a great favour and as a token that I would definitely see them the next day, I asked the prettier of the two to give me her rosary, which was gilded. They made a fuss about giving me it so, as surety, I offered them the hundred *escudos* and they told me where they lived. They thought they could swindle some more out of me so they became more confident and asked me where I was living. They explained that I couldn't send servants to their place at any time of the day or night because they were respectable ladies. I took them along the Calle Mayor and as we turned into the Calle de las Carretas I picked out the house which seemed the biggest and best to me, with a carriage without horses at the door, and said that was my place, and the owner and the coach were theirs to command. I said my name was Don Alvaro de Córdoba and, as they watched, I walked in through the door. And now I remember that, when we left the shop, I called one of the servants and beckoned him very authoritatively with my arm. I made out as if I were telling him that they should all stay and wait for me there. Actually the fact is that I asked him if he worked for my uncle the Comendador. He said he didn't. That is how I took an interest in the welfare of other men's servants as a proper gentleman should.

When it grew dark we all came back to our quarters. I went in and found the soldier dressed in rags. He had a wax torch that he'd been given to walk with in a funeral procession and brought home with him. His name was Magazo and he came from Olías; he'd been a soldier, in a play, and fought the Moors, in a dance. When he spoke to men who had been in Flanders he said he'd been in China, and he told the China veterans he'd been in Flanders. He was trying to form a regiment, but spent most of the time killing his fleas. He let drop the names of several castles but he'd hardly seen one, even on coins. He made a big thing about honouring the memory of Don Juan, the victor of Lepanto, and I often heard him say that Luis Quijada was an honourable friend. He was always on about Turks, galleons and captains, but he got it all from a few songs about them. He didn't know a single thing about the sea; the only naval thing he knew was navel oranges, so when he talked about Don Juan and the Battle of Lepanto he said that Lepanto was a very fierce Moor. As the poor devil didn't know it was the name of the sea we had some funny hours at his expense.

The next to come in was my own companion, with his nose bashed in and his head bandaged, covered in blood and filthy. When we asked him what had happened he said he'd been to the soup kitchen at St Jerome's and asked for a double portion on the pretext that it was for some poor but honest people. They deprived the other beggars of their rations to give them to him. The others followed him and saw him slopping it in as fast as he could in a corner behind the door. They shouted and told him it wasn't right to tell lies just to stuff himself and do others down, and then they started knocking him about and thumping him and raised bumps on his poor head. Then they hit him with their jugs and his nose was broken by somebody giving him a wooden spoon to smell quicker than he should have done. They took his sword away. Hearing the shouting, the porter came out, but he couldn't calm them down. At last my poor mate was in such a dangerous position that he said:

'I'll give you back what I've eaten.'

But even that wasn't good enough, because what annoyed them was that he was pretending to beg for others as if he were ashamed of doing it for himself.

'Look at him, all done up in rags like a kid's doll, as miserable as a pastry-shop in Lent. He's got more holes than a flute, more patches than a dapple mare, more stains than a cook, and more darns than a dustman,' said one of the students who collect old bread and left-overs in their hoods like magpies. 'Some of us who accept the blessed saint's soup might be bishops or some-

166

thing one day and this snob doesn't want to eat with us. I'm a graduate from Sigüenza, I am.'

The porter separated them because a little old man who was watching it all said that, even though my companion did come for the free soup, he was a descendant of the great Captain* and had important relatives.

That's all I've got to say because my mate had got away and was tenderly feeling his bones.

* Gonzalo de Córdoba, Spanish soldier of the sixteenth century.

CHAPTER THREE

⤙⤚

I N came Merlo Díaz with his belt looking like a necklace of jugs and glasses which he had knocked off, as he went around asking the nuns for a drink of water.

But he finished second to Don Lorenzo del Pedroso who came in with a really good cape which he'd 'swapped' in a billiards saloon for his own, which was so worn that it would be about as useful as a handkerchief to whoever picked it up. Don Lorenzo used to take off his cloak as if he was getting ready for a game, put it together with the others and then decide not to play, go to get his cloak, take the one which seemed in best condition and leave. His manor was usually a game of bowls or skittles.

But all this was nothing compared with Don Cosme's entrance. He came in surrounded by boys with scrofula, cancerous sores and leprosy, open wounds and missing arms or legs. He'd made himself a magic healer with the aid of some passes and prayers he'd learnt from an old woman. He earned as much as the rest of us put together because if a client didn't come along with a parcel under his cloak or money didn't jingle in his pocket or a pair of capons couldn't be heard, then he'd had it – no cure! He'd ruined hundreds of people. He could make anybody believe anything he wanted them to; he was the greatest liar of all time. In fact he didn't even tell the truth when he got careless. He talked about the Infant Jesus; it was 'Deo Gratias' every time he went into someone's house; then came 'May the Holy Ghost be with you all.' He had the full set of hypocrite's equipment; a rosary with double-size beads. Then he would, as if by accident, let people see the lashes of a whip hanging under his cloak. They were clotted with blood but the blood was from his nose. He wriggled to make them believe his fleas were really a hair-shirt

168

and that his hunger was voluntary fasting. He talked about his temptations. If he mentioned the Devil, he would say:

'God protect and spare us.'

As he went into church he kissed the ground and said he was an unworthy sinner. When it came to women he didn't raise his eyes, but that didn't apply to their skirts. People were so taken in by him that they put themselves into his hands completely and they might just as well have been entrusting themselves to the Devil because, as well as being a gambler, he was a crook – what is usually known as a front man in card-sharp swindles. Sometimes he took the Lord's name in vain and other times he swore for no reason at all. As far as women were concerned he had kids all over the place and had knocked up two pious ladies. In other words, whatever commandments of God he didn't break he split down the middle.

Then in came Polanco with a lot of noise and demanded a dun-coloured bag, a large cross, a long false beard and a bell. He used to walk about at night dressed like this and say:

'Remember death and help the poor souls in Purgatory!'

In this way he picked up a lot of contributions. He used to go into any house with an open door and, if nobody could see him or interrupt him, he took whatever he could lay his hands on. If he was discovered, he rang his bell and said, in a very false penitent voice:

'Remember, my friends, etc.'

In one month they taught me all these tricks and strange ways of stealing. Now I want to get back to what I was saying before. I told them the story and showed them the rosary. They praised my trick no end and the old woman accepted the rosary and said she would try and sell it. She went round people's houses and told them it belonged to a young lady who was very poor and who had to sell it for food. She had her individual trick and swindle for every situation. She wept all the way along; she clasped her hands and sighed at the bitterness of life; and she called everyone her child. Over an excellent chemise, jacket, skirt, sash and shawl, she wore a torn sackcloth robe belonging to a brother who was a hermit on the hill near Alcalá. She controlled our flock, advised them and covered up for them.

Now the Devil is never idle in matters to do with his servants, so he arranged that one day when she was trying to sell some clothes and some other bits and pieces at a house, somebody found out about her business. He fetched an inspector to arrest the old woman, whose name was Old Lebrusca. Then she confessed everything and told them how we all made our living and that we were gentleman thieves. The inspector left her in prison and came to our house and there he found all my companions and me with them. He brought half a dozen other policemen with him and the whole school of thieves ended up in prison, where our gentlemanly qualities did not flourish.

CHAPTER FOUR

→→←←

W H E N they threw us in gaol they put two pairs of irons on each of us and shut us up in an underground cell. When I saw how things were I decided to use the money I had on me. So I took out a doubloon and said to the warder:

'Excuse me, sir, can I have a word with you – in private?'

I showed him an *escudo* to make my meaning clearer and when he saw it he kept me on one side.

'I beg you, sir,' I said to him, 'to have some feelings for a gentleman.'

I felt for his hands. Their palms were used to bearing dates, so he closed his fist over the twenty *reals* and said loudly:

'I'll find out what's the matter with you and if it's not serious you'll go into the stocks.'

I caught on to his hint at once and answered very respectfully. I was left outside but my friends were pushed down below.

I forgot to say how everybody laughed at us as we were led through the street and into prison. You see, we were tied up and they were shoving us along. Some of us hadn't any cloaks and the others wore them trailing behind them on the ground, so it was quite a sight to see us all in our patches, wearing clothes that suited each other about as well as a mixture of red and white wine. Some had clothes which were falling to pieces so the policemen had to grab their bare flesh to be sure of a firm hold. Even then their grip wasn't very firm as the flesh was rotting away out of hunger. Others left bits of their shirts and breeches in the policemen's hands as they went along. We were all strung on a rope and when they released us it was left festooned with rags.

However, to get back to the story, when night came I was allowed to sleep in the part of the gaol reserved for paying guests and they gave me a camp-bed. It was quite an experience to see some of the prisoners go to sleep just as they were, without taking anything off at all; others took everything off altogether, and some of them played cards. Then the lights were put out and we were locked in. We all forgot about our leg-irons.

Now the chamber-pot was just behind my bed and all night prisoners came and released their loads. When I first heard the noise I was scared because I thought it was a thunderstorm, so I kept crossing myself and praying to St Barbara. But when I noticed the smell I realized that the thunder wasn't in the best of taste. The stink was so bad that I had to hold my nose and bury my head under the blankets. Some of them had diarrhoea and others constipation. In the end I had to ask them to move the chamber-pot somewhere else, and as a result there was a row. I decided that I'd better get in first so I hit one of them around the face with my belt. He got up in a hurry and knocked the chamber-pot over and that woke everyone up. Then they all began to shout at the tops of their voices and the governor ran up with his screws, thinking he was losing the whole nick. He arrived, opened the door, lit a candle and found out what was going on. They all said it was my fault. I said that with their shitting all night I hadn't been able to get a wink of sleep. The warder ordered me downstairs to the underground dungeon; he thought he'd get more cash out of me for keeping me out of that stinking hole. I did as he ordered rather than dip into my pocket again. So I was taken down to be greeted with shouts of joy from my friends.

I passed rather a chilly night. Day came and we were taken out. We looked at each other's faces and the first thing the other prisoners told us was that we had to contribute for 'cleaning' (which was nothing to do with the Immaculate Virgin, either) or else we'd get properly sorted out. There was a man in the prison who was tall and one-eyed. He was a mean-looking fellow with a moustache and broad shoulders covered with whip scars. He wore more iron than there is in the entire Basque country: two pairs of leg-irons and a ball and chain. They called him the Giant, and he was in prison for something to do with wind, so I thought he had stolen some bellow or musical instrument or even fans. When people asked him if it was anything like that he said no; it was for posterior crimes. I thought that he meant old crimes, but at last I realized it was because he was a queer. If the governor told him off for some offence or other, he called him 'hangman's nark' and 'cesspit'. Sometimes the governor threatened him by saying:

'You poor fool, don't you know you can be burnt at the stake? I hope for your sake they'll strangle you first.'

He had confessed, and we hated and feared him so much that we all wore protectors round our arses like dog-collars, and nobody dared fart in case they reminded him where their backsides were. He got friendly with another prisoner called Robledo, who was also called the Climber. He said he was in prison for being too free and easy. When we pressed him it transpired that he stole everything he could lay his hands on. He knew the whip better than any coach-horse, as every public flogger had tried his hand on him. He had so many razor-slashes on his face that if you took the stitches away there wouldn't be anything left. He only had half his share of ears. His nose had been split and put together again, but it hadn't been made as well as the knife that had done the first job.

As well as these there were another four, as rampant as lions on a coat of arms, all loaded with irons and condemned to the galleys. They said that in a short time they could say they had served the King on land and sea. I couldn't understand why they were looking forward to their fate so cheerfully.

Now all these men were narked that my friends hadn't made their contributions, so that night they planned to set about them with a rope's end that they kept for that precise purpose. Night came and we were all shoved into the deepest cell in the place. The light was put out and I hid straight away under the planks that were my bed. Then two of the men began to whistle and a third began to lay about him with the rope. When my gentlemen friends saw that they were in trouble they squeezed themselves into a corner underneath the bed. This wasn't too difficult, what with their 'fasting' and the fact that the mange and the lice had taken most of the flesh from their bones; they were like nits in your hair or bugs in a bed. The rope thudded down on the boards but my friends didn't say a word. When they realized they weren't even groaning, the other blackguards put down the rope and began to throw bricks, stones and rubbish which they collected specially for the purpose. It so happened that someone scored a hit on Don Toribio's neck and raised a nasty bump on it. He began to scream blue murder and, so that the guards shouldn't hear, the toughs began to sing in chorus and rattle their chains. Don Toribio grabbed everybody else to try to get underneath the bed. You should have heard it; the noise their rattling bones made was like the clappers beggars use. Their 'clothes' fell to bits; every rag bit the dust. The rubble and the stones flew so thick and fast that Don Toribio had more bumps on his head in a minute than a nobbly walking-stick. He couldn't find any shelter from the hailstorm which was falling on him and he saw he was about to enjoy martyrdom, though he wasn't even a good man, let alone a saint, so he asked to be left out. He promised to pay in time and leave his clothes as security.

The toughs agreed to this and, in spite of the others, who tried to dissuade him, he got up half-stunned, as best he could, and came over to my side. The others had more bumps on their heads than hair but they didn't waste any time in promising to pay as well. They offered their clothes in lieu of an entrance fee, for they realized that they were better off if they had to stay in bed because they were naked than because they were injured. That night they were left in peace but in the morning they had to take their clothes off. They stripped, but all their clothes together wouldn't have made a wick for a candle. They stayed in bed, or rather wrapped up in a blanket apiece, which was in fact the rough old prison blanket they deloused themselves under.

Soon they began to feel some life in the blankets, because the fleas were starving; some of them hadn't eaten for a week. Some of the fleas were enormous and others could easily have jumped into a bull's ear. My friends thought they'd be eaten alive that night. They threw off the blankets and swore violently and scratched till the blood ran. I got out of the cell and asked them to excuse me for not staying with them but it was rather important for me not to do so. I slipped the warder a few doubloons again and found out who was drawing up the charges against us; then I sent a boy along to fetch him. When he came I got him into a private room and we talked about the trial. Then I started telling him about the money I had. I begged him to look after it for me and, as far as he could, to look favourably on the case of an unfortunate gentleman who had been deceived into a life of crime.

'Believe me, sir,' he said, after taking the hint, 'it all depends on us. If anybody turns out bad, he can do a lot of harm. I've sent more innocent men to the gallows for pleasure than there are letters on your charge-sheet. Now trust me and I'll get you out safe and sound.'

He said his piece and cleared off. When he got to the door he turned round and asked me to give him something for good old Diego García, the Chief Constable, as he had to have his mouth shut with a silver gag. He also went on about something to compensate the Clerk of the Court for the expenses he would incur in not reading an entire paragraph of the indictment.

'A Clerk of the Court,' he said, 'only has to arch his eyebrows, raise his voice or stamp on the floor to attract the attention of a day-dreaming judge (most of them are miles away). With one little action or gesture he can destroy a man.'

I said I quite understood and added another fifty *reals*. As a receipt he advised me to turn up the collar of my cape and told me two more ways of curing the cold I had caught in that clammy cell. Lastly he said:

'Now you've no need to worry. If you give the gaoler eight *reals* he'll soften. People like him won't do anything for nothing.'

I thought that this last piece of advice was rather funny, coming from him. He went at last and I gave the gaoler an *escudo*; he removed my leg-irons and let me into his quarters. He had an elephant of a wife and two horrible daughters, ugly and stupid and, in spite of their faces, whores. His name was Something Blandones de San Pablo, and his wife's was Ana Moráez. One day he came in to dinner, while I was eating, in a rage and purple-faced. He refused to eat. His wife realized he had something serious on his mind, so she went up to him and annoyed him so much with her usual nagging that he said:

'What do you think's the matter? That bleeder Almendros had a row with me about the prisoners' lodging that he looks after, and he told me you weren't clean.'

175

'The bugger hasn't caught anything off me,' she said. 'God Almighty, you're not much of a man or you'd have pulled his beard out of his face. Do I ever ask his servants to clean for me?'

She turned to me and said:

'Thank God nobody can say I'm Jewish like him. His grandparents are scum on the one side and Jews on the other. By God, Don Pablos, if I heard him I'd remind him that the Inquisition's got its eye on him.'

The gaoler was very upset and said:

'Oh, Ana, I didn't want to tell you but he said you weren't all that Christian either. When he meant dirty he didn't mean like a pig. He meant not eating pig-meat.'

'So he said I was Jewish, did he? And you just listened to him, I suppose? Isn't it marvellous? Is that how you feel about my honour? Everybody knows I'm Doña Ana de Moráez, daughter of Estefanía Rubio and Juan de Madrid and God knows it's true.'

'What do you mean,' I said, 'the daughter of Juan de Madrid?'

'Juan de Madrid,' she said, 'from Auñón. By God I swear that bastard is a Jew, a queer and a cuckold.'

I faced them and said:

'Juan de Madrid, God rest his soul, is in Heaven. He was my father's first cousin and I can prove who he was and I'll make it my business, if I get out of prison, to make the bastard say he was mistaken a hundred times. I've got a family tree back home written in gold letters which concerns us both.'

They were very happy with their long-lost relative and cheered up when they learned about the family tree. Of course I didn't have one and I hadn't the slightest idea who *they* were. The husband began to go into details about our relationship. I didn't want him to catch me out so I pretended to lose my temper and stormed out, cursing and swearing. But they stopped me and said I wasn't to worry or think about it any more. Every now and then I pretended to forget myself and shouted:

'Juan de Madrid! You should just see the details I've got on him.'

At other times I said:

'Juan de Madrid, the older one? His father was married to Juana de Acebedo, the fat one.'

Then I'd keep quiet a little longer.

So, what with all this, the gaoler let me sleep and eat in his quarters and the Prosecutor (good luck to him), at his request and with my money, arranged things so well that they led the old woman out tied to a horse's tail, with a death-march band in front. The cry went up:

'This woman is being punished for theft!'

The executioner laid into her in time with the music as the gentleman of the court had instructed. Then came all my companions on dray horses, hatless, exposed to public humiliation.

They suffered public humiliation and private exposure (as their privates were exposed) and were exiled from Madrid for six years. I got out on probation thanks to the Prosecutor; and the Clerk of the Court did his bit too, because he changed the tone of his voice, spoke quietly, skipped a bit and swallowed some paragraphs whole.

CHAPTER FIVE

-◄-►-

WHEN I got out of prison I was quite alone and friendless. My friends told me they were going to make their way to Seville at the expense of charitable people but I didn't want to follow them. So I went to an inn where I found a girl with fair hair and a white skin, sharp eyes and a cheerful nature, sometimes inquisitive and sometimes plain randy. She lisped a bit, was scared of mice, and was very proud of her hands, so she did things to show them off like snuffing the candles, serving up the food, and always clasping them together in church. In the street she kept pointing out whose house was whose and so on. In the drawing-room she was always having to push a pin back into her hat; and if she played a game it was 'pizpirigaña', which you play by turning your hand around and around.

She yawned on purpose, even when she wasn't tired, just to show her teeth and make the sign of the cross over her mouth. In other words there was so much of her hands all over the house that it was even beginning to annoy her parents. They were very good to me there because they earned their living from letting furnished rooms to three lodgers: me, a Portuguese and a Catalan. They really made me feel at home. The girl looked all right for a bit of you know what, especially as it was very convenient her being in the same house as me. I stared at her all the time; I told them all stories that were meant to be amusing. I always had news even if I had to invent it. I did everything I could for them so long as it didn't cost me anything. I told them I knew some magic spells, that I was a magician, and that I could make the house appear to sink into the ground or burst into flames and lots of other things that they were credulous enough to swallow without question. I felt that they were all very well-disposed towards me but had no real respect for me. They didn't take any special notice of me because I wasn't as well dressed as I ought to have been. Mind you, I'd improved my outfit somewhat with the gaoler's help. I visited him constantly and kept my blood healthy with the good red meat and bread I wormed out of him.

I wanted them to think I was a rich man hiding the fact, so I arranged for friends to call at the house and ask for me when I was out. The first one came and asked for Don Ramiro de Guzmán; that's the name I gave, as my friends said it was cheap enough to change your name and very useful sometimes. Anyway the man asked for Don Ramiro, a business man who had two good government contracts in his pocket. The women in the house didn't recognize me from that description and told my friend that there was a Don Ramiro de Guzmán living there, with more rags to his name than riches, stunted, ugly and poor.

'That's him,' he answered; 'that's the one I mean. I'd be happy enough with his two thousand ducats a year.'

He told them a lot more lies; they were stupefied and he left them a forged bill of exchange that I was due to pay for nine thousand *escudos*. He told them to give it to me to sign and cleared off. Mother and daughter believed I was a wealthy man and marked me down straight away for a husband. I came in pretending I didn't know what had happened, and as they gave me the bill, they said:

'You can't hide money *and* love, Don Ramiro; why do you hide your real identity from us? After all, you do owe us a lot.'

I pretended to be annoyed about the bill of exchange and went off to my room. It was quite striking how their attitude to me changed when they thought I had money. They hung on my every word; nobody was as witty as me. When I saw I had got them well set up I told the girl how I felt about her and she heard me out delighted, whispering sweet nothings all the time. We separated and one night I shut myself up in my room which was divided off from theirs by just a thin partition. I wanted to convince them I was well off, so I took out fifty *escudos* and counted them so many times that they thought they heard me count up six thousand. It was ideal for me that they should think I had so much money because they worried all the time about how to make me happy and comfortable.

The name of the Portuguese was Senhor Vasco de Meneses, Knight of the Hymn-books, I mean, the Order of Christ. He wore a black cap, boots, a small collar and big moustaches. He was madly in love with Doña Berenguela de Rebollo (that really was her name). He courted her with long conversations and sighs deeper than those of a nun in Lent. His singing was awful and he was always quarrelling with the Catalan who was the most wretched and miserable worm God ever created. He ate like the tertian fever, once every three days, and the bread was so hard that, however cutting you might be, you'd never sink your teeth into it. He pretended to be quite a lad; in fact all he needed was eggs to make him a hen, because he cackled all the time. The two of them saw how well I was getting on, so they began to slander me. The Portuguese said I had fleas, was a scoundrel and hadn't a penny to my name. The Catalan said I was cowardly scum. I knew all about this and even heard them sometimes, but I wasn't really brave enough to do anything about it.

Well, in the end the girl agreed to go steady with me and accept my little love letters. I began in the usual way: 'My darling, your great beauty ...' I said all that stuff about burning with passion, trying to atone, and offering myself as her slave, and I signed with a heart transfixed with an arrow. At last we began to call each other tú and, to make them believe even more that I was somebody, I went out and hired a mule; then, all muffled up and disguising my voice, I went to the inn and asked for myself, inquiring if His Grace Don Ramiro de Guzmán, Squire of Valcerrado and Vellorete, lived there.

'There is a gentleman of that name living here,' replied the girl, 'he's rather small.'

I said I knew it was him by her description and asked her to tell him that Diego de Solórzana, his steward of accounts, was on his way to collect rents and had called to kiss his hand. Having said my piece I rode off and returned home a little later.

They were smiling all over their faces when I got back and asked me why I had hidden the fact that I was Squire of Valcerrado and Vellorete. They gave me the message. At this stage the girl decided to hurry things up as she was all out to land a rich husband, and she arranged that I should meet her at one o'clock in the morning. I'd have to go along a corridor and up on the roof and get into her room through the window. Now the Devil keeps a sharp eye on everything, so he arranged matters so that, when night came, I should be looking forward to seizing my chance. I went along the corridor, but as I was climbing on to the roof, I slipped and came down on the roof of the lawyer who lived next door. I fell with such a bump that I broke all the tiles and got them imprinted on my body. Half the household woke up at the noise and, as lawyers are always on the lookout for thieves, they thought I was one.

When I saw what was going to happen, I hid behind a chimney, but that made their suspicions worse, and the lawyer and his two servants and his brother worked me over properly and tied me up in front of the girl's eyes. It was no use my protesting. In fact she thought it was very funny because I'd told her that I could do magic and disappearing tricks. She'd thought I'd fallen on purpose as a sort of performance for her benefit and kept telling me that a joke was a joke and I should get up now. When I heard this, and what with the kicks and punches I had received, I began to howl and that girl still thought I was acting and nearly choked with laughter. Then the lawyer began to try me. There were some keys rattling in my pocket, so he said, and he wrote down that they were skeleton keys, even though he saw them and it was obvious that they weren't. I told him I was Don Ramiro de Guzmán and he thought that was very funny. I was very miserable as I'd been knocked about in front of my girl and now I was being arrested shamefully and without reason. I didn't know what to do. I knelt down before the lawyer and begged him for the love of God but nothing could move him to let me go.

All this was happening on the roof. It didn't matter that they were a little nearer Heaven; they still told lies. I was taken down through the window of a room that was used as a kitchen.

CHAPTER SIX

◄─┼─►

I DIDN'T sleep a wink all night thinking how unlucky I was not to land on the roof but to fall into the hands of the cruel and merciless lawyer. And when I remembered how he'd found the so-called skeleton keys in my pocket and how he'd scribbled out pages and pages of indictment, I realized that nothing grows as fast as your guilt when you're in a lawyer's hands.

I spent the night making plans and rejecting them. Sometimes I decided to beg him for mercy for the sake of Our Lord Jesus Christ but, when I thought what He'd had to put up with from lawyers when He was alive, I didn't dare. I kept trying to free myself but he soon heard me and came running down from bed to check the knots. In fact he was even more concerned about pushing through his trumped-up case than I was in getting safely away.

He got up at dawn and dressed so early that only he and the witnesses were up. He got his belt and gave me another good walloping. He reproved me for the evil habit of stealing – he knew plenty about it. I'd just reached the point where I was about to offer him money to stop (that's the only thing to cut diamond-hard hearts like his) when, urged on by the shouts of my girl, who'd seen me fall down and get knocked about and realized I wasn't playing around, in came the Portuguese and the Catalan.

As soon as the lawyer saw them talking to me, he drew his pen to try and skewer them as accomplices to my crime. The Portuguese wasn't going to stand for this and started abusing him. He said that he was a noble in the King's household and I was a very noble gentleman (all in Portuguese) and that it was disgusting to keep me tied up like that. He began to untie me and the lawyer promptly bellowed for help.

Two of his servants, half private police and half porters, trod on their cloaks and tore their clothes, as they usually do to show they've had to fight when they haven't, and called for help in the King's name. Anyhow, the Portuguese and the Catalan got me free, and when the lawyer saw that nobody was going to help him, he said:

'By God, I'm not going to put up with this, and if Your Graces weren't who you are it would cost you dear. Just satisfy the witnesses and take note that I'm not expecting to get anything out of it.'

I took the hint at once, got out eight *reals*, and gave them to him. I was even in mind to pay him back in his own coin for the beating he had given me; but I didn't as I'd rather nobody knew I'd had one. So I went off with my friends and thanked them for getting me released. My face was cut and grazed and my shoulders pretty sore. The Catalan laughed his head off and told the girl she ought to get married to me to turn the proverb round: instead of 'cuckolded and then beaten' it would be 'beaten and later cuckolded'. He said I was a hard nut and that the misadventure had opened my eyes to things. These remarks annoyed me. If I went to see them he'd start talking about knocking, or firewood or timber. I saw how I'd lost face and how I was being insulted, and that they were beginning to realize that I wasn't a rich man, so I began planning to leave.

I didn't intend to pay for my board and lodging, so I made an arrangement with a man from Hornillos called Brandalagas, and two friends of his, to come and arrest me one night. They came in the night and told the landlady that they were from the Holy Inquisition and that she mustn't say anything. They were all terrified because I'd made out I was a magician. When I was brought down they didn't say anything, but when they saw my baggage, they asked if they could keep it for what I owed them. But my friends said that it all became the property of the Inquisition and nobody on earth could dispute that. They let me go and said they were always afraid something like that was going to happen. The 'inquisitors' told the Catalan and the Portuguese that the people who'd asked for me were devils and I had a familiar. About the money I had been counting, they said it might look like money but it certainly was not. The women were convinced, and I got my clothes away and my food free into the bargain.

Helped by my friends, I managed to change my style of clothes and to wear fashionable breeches and large collars; I also hired a servant and a couple of little boys as pages; that was what a gentleman needed in those days. My friends urged me on and pointed out how useful it would be to have the appearance of a wealthy man when I looked around for a wife: after all, marriages are often made like that in Madrid society. They even went so far as to offer to show me the right way to the gold mine. Well, I was cunning and rotten with greed and made up my mind to look for a rich woman. I went round all the second-hand shops and bought my wedding outfit. I found a place where they hired out horses and began to cut a fine figure on one straight away. But I couldn't find a servant. So I went down to the Calle Mayor and stood in front of a saddler's, as if I were thinking of buying something. Up rode two gentlemen who asked me if I was thinking of buying the saddle I was holding, which was chased with silver. I put it down and engaged them for some time in flattering conversation. In the end they said they were thinking of having a little bit of fun in the Prado gardens and I said I'd go with them, that is, of course, if they didn't mind. I left a message with the shopkeeper that if my pages and a lackey appeared, would he please send them to the Prado? I described their uniforms; then I rode off between the two gentlemen. It occurred to me as I rode along that nobody who saw us could tell whose were the pages or footmen with us, nor which of us didn't have any. I began to talk in a very self-assured manner about the jousting at Talavera and a white horse I'd had; I boasted a lot about the war-horse I was expecting from Córdoba. Every time we passed a page, a horse or a servant I made them stop, asked them who their master was, went over the horse's points and asked if it was for sale. I made the horse trot up and down the street twice, and even if it was perfect I pointed out some fault in the bridle and told the man how to put it right; as it happened, I had plenty of opportunities of doing this. Now the other two were wondering and, as I thought, asking themselves:

'Who on earth is this country bumpkin who's sticking to us like a leech?'

You see, one of them had a noble insignia on his chest and the other a diamond chain – that's insignia and estate lumped together, or as good as – so I said I was looking for a couple of good horses for myself and a cousin of mine as we'd put our names down for some events in a competition. We reached the Prado and, as we were going in, I took my foot out of the stirrup and let my horse walk slowly with my feet hanging loose. I wore my cape over one shoulder and carried my hat in my hand. Everybody stared at me. Some said:

'I've seen that one walking,' and others:

'Pretty bugger, isn't he?'

I pretended not to hear any of it, and swaggered on.

The two gentlemen rode up to a coach full of ladies and asked me to keep them amused with my chatter for a time. I left the side where the young ones were and went round to the mother and the aunt.

They were a cheerful pair of old girls; one was fifty and the other a bit younger. I told them no end of nonsense and they listened to me. However old a woman is she's got more vanity than years in her. I promised to buy them presents and I asked them about the girls. They said they weren't married: I could tell that from the way they talked. I said the usual thing, that I hoped the old ladies would see them well matched, and they thought 'well matched' was a very smart way of putting it. Then they asked me how I spent my time in Madrid. I told them I was running away from my mother and father who wanted to marry me off against my will to an ugly, stupid, common woman, just because she had a large dowry.

'And I, ladies, prefer a clean woman without a rag to her back to a rich heiress. You see, God be thanked, my inheritance is worth a good forty thousand ducats a year and, if I win a case which looks pretty favourable for me, I shan't need anything.'

Up jumped the aunt (a right old bitch), and said:

'Oh, young man, I do so think you're right! Don't get married unless you love the girl and she's in your class. I can tell you that although I'm not well off, I've refused my niece to lots of rich men because they didn't have any class. She's poor – she's only got a dowry of six thousand ducats – but as far as blood's concerned, she can look anybody in the eye.'

'I'm sure of that,' I replied.

At that point the girls put an end to our conversation by asking my friends to buy them a snack.

> Each man looked at his brother;
> Every jowl began to shudder.

I saw my chance and jumped in. I explained that I really missed having footmen to send home for some hampers I had. They thanked me for my kind intentions and I begged them to go to the Casa del Campo (a well-known park) the next day and I'd have some cold delicacies sent out to them. They accepted on the spot; they told me their address and asked for mine, and then their coach moved off and I and my companions began to make our way back. They saw how open-handed I'd been about the ladies' picnic so they began to feel more friendly and invited me to have supper with them that night. I made them ask me several times, but not too many, and then I went and had supper with them. I kept sending out people to fetch my servants and swearing I'd give them the sack. The clock struck ten and I said I had an appointment with a lady and would they mind if I left. Off I went, after arranging to meet them the next afternoon in the Casa del Campo.

I rode back and gave my horse in at the livery stables, and then I went home where I found my friends playing Four of a Kind.* I told them what had happened and the arrangement I had made, and we decided to send the ladies the picnic without fail and spend two hundred *reals* on it. Having made up our minds, we went to bed. I must confess I didn't sleep a wink all night worrying about how I'd spend the dowry, but I really couldn't decide whether to build a house with the money or invest it in an annuity. I didn't know what would be best for me.

---

* A card game, the object of which is to make a trick with four cards of the same suit.

CHAPTER SEVEN

-<+>-

DAY came and we got up to go and find servants, chinaware and the cold lunch. In the end, as money can buy anything and nobody is rude to hard cash, we bribed a nobleman's butler to give us the dinner service and he and three servants agreed to serve the meal. We spent the morning getting everything ready and by the afternoon I had hired a nag. At the agreed time I rode out towards the Casa del Campo. My belt was stuffed with papers, like a big business man's, and half a dozen of my doublet buttons were open with papers peeping out from underneath as well.

When I arrived the ladies and gentlemen and everything else were already there. The ladies received me in a friendly way and the gentlemen called me *vos* to show that we were all good friends. I had said that my name was Don Felipe Tristán and all day it was Don Felipe this and Don Felipe that. I started telling them that I had been so taken up with His Majesty's service and business connected with my inheritance that I'd been afraid I shouldn't be able to come, and they mustn't expect more than a scratch cold lunch. As I said this the butler arrived with his equipment, the dinner service and the servants; the gentlemen and the ladies just sat there, speechless, staring at me. I told the butler to go to the eating-place and lay everything there while we went to the fishponds in the meanwhile.

The old women made a great fuss of me and I was glad to see the girls hadn't any veils on, because since I was born I swear I've never seen anything so lovely as the one I'd planned on marrying. Her skin was pink and white, her lips were ruby-red, her tiny teeth were even, her nose was straight, her eyes green and almond-shaped, she was tall, her hands were well formed and she had a delicious lisp. The other one wasn't bad but she was a little more self-assured and I reckoned she'd been around a bit too much. We went to the fishponds and saw everything. By the way she talked I saw that if my fiancée had been living in Herod's day she'd have been done away with as one of the Innocents; she was dead simple. Still, as I don't need women to give me advice or make me laugh but just to go to bed with – if they're ugly and intelligent I might just as well be in bed with Aristotle or Seneca or a book – I usually pick them as being good for a roll in the hay. This consoled me. We came to the picnic-spot and, as we passed through a thicket, my collar-lacing was caught by a twig which tore it a bit. The girl came up to me and sewed it up again with a silver needle and the mother told me to send the collar to her house the next day and Doña Ana, that was the girl's name, would repair it properly. I did everything just right: plenty to eat, hot and cold meat, fruit and desserts. They cleared the table and just then I saw a gentleman with two servants coming through the park towards me. You can imagine the shock I had when I saw it was my old friend Don Diego Coronel! He came up to me and just stared at me, seeing me dressed as I was. He spoke to the woman, calling them cousins, and he kept turning round to look at me all the time. I talked to the butler while Don Diego's other two gentlemen friends were deep in conversation with him. He asked them my name (I found this out later) and they said I was Don Felipe Tristán, a very noble and wealthy gentleman. I saw him cross himself. Finally, in front of everybody, including the ladies, he came up to me and said:

'Sir, I beg your pardon. I swear by God that until I was told who you were I thought you were a very different person from what you appear to be. I've never seen anybody look so much like a servant I had in Segovia, a fellow called Pablillos whose father was a barber there.'

They all laughed loudly and I forced myself to do so as well, otherwise my red face would have given me away. I told him I'd like to see that Pablillos because lots of people had told me he was the spitting image of me.

'Christ!' exclaimed Don Diego, 'I should say so! Your height, the way you talk, your movements; I've never seen anything like it. Let me tell you, my friend, it's uncanny. I've never seen anything so striking!'

The old women, that is the aunt and the mother, asked me how it came about that such a noble gentleman could look so much like a common man of that sort. Then they realized it might reflect on them, so one of them said:

'I know Don Felipe very well. He put us up at Ocaña when my husband asked him to.'

I took the hint and said that all I wanted to do within my limited power was and would be to be entirely at their service everywhere. Don Diego gave me his hand and apologized to me for the insult in thinking I was a barber's son, and he added:

'You won't believe this, sir, but your mother was a witch, your father a thief and your uncle a public executioner, and he was the worst and most unpleasant man you ever saw.'

You can imagine how I felt when he made such insulting remarks to my face. I hid my feelings, but I was burning with rage. We decided to go back to town. I and the other two gentlemen took our leave and Don Diego got into the coach with the ladies. He asked them what the cold lunch had been like and what they thought of my company, and the mother and aunt repeated that I was due to inherit an income of so many ducats and that I wanted to marry Anica; they asked him to go into the matter and said he would see, not only that they were right, but that the marriage would bring honour on all their family.

So they whiled away the journey till they got to their house in the Calle del Arenal in the parish of San Felipe. I and my companions went home together as we'd done the other night. They suggested cards as they reckoned they could get my shirt off my back. I saw what they were after and sat down. They took out some packs of cards that were about as genuine as a wig. I lost one hundred *reals*, said good-bye and went home. There I found my friends Brandalagas and Pero López, practising some new cheating tricks with a pair of dice. When I came in they stopped and asked me what had happened all day, but all I told them was that I'd been in a pretty big fix. I told them how I'd bumped into Don Diego and what had transpired. They calmed me down and advised me to go on with the pretence and not to give up whatever happened.

Then somebody told us there was a game of Lansquenet on next door in the pharmacist's place. I had a pretty good idea of things because I was as sharp as a knife and had a good pack of marked cards. We decided to go and slay them (that's what we call cleaning-up) and I sent my friends on ahead. They went into the room and asked the people there if they'd like to play with a Benedictine friar who'd just come to have a rest with some cousins of his as he was ill. They added that he had plenty of pieces of eight and *escudos* on him. Their eyes all started to pop and they shouted:

'Let the friar come, he's welcome!'

'He's a serious man in a strict order,' retorted Pero López. 'As he's come out, he wants to enjoy himself, but of course it's mainly for the sake of conversation.'

'Let him come, whatever it's for!'

'So keep it quiet . . .' began Brandalagas.

'As good as done,' answered the host.

That way they were so sure of themselves that they swallowed the lie whole. Back came my acolytes. I already had a scarf on my head, my Benedictine habit – which had come into my possession on a certain occasion – a pair of spectacles and a beard, which helped even if it was trimmed. In I walked very humbly and took my seat. We began to play. They picked up some good cards and the three of them set themselves against me. But the three of them were defeated, I'm happy to say, because I was sharper than them and gave them such a skinning that in three hours I took more than thirteen hundred *reals* off them. I threw them a few coins and cleared off with my 'God be praised,' reminding them not to be scandalized at seeing me gamble, as it was only for amusement and not serious.

The others cursed roundly as they'd lost all they had. I said good-bye and we left. We got back home at half past one and went to bed after sharing out our winnings. That cheered me up a little after what had happened, and next morning I got up and went to get another horse. But I couldn't find one for hire anywhere. So I realized that there were a good many others like me, as it doesn't look good to be seen walking nowadays, and looked even worse in those days. I went to San Felipe and met up with a lawyer's servant. The man was looking after a horse as his master had just dismounted and was hearing Mass; I slipped him four *reals* to let me take the horse while his master was in church and let me ride it up and down the Calle del Arenal where my lady lived. He agreed, so I mounted and rode up and down the street a couple of times but didn't catch a glimpse of her; however, the third time, Doña Ana looked out of her window. I saw her and wanted to show off my riding to her, but I didn't know the horse's tricks and I wasn't a good rider. I hit it twice and pulled hard on the reins; it reared up, kicked out and bolted, throwing me head first into a puddle. When I saw the state I was in, surrounded by kids who had run up to look, and under my lady's eyes, I began to curse the horse:

'Bleeding old carthorse! This sort of trick will be the end of me some day. I knew what your little game was. I should have known better.'

The horse had stopped and the servant brought it back to me. I got on again. Don Diego Coronel, who lived in the same house as his cousins, had looked out of the window on account of the noise. I changed colour when I saw him. He asked me if I was hurt, and I replied that I wasn't, though there was something wrong with my leg. The servant was telling me to get a move on as he didn't want his master to come out and see what was going on, because the lawyer had to go to court. I'm so unlucky that just as the servant was saying we should go, along came the lawyer from behind, recognized his nag, and started clouting his servant, shouting all the time what the hell he was doing to let somebody else ride his horse. The worst thing was that, in front of Don Diego and my lady, he told me to be so good as to get off *his* horse, and in a pretty rough way into the bargain. I've never been so ashamed in my life; it was worse than getting a public flogging. I was dejected, and had good reason to be, to have two such awful misfortunes happen in such a short time. Well, in the end I had to get off. The lawyer mounted and rode away. To make it look better, I stood there in the street talking to Don Diego.

'I never rode such a beast in my life,' I said. 'My white horse is near San Felipe. He gets wild and always starts to gallop. I was telling them how I could get him up to a gallop and then pull him up on the spot, and they pointed out a horse and said I'd never be able to do that with him. He belonged to that lawyer. I tried him out. He was very bony and the saddle was so bad it nearly killed me.'

'Yes, you're right,' said Don Diego. 'Whatever you say, I think your leg is hurting you.'

'Yes, it is,' I said, 'so I'd like to get my horse and go home.'

This performance satisfied the girl's doubts and I could see she was very upset about my fall. But Don Diego got very suspicious about the lawyer and what had happened in the street, and that was the major cause of my downfall, although I had a lot more troubles. The most serious one was that, when I got back home and went to have a look at the chest where I kept a little box with all the money I had left from my inheritance and my winnings at cards, except for a hundred *reals* that I kept on me, I found that my good friends Brandalagas and Pero López had taken the lot and disappeared. I felt like death and didn't know what to do next. I said to myself:

'It serves you right, relying on money that you got dishonestly. Easy come, easy go! Oh my God, what am I going to do?'

I didn't know whether to go after them or report the theft to the police. The latter idea didn't seem very good to me, because if they were caught they'd spill the story about my wearing a religious habit and a few other things besides, and I'd end up on the gallows. But how could I go after them if I didn't know which way they'd gone?

In the end I made up my mind to stay and press my suit, so that I shouldn't lose the girl as well. After all, the dowry would easily make up for my loss. I had lunch and hired a pony in the afternoon and rode towards my lady's street. I didn't have a servant and didn't want her to see this, so I waited at the street-corner for a man who looked like a servant. Then I rode behind him as if he were working for me. When I reached the end of the street I again waited behind the corner for someone else to turn up and then I did the same thing again.

I don't know whether truth was so strong that it came out that I was the good-for-nothing Don Diego thought I was, or whether it was his suspicions about the lawyer and his servant, or what it was, but he started spying on me and making inquiries about who I was and where I got my income from. He busied himself so much that in the end he found out the truth; but by the oddest route. I was trying for the girl as hard as I could, besieging the mother and the aunt with letters, and he was being nagged by them to help put an end to my importuning. So, one day while he was out looking for me, he met Sharp (the university man who invited me to dinner when I was with the gang of 'gentlemen'). Sharp was annoyed because I'd dropped him, so as he knew I'd been Don Diego's servant, he told him what my social position had been when he took me off to eat. He also said that only two days before he'd met me on horseback looking very well off, and that I'd told him I was going to marry a lot of money. Don Diego didn't stay to hear any more but went straight back home. On the way he met my two latest friends (the ones with the noble insignia and the jewelled chain) in the Puerta del Sol and told them all about me. He told them to arm themselves and to waylay me that night in the street and knock my teeth through my head. They'd recognize me because he'd arrange for me to wear the cloak he was wearing then. They made their plan and then, soon afterwards, met me in the street. The three of them hid their feelings so well that I was never so convinced of having three first-class friends. We spent some time discussing how to amuse ourselves until it was time for the evening Ave Maria. The two excused themselves and rode down the street and Don Diego and I rode off towards San Felipe. When we got to the top of the Calle de la Paz, Don Diego said:

'I say, let's swap cloaks, Don Felipe; I've got to go down here and I don't want anybody to recognize me.'

'Right,' I said.

I took his cloak in all innocence and gave him mine, which he took in all cunning. I offered to back him up, but his plan was to break my neck so he said he had to go alone and would I mind going away?

No sooner had I left him, wearing his cloak, than it was just my bad luck that a couple of fellows who wanted to beat him up over a woman, ran up and rained blows on me with clubs. When I shouted they looked at me more closely and realized I wasn't him. They ran off and left me in the street with my bruises; I did my best to hide three or four bumps and stopped there for some time as I was dead scared of walking down the street. At last, at twelve o'clock, which was when I usually courted the girl, I rode up to the door. One of the two men to whom Don Diego had spoken came up close to me and hacked me over the shins with a cudgel. Down I went on the ground. Up came the other and slashed me from ear to ear. They took my cape and left me there on the ground, saying:

'That's for being a lying bastard!'

I began to scream and yell for a priest to confess me; I didn't know who had attacked me, though from what he said I reckoned it might be the landlord I hadn't paid because I'd pretended I was being arrested by the Inquisition, or the gaoler I'd tricked, or my companions who had disappeared. In fact I expected to be knifed by so many people that I didn't know who to blame it on; but I never suspected Don Diego nor what it was for. I shouted:

'Stop them! They've taken my cloak!!' At that shout the watchmen ran up. They picked me up and saw a slash as long as a hand on my face. They took me away, without my cloak or finding out what had happened, to be treated. They took me to a barber who sewed me up. Then they asked me where I lived and took me home.

I went to bed and worried all night. My face was cut in half, I was covered in bruises, and my legs were so lame from the blows that I couldn't stand up or even feel them. So there I was, wounded and robbed; I couldn't get hold of my friends, or do anything about getting married; and I couldn't stay in Madrid or go away.

CHAPTER EIGHT

◀◀▶▶

U P popped the sun and so did my landlady, by my bedside. She was a ripe old girl, fifty-five if she was a day, with a great big rosary and a face like a piece of dried fruit or a walnut shell, furrowed like a ploughed field. She was well thought of locally and anybody who fancied her could hop into bed with her. She gave great satisfaction. Her name was Something de la Guía, she let rooms in her house and acted as an agent for other houses. Her place was always full, all the year round.

It was quite a sight to watch her teaching a young girl how to conceal her features and how to reveal those parts of her face which she should show first. She told girls with good teeth to laugh all the time, even if they were expressing their sympathy at somebody's death. Girls with fine hands she taught how to show them to best advantage. She told the blondes to wear their hair loose and always to have some locks peeping out from under their hats and over their cloaks. Girls with nice eyes should keep flashing them, lowering the lids for the sleepy look or showing the whites by looking upwards. She was also a specialist in cosmetics. Sometimes a real old crow would turn up and the landlady would repair her so that when she got home her face was so white that even her husband didn't recognize her. But her real speciality was repairing virgins and patching up young girls.

I only lived there a week and I saw she taught women how to pluck a man and what sort of things to say to him. She taught them how to get jewels: the girls had to use their charms, while the young women had to show that it was their right, and the old ones that they should be given presents as a mark of respect. She showed them how to ask for cash and how to get necklaces and rings. She quoted Señora Vidaña, her rival at Alcalá, and

195

Señora Planosa of Burgos, both past mistresses of the art. I've mentioned all this so that my readers will be sorry for me at having fallen into her hands and will think about the things she said to me. This is how she began (she always talked in clichés):

'If you take and don't put back, Don Felipe, my boy, you'll soon get yourself the sack. As ye sow so shall ye reap; you can't take out if you don't put in. I don't understand you, and I don't know how you make a living; you're only a lad and it wouldn't surprise me if you got up to some mischief or other without realizing that every minute, even while we're asleep, brings us nearer our end. I'm just a piece of human clay and can tell you this: What's this people tell me about you having spent your fortune without knowing how, and having been seen as a student, or a vagrant or a gentleman, and all because of the company you keep? Birds of a feather flock together, my boy; to each his own, and there's many a slip 'twixt cup and lip. Get along with you, you silly boy: if you're randy you know they all pass through my hands in this town, and I live on the commission. As I train them, we'll start them off here and keep them at home and you won't have to go running off with every ponce you see after every bit of skirt and crumpet that lifts her skirt to keep her man in ready cash. I can tell you you'd have saved yourself plenty of ducats if you'd come to me first, because I don't care very much about money. And I swear by my mother and father and all that's holy and God help me that I wouldn't even ask you for the board and lodging you owe me if I didn't need it for some little candles and a few herbs.'

You see, she wasn't a pharmacist but she did a little pharmacy on the side, and if you greased her palm well she'd grease herself and clear out at night like greased lightning.

I saw that she'd finished her lecture and sermon by asking for money (as it was her conclusion she ended with it and didn't start with it as most people do). So I wasn't surprised at her visit, even though she'd never come up before all the time I'd been staying there except once when she came to give me an explanation. She'd heard I'd been told that she cast spells, or something of the sort, and they were going to arrest her, because they said she made the house and the street disappear. She came to clarify matters and to say it was another woman also called Guía. I'm not surprised that with all those guides (that's what the name means) we all lost our way.

I counted out her money and, as I was giving it to her, it was just my bad luck, as always, that they came to arrest her for offences against public morals. They knew her fancy man was in the house, and they burst into my room. Seeing me in bed and her with me, they gave me half-a-dozen cracks over the head and dragged me out of bed. Two others were holding her, calling her a procuress and a witch (who would have thought that from the way I've described her?). Hearing the policemen shouting and me yelling in protest, my friend the fruiterer, who slept in the inner room, began to run for it. The police saw him and guessed, from what the other tenant was telling them, that I wasn't their man. They ran after the bugger and grabbed him and left me thumped and bruised. But though I was hurt I laughed at what the bastards said to the old woman, because one of them stared at her and said:

'You won't half look good with a penitent's hood on, Mum, and I'd love to be there to see two or three thousand turnips thrown at the cart, just for you!'

'The Mayor,' said another, 'has already chosen the feathers so you'll look nice and smart when you're done!'

Presently they brought her fancy man in and tied them both up. They apologized to me and left me to myself. I was quite relieved to see my good landlady reach the position she deserved, and the only thing I had to worry about was to get up in time to throw my rotten orange at her. But from what I was told by one of the maids who stayed in the house, I didn't trust her to be kept in prison, because the maid told me she could fly or something and a few other things that didn't smell very good to me. I stayed there a week getting better and even then I could hardly move out. I had twelve stitches in my face and had to use a pair of crutches.

I was completely broke as the hundred *reals* had gone on my board and lodging. I didn't want to get into any more debt, so I decided to hobble out of the house on my crutches and sell my doublets and collars and all my fine clothes. I did this, and with what I got for them I bought myself an old leather jacket, a thick doublet, a dirty old overcoat, patched and too long for me, heavy leggings and clumsy boots. The coat had a hood which I pulled over my head. I wore a large brass image of Christ round my neck and carried a rosary. I learnt all about how to pitch my voice and the proper sympathy-arousing phrases from a beggar well up in his profession; and so I began to exercise this trade in the street. I sewed the sixty *reals* which I had left into the lining of my coat, and I began to be a beggar, confident in my fluent tongue. I spent a week like that, whining along the streets, complaining, and using my new language:

'Good Christians, servants of the Lord, give to a poor old broken-down man.'

That's what I said on week-days, but on Sundays and holy days I used to do it like this and in a different voice:

'Faithful Christians, servants of the Lord, for the sake of the Princess of Heaven, Queen of the Angels, Mother of God, give to the poor man, the cripple, lamed by the will of the Lord.'

I'd stop a bit – that's very important – and then go on:

'A fever-carrying wind, curse the hour, caught me as I was working in a vineyard and did for my legs. I was healthy and whole as you are, and I hope you stay like that, God be praised.'

This brought the coins rolling in and I made a lot of money. I'd have made more if I hadn't had my pitch spoilt all the time by an ugly lout with no arms and only one leg who did the same streets as me in a cart and collected more charity even though his formula wasn't as elegant as mine. He had a hoarse voice and ended up with a scream.

'Remember, servants of Christ,' he said, 'remember God's punishment for my sins. When you give to the poor it's like giving to God.' Then he added: 'For Jesu's sake.'

He got fantastic sums. I took note and stopped saying 'Jesus': I removed the 's' and so made the public more devout. In other words, I changed my words and did very well out of the change. I kept both my legs tied up in a leather bag and used two crutches. I slept in the doorway of a surgeon's house with a local beggar, one of the biggest twisters I ever met. He was very rich, and was a sort of beggars' king. He earned more than any of us. He had a huge false hernia and used to tie a rope tight round his upper arm so that it looked as though his hand was all swollen up, as well as paralysed and inflamed at the same time. He used to lie down flat on his back on his pitch to show his hernia, which was as big as a football, and say:

'Look at me! See what God has done to a Christian man!'

If a woman passed by, he would say: 'Beautiful lady, God be with you,' and most women, feeling flattered, gave him money and deliberately went down that street although it was out of their way. If some dirty little soldier walked by, it was: 'Hey, Captain, Sir!' and if it was anybody else it was: 'Ah, Sir!' If anybody was riding in a coach, straight away he addressed him as 'Your Honour'. If it was a priest riding on a mule, then he said: 'Venerable Archdeacon'. What I mean is that he was a real boot-licker. He had a different style of begging on holy days.

I became very friendly with him; so much so that he revealed a secret to me which was that he had three little boys who all begged in the streets and stole what they could. They made up their accounts with him and he put all the money away. He also had a share in what two other children stole from the poor-boxes. With the advice of such a good teacher and the lessons he gave me, I began the same profession and the kids helped me along. In less than a month I'd made more than two hundred *reals* and in the end, because he wanted us to go off together, he told me his greatest secret and the craftiest trick any beggar ever knew. We did this between us. We kidnapped four or five children between us every day. The town-crier would announce their loss and a reward; we would ask for a description and say:

'Oh yes, sir, I saw him at such and such a time. If I hadn't caught him in time he'd have been run over by a cart; he's at my house now.'

They gave us the reward and we got so rich that I soon had fifty *escudos* and healthy legs, although I still kept them bandaged. I decided to leave Madrid and work my way down to

Toledo. I didn't know anybody and nobody knew me either. In the end I went. I bought an old brown suit, a collar and a sword and said good-bye to Valcázar (that was the beggar's name), and went round the inns to find some way of getting to Toledo.

CHAPTER NINE

꘎

A T a hotel I fell in with a company of actors who were making
for Toledo. They had three wagons and by good fortune one
of the actors had been a fellow student of mine at Alcalá. He'd
given up and gone to be a player. I told him I had to leave Madrid
to go to Toledo. The fellow could hardly recognize me with my
face all slashed and had to keep crossing himself as he talked
to me. In the end he agreed to be friends (with my money) and
find a place for me among the others. The men and women were
all mixed up together and one of them, the ballerina, who also
acted the Queen and serious parts in the plays, seemed to me a
right little tart. It so happened her husband was sitting next to
me and I really fancied her and didn't know who he was, so I
said to him:

'Tell me, how can I get a word with that woman? I wouldn't
mind spending twenty *escudos* on her, I think she's quite a
smasher.'

'Well, I oughtn't to say so, as I'm her husband,' said the man,
'and I shouldn't have anything to do with it, but, keeping my
feelings out of it (I haven't many in any case), she's worth plenty
because you won't find a nicer bit of crumpet than her anywhere.'

As he said this he jumped down from the cart and climbed
into another to give me a chance to speak to her. That's how it
looked to me, anyhow. I thought his answer was very funny.
One could see that he did have a wife, but might just as well
not have, a situation reversing the usual state of affairs among
actors. I took advantage of my opportunity. She asked me where
I was going and all about myself and my life. We talked a lot
but left the action for when we got to Toledo. Still, the journey
passed pleasantly enough.

Just by chance I began to recite bits of a play about St Alexis that I remembered from my boyhood, and I recited it so well that the actors took an interest in me. They already knew from my friend, who was one of the company, all about my bad luck and misadventures, and so they asked me if I wanted to join them. They told me what a marvellous life travelling actors led, and as I needed some support and fancied the girl, I made a two-year contract with the manager. I signed up with the company and he gave me a sum for expenses and also the parts I was to play. Then we came to Toledo. I was told to learn up two or three prologues and old men's parts that suited my deep voice. I prepared them very seriously and performed my first prologue there. It was about a ship which was (as they always are) wrecked and helpless; I recited the lines about 'this is the harbour', called the audience 'noble senate', asked them to keep quiet and excuse our shortcomings, and left the stage. My performance was applauded. I'd made an excellent theatrical début. We acted a play that one of our company had written. I marvelled that they could write poetry, as I thought only wise and learned men could do it, and certainly not people as ignorant as actors.

It shows how wrong I was that today any actor can write a play and any artiste his cheap comedy about the Moors and Christians. I remember that in the old days the only dramatists worth listening to were Lope de Vega and Alonso Ramón. To come back to the play, we put it on the first day and nobody understood a word. We began again on the second day and, just my luck, it began with a battle and out I went armed and holding a shield. It's lucky I held it, otherwise I would have been pelted to death with rotten quinces, cabbage roots and water melons. I never saw such a storm, but the play deserved it, because for no reason at all it dragged in a king of Normandy dressed as a hermit and two lackeys as comic relief, and the end of the enormously complicated plot was that everybody got married and that was that. In other words, we got what we deserved.

We gave our actor-author a rough time, but when I told him that we were lucky to get away with our lives and that he should be more careful in future, he said the play wasn't his at all, but that he'd nicked one act here and another there and patched up a real beggar's cloak. The only thing wrong was the design of the patchwork. He admitted that actors who wrote plays used everything they had ever acted in, which was very easy, and that they ran the risks for the sake of three or four hundred *reals*. The other thing he told me was that, as the actors passed through towns, authors used to read plays to them and the actors took the manuscripts away to read them; then they stole them, adding some nonsense and removing the good lines, and issued them as their own work. And he assured me that there had never been any actors who could write a few lines in any other way.

Actually, it seemed quite a good idea to me, and I must admit I felt some sympathy, as I fancied myself as a bit of a poet, especially as I had some knowledge of poetry, having read Garcilaso de la Vega. So I decided to try my own hand. I spent my time doing this, acting, and making love to the actress. By the time we'd been in Toledo a month, doing some very nice plays and making up for our early mistake, I had made quite a name for myself. I called myself Alonsete, because I'd said my name was Alonso, and I was also called the Cruel because I'd played a role of that name to the great approval of the mob standing in the pit. I already had three suits of clothes and some other managers were trying to lure me away. I claimed to know all about the theatre already, and I criticized famous actors, said Pinedo's facial expression was all wrong, gave my solemn opinion on Sánchez's solemn deportment and called Morales a pretty boy. They asked my opinion about scenery and stage-designing. If an author came to read his play I was the one to whom he read it. I was so puffed up with all this that I lost my innocence and wrote a short ballad and then a curtain-raiser which wasn't too bad.

Next I ventured on a play, and to keep it proper I wrote it on the theme of Our Lady of the Rosary. It began with flageolets, and there were souls in Purgatory and demons who yelled 'Bu! Bu!' when they came on and 'Ri! Ri!' when they went off. They liked the name of Satan that I put into my verses and then the discussions as to whether he fell from heaven and so on. In other words, my play was acted and very well received.

I didn't have enough hours in the day, because next I had all the young men running up asking for verses about their girls' eyebrows or eyes or hands or hair or something. Everything had its price; there were other shops but my charges weren't high, as I wanted the business. And as for hymns, the place was soon crawling with sacristans and convent messengers. Blind men kept me going with prayers at eight *reals* each, and I remember that was the time I wrote the one called *The True Judge*, a grave and sonorous piece which was good for making faces. I wrote the lines which begin as follows for a blind man who then claimed them as his own:

> 'Mother of the Word made man,
> Daughter of divine Father,
> Give me thy grace, virginal,' etc.

I was the first one to introduce endings to poetry like sermons, consisting of 'Grace here and hereafter Glory.' I did it in this verse about a Christian held captive by Moors in Tetuan:

> 'Let us beg with honesty
> Of the king without fault
> Who sees our perfidy
> That he give us his Grace
> And hereafter save us, Amen!'

I was forging ahead with all this; I was rich and prosperous and aiming at having my own troupe of actors. I had a very nicely furnished house because, to decorate it cheaply, I'd had the crafty idea of buying up saddle cloths from inns and putting them on my walls. They cost me twenty or thirty *reals*, and they looked better than the King's as you could see anything through them whereas his block out the light.

One day a really funny thing happened to me. I'll tell you about it, though it doesn't show me in a very good light. I was writing a play and had shut myself away in the attic. I stayed there all day and the maid used to bring me my meals and leave them. My habit was to speak the lines aloud as I wrote, just as if I were on the stage. My luck had it that, just at the very moment the maid was coming up the staircase, which was narrow and dark, with two plates and the pot, I was writing a scene about a hunt and was bawling out the play as I wrote it. It went like this:

> 'Watch out for the bear, the bear,
> It's torn me to pieces and left me all bare,
> And it's after you now, so beware, beware.'

What did the girl, a thick-headed Galician, think when she heard: 'It's torn me to pieces' and 'It's after you now'? She thought it was true and that I was warning her. She turned to run, and in her panic tripped over her skirt and tumbled down the stairs. She dropped the pot and broke all the plates and ran into the street screaming that a bear was in the house killing a man. And before I could get down, the whole neighbourhood was up in my room asking where the bear was. Even when I explained how stupid the girl had been and what had actually happened, they still refused to believe me. I didn't eat at all that day.

My companions found out what happened and the story went all over the city. Many things like that happened to me while I insisted on being a playwright and refused to give up that wicked profession.

Well, as always seems to happen, people got to know how well my manager was doing in Toledo, so they summonsed him for some debt or other and threw him into gaol. As a result the company broke up and everyone went his own way. As far as I was concerned, although the others wanted to help me get into some other company, I had no real interest in the profession and had only taken it up to tide me over a difficult patch. I had money now and was well set up and so all I thought of was having a good time. I said good-bye to everyone; they went away and I made up my mind to improve my morals by leaving the acting profession altogether.

I hope this doesn't annoy Your Honour but I became a barred-windows Johnny, after a bit of coif. What I mean is I became a follower of Antichrist which is the same as saying that I began to chat up nuns. My opportunity to begin was when I learnt of the Venus-like beauty of a certain nun, for whom I had written quite a lot of little hymns. She took a fancy to me when she saw me acting St John the Apostle in a Corpus Christi play. The woman was very kind to me and she told me that the only thing she didn't like was that I was an actor. She felt sorry for me as I'd told her my father was a great nobleman. After thinking it over I decided to write her this note:

'I've left the company, more to please you than for my own convenience. You see, any company but yours is loneliness to me; the more I am free the more I shall be yours to command. Let me know when you can talk to me and then I shall know when I shall be happy,' etc.

The convent messenger took the note. You can't imagine how happy the pretty nun was at my leaving the theatre. This is what she replied to my message:

'I feel happier for myself than for you at the good news. I would be ashamed if my desire and your prosperity were not the same thing. We can say that you have found your soul again. All you need to do is persevere and I shall try to help you. I don't think we'll have a chance to talk today but be sure to come at vespers and we'll see each other then and afterwards through the windows. I might even be able to pull the wool over the abbess's eyes. Good-bye for now.'

This letter made me very happy as the woman was intelligent as well as beautiful. I ate, and put on the suit I usually wore to play the handsome young man on the stage. I went to church, said my prayers and then began to watch all the twists and turns in the convent grille to see if she was coming. Then by God and good luck – or rather the Devil and bad luck – I heard the well-known signal, I began to cough and a whole barrage of hacking followed. It was like trying to clear catarrh or as if someone had thrown pepper around the church. At last I couldn't cough any more and up at the grille pops an old woman, coughing away, and I realized my mistake. It's a very dangerous signal to use in convents because it may be a signal for girls, but it's a habit in old women, and many men think they've wooed a nightingale and all they've got is an ugly old barn-owl. I spent a long time in the church, in fact until they began vespers. I stayed the whole service. That's why they call nuns' young men 'devout lovers' and they're always on the eve of delight because the day never comes. You won't believe how many services I attended but my neck was a couple of yards longer than it had been before I started the affair just because of stretching it to try and catch a glimpse of the nun. I became a great friend of the sacristan and the acolyte, and the priest, who had a great sense of humour, always had a smile for me. He walked so stiffly that he looked as if he fed on roasting-spits and iron bars.

I went at 'viewing-time' and, as there was quite a large court-yard there, you had to send a boy to reserve a place for you by noon, just like for the first performance of a play. The place was crawling with worshippers. I used to edge in where I could and it was quite a sight to see the different postures adopted by the lovers. Some stared without blinking, others clutched their swords in one hand and their rosaries in the other and stood like graveyard statues. Others held their arms stretched out like seraphs. Others said nothing but stood there with their mouths open like begging women, showing their guts to their beloved through their throats. Others held the wall up but pushed the bricks out of place as they did so. Some walked up and down like mustangs showing off their virile bearing. Others with their *billets-doux* in their hands looked like hunters luring on their falcons with pieces of meat. The jealous lovers were a different lot; some stood in groups laughing and looking for the girls, others were reading their verses and passing them around. Some, to annoy the others, were walking up and down the parade arm in arm with a woman and others were talking to maids secretly sent with messages. This was all taking place where we were, in the yard. But up above, where the nuns were, there was also a sight worth seeing, as their place was a little tower full of slits and a wall so full of holes that it looked like a sieve or a pomander-box. The holes were like eyelets through which to peep. Here was an arm or leg, there a hand and there a foot. Here there were extremities, heads, mouths. There weren't any brains, though. The other side was like a pedlar's pack, here a rosary, there a handkerchief, there a glove, here a green ribbon. Some of the nuns talked loudly, other coughed. Some made signs with their hats as if they were scaring away spiders with the whoosh-ing sound.

You should see how the men don't just warm themselves in the summer sun; they roast. It's quite funny to see them so red and the nuns so pale. In winter it's so damp that some of us grow shoots and give out roots standing there. We don't escape any flake of snow or drop of rain and, in the end, it's all just to see a woman behind iron grilles and glass like the holy relics of a saint. If she speaks it's like falling in love with a caged thrush, and if she doesn't it's like falling in love with a picture. Any favours are all touch and no go, a bit of finger-fluttering. They lean their heads against the bars and fire their witty remarks through the holes. They love intrigue. Just think of the men who have to keep their voices down as if they're praying, and put up with nagging old women, bossy porteresses and lying messenger-girls. And to crown it all, the nuns are jealous of women outside the convent and say that theirs is the only true love and what complicated arguments they use to prove it!

In the end I was calling the abbess 'ma'am' the priest 'father' and the sacristan 'brother'. These are things that a desperate man will do when time and his patience are running out. I got rather tired of the messengers sending me away and the nun keeping me on the hook. I began to think that, if I was going to Hell, it was a pretty difficult journey which others made much easier, and the way I was going on, I saw I was well on my way to Hell just for indulging my sense of touch. When I spoke to her I pushed my face so close to the grille, so that the others shouldn't hear me, that I had marks on my forehead for the next two days. She spoke so quietly I had to use an ear trumpet to find out what she was talking about. Everybody who saw me called me a convent-crawling bastard or worse.

All of this kept me worrying about what to do and I almost made my mind up to leave the nun even though I'd have to give up my comfortable life. So I made up my mind to leave on St John the Apostle's day because I'd found out what nuns are really like. All I can tell Your Honour is that the Baptist's followers started howling and moaned the Mass instead of singing it. They didn't wash and wore mourning. Their lovers, to pour scorn on the Holy day, brought stools into Church instead of chairs and plenty of riff-raff from the street markets. When I saw some acclaiming one saint and the others screaming obscenely at them for doing so, I got fifty *escudos* from my nun by promising to raffle some needlework, silk-stockings, amber bags and sweets for her, and did a flit to Seville where I thought the field for my special talents was wider. What the nun felt about losing her property rather than losing me, I'll leave the pious reader to infer for himself.

CHAPTER TEN

❧❧❧❧

I DID quite well for myself on the journey from Toledo down to Seville. You see I was quite the little swindler by now and had my own set of dice, loaded for both high and low scores. I could palm one of the dice, that is pick up four and only throw down three. I had my own supply of specially broad and narrow cards, so I could pick out the ones I pleased from the pack. I never lost the chance of making some money. I won't mention all the other tricks or people will think I'm more of an acrobat than a man or, worse still, somebody might be tempted to imitate me and practise vices that are generally disapproved of. Still perhaps if I give an account of some tricks and thieves' slang the ignorant may be forewarned, and it will be his own fault if anybody is caught out after reading my book.

Don't think, my friends, that you'll be safe if you use your own pack of cards, because they'll swap it as quickly as you can blink. Watch out for cards which feel rough or scratched, because that's how they recognize the suits. If you must gamble, friend, you'd better know that in the stables and kitchens they use a pin to prick cards, or bend them so that they can recognize the suits. If you like playing with better-off people, watch out for cards which were actually conceived in sin at the printer's and have water-marks in them for their owner's own benefit. Don't trust a clean card because even the best washed one is dirty for a player who's got good eyes and a good memory. Watch out when you're playing Lansquenet that the dealer doesn't bend the picture cards over, except the kings, more than the other cards, because, if he does, you can say good-bye to your money. Watch you don't get dealt any cards the dealer himself wants to discard and watch out for players who show what cards they want by tapping with their fingers and using the first letters of words. That's all I want to tell you and it's quite enough for you to know how to take care of yourself, although I could have told you a great deal more. When they take your money they call it 'making a killing' and rightly so; 'twist' means cheating your partner, and the game is so twisted nobody can follow what's going on. 'Doubles' mean simple people brought in to be fleeced by these swindlers. 'White' means someone who is innocent and simple and 'black' is someone who just pretends not to know anything.

So, well primed about this language and these tricks, I reached Seville. I won the hire of the mules from my friends, and food and money from the landlords of the inns along the road. I went and put up at the Moor's Head inn where I met a fellow student of mine from Alcalá called Mata but he didn't think it was much of a name so he changed it to Matorral. He dealt in men's lives and bought and sold knifings, which suited him well. He had samples on his face and calculated the length and depth of the slashes he gave from the ones he received.

'There's nobody as skilled,' he used to say, 'as a well-cut man.'

And he was right as his face was as seamed as a leather jacket and he was a walking leather wine-skin. He told me to come and have supper with him and some mates of his. They'd see I got back to the inn afterwards.

We arrived at his place and he said:

'Come on, boy, off with your cloak. Try to look like a man. Tonight we'll see all the likely lads in Seville. You don't want them to think you're a queer, do you? Well, take off that fancy collar and don't stand so stiff. Hang your cape off your shoulders – we always wear it like that. Twist your face, gesticulate more, and don't forget to make your g's like h's and your h's like g's as we do in the south.'

He gave me a whole set of words to learn off by heart, and lent me a dagger which was as wide as a scimitar and as long as a sword.

'Drink this quart of wine,' he said. 'There's no water in it. Nobody will respect you if you don't stink of wine.'

At this point, with me half tight with the wine, in came four of them with faces like old slippers and a rolling walk. They didn't wear cloaks. They had sashes round their stomachs, and their hats pushed up high on their foreheads with the brims turned up so that they looked like they had crowns on. Each one had a mass of ironmongery: daggers and swords in ornamented scabbards knocking against their ankles. Their eyes were expressionless, but stared at you. Their moustaches were turned up at the ends and they had beards pointing out like Turks. They muttered something to us and then said to my friend, gruffly and clipping their words:

'Lo, Mate.'

'Lo, Boy,' replied my guide.

They sat down. They wanted to know who I was but they didn't say a word. One looked at Matorral and then at me, pushing out his lower lip, and then at Matorral again. The master of novices answered him satisfactorily by tugging his beard and looking down. Then they all cheered and stood up, embraced me and clapped me on the back, and I did the same to them and it was just like sampling four different wines.

Supper time came and we were waited on by four great toughs of the type that are called strong-arm men. We all sat down at the table together and up came a dish of pickled capers. As I was the new man they all drank to my honour. Until they drank to it I didn't know I had so much. In came fish and meat, all highly seasoned to make us drink more. There was a great barrel on the floor, full of wine, and anybody who was thirsty stuck his head straight into it and drank. I thought it was quite an original little jug. They began to talk about fighting; they swore foully. Twenty or thirty men were done away with every time they had a toast. The police-chief was sentenced to be carved up and a toast was drunk to the memory of the toughs called Domingo Tiznado and Gayón. The wine flowed like blood to the memory of Escamilla. The ones who were maudlin wept over the unfortunate Alonso Alvarez. My companion didn't know where he was by now, and taking a loaf in his hands, he said hoarsely:

'I swear by this, which is the face of God, and by the light that came from the angel's face (looking at the candle) that tonight, if you like, we'll get the copper that got poor One Eye.'

They set up a toneless shout, and taking their daggers out, swore it, putting their hands on the edge of the barrel of wine. Next they stuck their heads into it and said:

'As we drink this wine, so shall we drink every traitor's blood!'

'Who was this Alonso Alvarez?' I asked. 'And why are they so upset over *his* death?'

'A fine lad,' said one, 'a fighter with guts. He was a champion and a good friend. Come on everybody, the devil's calling me.'

So we left the house and started to hunt out coppers.

I was dead tight and didn't know what I was doing. So I didn't realize the risk I was running. We got as far at the Calle de la Mar when the police-patrol met us. As soon as my companions saw them, they unsheathed their swords and attacked them. I did the same and released two souls from their evil bodies at the first attack. The sergeant took to his heels and shouted for help up the street. We couldn't follow him as we were already engaged. At last we took sanctuary from the rigours of justice in the Cathedral, and we slept soundly enough to let the effects of the wine on our heads wear off.

When we came to I realized with astonishment that two men and the sergeant had been killed or had run away from our wretched little mob. We had a good time in the Cathedral because, at the smell of criminals on the run came plenty of whores who stripped to cover our nakedness. One called Grajales took a fancy to me and dressed me in her new finery. I liked being with her better than anything that had happened to me before, and so I made up my mind to spend the rest of my life with Grajales in this vale of tears. I took a good look at Seville low life and in a few days I was the gang leader. The law wasn't lazy in trying to catch us. They patrolled our hideouts but even so, after midnight we slipped out and went where we liked in disguise.

When I saw that this situation was going to be more or less permanent and that bad luck was dogging my heels, I made up my mind, not because I was intelligent enough to see what was going to happen but because I was tired and obstinate in my wickedness, to go to America with Grajales. I consulted her first; I thought things would go better in the New World and another country. But they went worse, as they always will for anybody who thinks he only has to move his dwelling without changing his life or ways.

Discover more about our forthcoming books through Penguin's FREE newspaper...

Penguin
Quarterly

It's packed with:

- exciting features
- author interviews
- previews & reviews
- books from your favourite films & TV series
- exclusive competitions & much, much more...

Write off for your free copy today to:
Dept JC
Penguin Books Ltd
FREEPOST
West Drayton
Middlesex
UB7 0BR
NO STAMP REQUIRED

READ MORE IN PENGUIN

In every corner of the world, on every subject under the sun, Penguin represents quality and variety – the very best in publishing today.

For complete information about books available from Penguin – including Puffins, Penguin Classics and Arkana – and how to order them, write to us at the appropriate address below. Please note that for copyright reasons the selection of books varies from country to country.

In the United Kingdom: Please write to *Dept. JC, Penguin Books Ltd, FREEPOST, West Drayton, Middlesex UB7 OBR*

If you have any difficulty in obtaining a title, please send your order with the correct money, plus ten per cent for postage and packaging, to *PO Box No. 11, West Drayton, Middlesex UB7 OBR*

In the United States: Please write to *Penguin USA Inc., 375 Hudson Street, New York, NY 10014*

In Canada: Please write to *Penguin Books Canada Ltd, 10 Alcorn Avenue, Suite 300, Toronto, Ontario M4V 3B2*

In Australia: Please write to *Penguin Books Australia Ltd, 487 Maroondah Highway, Ringwood, Victoria 3134*

In New Zealand: Please write to *Penguin Books (NZ) Ltd,182–190 Wairau Road, Private Bag, Takapuna, Auckland 9*

In India: Please write to *Penguin Books India Pvt Ltd, 706 Eros Apartments, 56 Nehru Place, New Delhi 110 019*

In the Netherlands: Please write to *Penguin Books Netherlands B.V., Keizersgracht 231 NL–1016 DV Amsterdam*

In Germany: Please write to *Penguin Books Deutschland GmbH, Friedrichstrasse 10–12, W–6000 Frankfurt/Main 1*

In Spain: Please write to *Penguin Books S. A., C. San Bernardo 117–6° E–28015 Madrid*

In Italy: Please write to *Penguin Italia s.r.l., Via Felice Casati 20, I–20124 Milano*

In France: Please write to *Penguin France S. A., 17 rue Lejeune, F–31000 Toulouse*

In Japan: Please write to *Penguin Books Japan, Ishikiribashi Building, 2–5–4, Suido, Bunkyo-ku, Tokyo 112*

In Greece: Please write to *Penguin Hellas Ltd, Dimocritou 3, GR–106 71 Athens*

In South Africa: Please write to *Longman Penguin Southern Africa (Pty) Ltd, Private Bag X08, Bertsham 2013*

READ MORE IN PENGUIN

A CHOICE OF CLASSICS

READ MORE IN PENGUIN

A CHOICE OF CLASSICS

William Hazlitt	**Selected Writings**
George Herbert	**The Complete English Poems**
Thomas Hobbes	**Leviathan**
Samuel Johnson/ James Boswell	**A Journey to the Western Islands of Scotland and The Journal of a Tour of the Hebrides**
Charles Lamb	**Selected Prose**
George Meredith	**The Egoist**
Thomas Middleton	**Five Plays**
John Milton	**Paradise Lost**
Samuel Richardson	**Clarissa**
	Pamela
Earl of Rochester	**Complete Works**
Richard Brinsley Sheridan	**The School for Scandal and Other Plays**
Sir Philip Sidney	**Selected Poems**
Christopher Smart	**Selected Poems**
Adam Smith	**The Wealth of Nations**
Tobias Smollett	**The Adventures of Ferdinand Count Fathom**
	Humphrey Clinker
Laurence Sterne	**The Life and Opinions of Tristram Shandy**
	A Sentimental Journey Through France and Italy
Jonathan Swift	**Gulliver's Travels**
	Selected Poems
Thomas Traherne	**Selected Poems and Prose**
Sir John Vanbrugh	**Four Comedies**

READ MORE IN PENGUIN

A CHOICE OF CLASSICS

READ MORE IN PENGUIN

A CHOICE OF CLASSICS

Molière	**The Misanthrope/The Sicilian/Tartuffe/A Doctor in Spite of Himself/The Imaginary Invalid**
	The Miser/The Would-be Gentleman/That Scoundrel Scapin/Love's the Best Doctor/Don Juan
Michel de Montaigne	**Essays**
Marguerite de Navarre	**The Heptameron**
Blaise Pascal	**Pensées**
	The Provincial Letters
Abbé Prevost	**Manon Lescaut**
Rabelais	**The Histories of Gargantua and Pantagruel**
Racine	**Andromache/Britannicus/Berenice**
	Iphigenia/Phaedra/Athaliah
Arthur Rimbaud	**Collected Poems**
Jean-Jacques Rousseau	**The Confessions**
	A Discourse on Inequality
	Emile
Jacques Saint-Pierre	**Paul and Virginia**
Madame de Sevigné	**Selected Letters**
Stendhal	**Lucien Leuwen**
	Scarlet and Black
	The Charterhouse of Parma
Voltaire	**Candide**
	Letters on England
	Philosophical Dictionary
Emile Zola	**L'Assomoir**
	La Bête Humaine
	The Debacle
	The Earth
	Germinal
	Nana
	Thérèse Raquin

READ MORE IN PENGUIN

A CHOICE OF CLASSICS